Steadfast Love

STEADFAST *Love*

CAROL GENENGELS

Torchflame Books

Vista, CA

ISBN: 978-1-61153-695-9 (paperback)

ISBN: 978-1-61153-696-6 (ebook)

ISBN: 978-1-61153-697-3 (large print)

Library of Congress Control Number: 2025913357

Steadfast Love is published by Torchflame Books, an imprint of Top Reads Publishing, LLC, 1035 E. Vista Way, Suite 205, Vista, CA 92084, USA

www.torchflamebooks.com

Unless otherwise noted, all scripture quotations are from the King James Version. The King James Version is in the Public Domain.

Scripture quotations marked (ESV) are from the ESV® Bible (The Holy Bible, English Standard Version®), © 2001 by Crossway, a publishing ministry of Good News Publishers. ESV Text Edition: 2025. The ESV text may not be quoted in any publication made available to the public by a Creative Commons license. The ESV may not be translated in whole or in part into any other language. Used by permission. All rights reserved.

Cover design and interior layout: Jori Hanna

The publisher is not responsible for websites or social media accounts (or their content) that are not owned by the publisher.

This is a work of fiction. Names, characters, places, and incidents are either the product of the author's imagination or used fictitiously, and any resemblance to actual persons, living or dead, business establishments, events, or locales is entirely coincidental.

To the Encouragers who make the world a better place

Prologue

SEATTLE, WASHINGTON, 2010

J ohn Beaumont closed his journal. Questions flooded his notes lately. What did he want anyway? Despite a successful career running his family's corporation, something was missing. Why wasn't he married? Some of his friends feared commitment; was that his problem? Was he destined to remain single? John leaned forward as he reflected on college days. His desire to attend seminary was out of the question. He visualized his father's stern face. "John, you can still serve God as a businessman. Running our stores is the opportunity of a lifetime. You would be crazy to turn your back on it. As my only son, I'm counting on you to take the helm. Everything depends on you."

The stores turned a greater profit than ever under John's capable hands. He was good at what he did. Things usually came easily for him, whether it be sports, music, academics, or women. People liked him, and he liked people. His customers felt special when he took time to educate them on the virtues of investing in fine furniture. His favorite quote was: *"Long after the sweet taste of a bargain price is gone, the bitter taste of poor quality remains."*

His demanding career left little time for ministry or dating. That's one of the reasons he agreed to help his friend lead a Bible study for single adults. At least he would be in church on a regular basis. Even though he loved teaching, his prayers for direction seemed to smack the brick wall in front of him and sink into the mortar. He tucked his journal in his briefcase. "Thank you, Lord, for another morning; please guide our class and let me be a blessing to somebody today."

One

SEATTLE, WASHINGTON, 2010

Beth Delaney debated whether or not she should join a Bible Study class for single adults. She was still dealing with the trauma of the last two years. Beth coped by working as many hours at the hospital as possible. With the current nursing shortage, overtime was no problem. However, she realized drudgery wasn't the cure for her aching heart. She needed fellowship with people her own age. Her married friend, Carlene, encouraged her to "give it a try."

After parking her car, Beth checked her image in the visor mirror. She touched up her lipstick and reached for her Bible. A gust of wind stung her eyes as she exited the car. She saw her breath in the air as she gingerly made her way across the icy parking lot. As she entered the church foyer, warmth and music embraced her like an old friend. The 8 o'clock church service was already in session.

The assistant pastor was talking to a small group nearby. He smiled and waved. "Morning, Beth, glad you could make it." She loosened her hood as dark hair spilled past her shoulders. "Good morning, Pastor Phil."

Phil Stevens left the group to shake her hand. "Follow me,

I'll show you where we meet." Beth removed her gloves as they walked the corridors. Phil stopped and opened the door to the fireside lounge. An aroma of coffee permeated the room that buzzed with chatter. "Hey class, listen up! We have a newcomer. Let's welcome Beth Delaney on this fine January morning."

Applause and warm smiles greeted her. She recognized one woman and smiled. The pastor asked the class to give their names. "Don't worry," he whispered, "There won't be a test afterward." Nine women and eight men gave brief introductions. Afterwards, Phil pointed out the snack bar and encouraged Beth to help herself. She had just settled down with a cup of coffee when another woman dashed into the room and sat next to her. She flipped her dark hair back and extended her hand. "Hi, you must be new. My name is Janet."

"It's nice to meet you. I'm Beth."

Pastor Phil asked John Beaumont to open with prayer. Heads bowed as John began. After praying, he moved to an upright piano and accompanied the group as they sang a few choruses. Beth hugged her jacket around her. Though flames danced in a cozy fireplace, ice crystals circled the outside windowpanes. The pastor started a video that grabbed her attention. Beth sipped coffee while scanning the faces watching the video. The students appeared to range in age from early twenties to late thirties. One person particularly caught her attention: the man who played the piano. The blond, blue-eyed man was extremely handsome. She tried not to stare.

Beth relaxed as the subject matter drew her in. The video was followed by lively discussion as they formed small groups. Beth was surprised to learn that Janet was also a nurse. Len managed a sporting goods store. Mindy, a bubbly blonde, worked for U.S. Bank.

Time passed quickly as the groups hashed over their lesson. As the discussion ended, Beth bid her classmates goodbye. To her surprise, she found herself looking forward to the next Sunday.

As the weeks progressed, Beth and Janet became friends, often chatting in their free time and confiding in one another. Janet learned that Beth carried emotional baggage from a broken engagement a year earlier. As a result, she wasn't interested in moving forward with any guy.

Their visits usually ended with a prayer for Janet's fiancé, David, stationed overseas.

The singles' group often enjoyed fellowship events like bowling, video games, pizza parties, skating, or movies. Though a few men approached Beth for private dates, she politely turned them down. Group events were fine, but she was not interested in dating.

Gradually, harsh winter winds and sleet yielded to March storms and April showers. The days grew longer and warmer as winter lost its firm grip. Green leaves sprouted on the trees, along with fragrant pink and white blossoms. The scent of freshly mowed lawns added to the perfume. Goldfinches flitted from tree to tree. Beth felt content as the beauty of spring lifted her heart.

The Bible class proved to be a blessing. Beth appreciated her classmates, and they filled a void in her life. The students challenged one another in hot-topic debates, which Beth thoroughly enjoyed. She felt safe and secure within her new circle of friends.

John Beaumont and Pastor Phil took turns leading the discussions. Despite Beth's resolve, she fought a growing attraction to John. His smile brightened any room. It wasn't just his looks that impressed her; it was the depth of his faith, his sense of humor, and the way he treated others with kindness and respect. The light in his captivating blue eyes came from deep within.

After church one afternoon, Beth went to Janet's place for

lunch. After their meal, they sat on the floor sorting through a pile of videos. Beth casually asked a question. "What do you think of John Beaumont?"

Janet leaned against the sofa. "John?"

Beth shrugged. "Yeah."

Janet looped her fingers like a tent. "Hmm . . . Well, let me put it this way: if you looked up the meaning of the word 'gentleman' in the dictionary, you'd find John's name there."

Beth laughed. "He is nice, isn't he?"

"And handsome too! Truthfully, John is one of the coolest guys I know. Next to David, of course." Beth set a video aside. "I like the way he explains things. He never uses notes and his eye contact; it's like he sees right into my soul."

"I know what you mean; as a teacher, he rocks."

"Is it true he manages a furniture store?"

Janet shot Beth a side glance. "I think it's more than one. Why are you asking, anyway?"

"Just curious."

Janet rolled her eyes. "Don't tell me you're falling for him, too." Beth felt heat creep up her neck. "What are you talking about?"

"Surely you've noticed how women flock around him after class."

Beth jerked her head back. "I have no intention of getting entangled with anyone."

Janet playfully punched her arm. "Yeah, sure."

Several days later, Beth and her father dined at a family restaurant. In the middle of the meal, she noticed John across the room sitting opposite a beautiful blonde. They seemed to be having a good time laughing and writing something down. Beth felt a twinge of disappointment that she immediately tried to quash. Why wouldn't a guy like him have a girlfriend? She watched them leave the restaurant, trying to tell herself that whether or not John Beaumont had a girlfriend was none of her business.

Two

The Bible class planned a daylong hike, and Janet and Beth signed up. A week before the event John caught Beth after class. His grin highlighted his dimples. "I see you've signed up for the hike." She closed her purse and looked up. "Yes, are you going?"

"It sounds like fun. I hope to make it."

Beth smiled. "See you next Saturday then."

Why had he singled her out? Was he just being friendly? She gathered her things. Yes, John was a friendly guy—a friendly guy with a girlfriend. Beth didn't think most women realized that, considering how they fussed over him. Marla, a buxom blonde, made no effort to hide her feelings, often sitting next to him, though he seemed oblivious.

The following Saturday morning, Beth awoke early, grateful for sunshine streaming through her windows. She stretched and yawned before leaving the comfort of her bed. After showering, she dressed in jeans, a red T-shirt, and a blue sweatshirt jacket. She pulled her hair into a ponytail and finished filling her daypack. The house she shared with her father was silent. After gathering her things, she headed for the garage. Beth sang along with her car's radio on the drive across town. As she approached the church, her phone rang. She glanced down. "Hi Jan."

"Hey, I'm sorry, but I need to bail. My boss called at the last minute."

"Bummer, we'll miss you," Beth said as she parked in the church lot.

Janet sighed, "We're swamped. At least the overtime comes in handy. It goes into my wedding fund."

"I understand, duty calls. Don't work too hard."

Beth decided to make the best of it. She transferred her wallet to the backpack and locked her purse in the trunk. She waved at the group waiting to enter the van. John wasn't there. Nine members joined hands as Pastor Phil led them in prayer. As Beth opened her eyes, a BMW sped into the parking lot. John emerged, and several women, including Marla, rushed up to him. He was cordial but scanned the crowd. He met Beth's eyes, grinned, and wove through the group towards her.

Beth smiled, "I'm glad you made it." They boarded the van, and John took the seat next to her. Sitting close to John proved to be an unexpected blessing. He had a good head on his shoulders, a very handsome one. Beth began to feel better about Janet's absence.

Phil played stereo instrumentals while he navigated the I-5 freeway. John and Beth leaned back to enjoy the music while they admired the scenery. They made a rest stop near Olympia before heading west. Towering evergreens, pink and red rhododendrons, and an abundance of yellow, Scotch Broom dominated the landscape. An hour later, Phil drove down a road leading to a lodge in a national park. The gang stared in awe at the rustic lodge before them. "Wow!" seemed to be the consensus of the travelers.

As they ventured inside, Beth joined the gals headed to the

restroom. Marla stood in front of the mirror, combing her hair. "Well, aren't you lucky? Snagging the seat next to John!"

"I wouldn't read too much into it, Marla. It just happened that way."

"Okay then, I won't," Marla snapped as she left the room.

Mindy exited a stall and washed her hands. "I think Marla has such a crush on John, she can't see that he has no interest in her at all."

"She has nothing to worry about. He's just a friend." Beth freshened her lipstick. "I'd like to explore this place before our hike."

Beth entered a huge lobby with aging cedar walls and floor-to-ceiling windows. Leather sofas and armchairs were placed around the lodge. A huge brick fireplace crackled. A mammoth stag head jutted out of the upper portion. John was sitting on a sofa with a trail map in front of him. "It's quite impressive, isn't it?"

Beth answered, "I'll say! It's a work of art." Marla sat nearby watching John. She tugged at her low-cut top and smoothed her jeans.

Mindy entered from the deck and called out, "Hey guys, come and check out this lake."

"I want to study the map for a few more minutes," John said.

Beth excused herself to join the outside group. She crossed a planked cedar deck with steps leading down to a walkway. The sidewalk meandered through manicured lawns towards a deep blue lake. Placid water reflected a line of evergreen trees, rugged mountain peaks, and a cloudless blue sky. A slew of rowboats and kayaks lined the beach where gentle waves lapped the shore.

Beth and Mindy admired the view while the others scattered along the pebbly shoreline. Beth prayed silently, *Thank you, Lord, for this beautiful place. Bless the hike and our fellowship. Keep us safe and in Your care.*

Rod approached and asked the girls to join him for a quick stroll along the lake. Beth said she wanted to check out the gift shop before the hike started. He turned to Mindy. "How about you?" She took him up on his offer.

Beth returned to the lodge to explore the quaint shop. She discovered an assortment of wildlife books, carved bears, sweatshirts, pants, rain gear, and handcrafted native American jewelry. She stood in line waiting to pay for a cup of coffee and a postcard when John walked up behind her. "We're gathering for the hike." After searching through her pockets, she panicked.

"Here, I've got it," John said as he dropped a bill on the counter. The clerk cheerfully took his money and made change. It wasn't until after he'd paid for her purchases that Beth remembered her wallet was in the daypack. "Thank you, John. I'll pay you back later."

He shrugged. "What's a cup of coffee and a postcard between friends? My treat."

Beth sipped her coffee and showed him the postcard. "Isn't it pretty?"

He studied the photo of jagged peaks behind an azure lake. "It's beautiful. Is it for anyone special?"

"Yes, someone very special." His smile slowly faded. She chuckled, "It's for my dad's scrapbook." John's smile returned.

They met Phil in the parking lot, locking the van; Beth and John's packs were on the ground. "Are you looking for these?" he asked.

"I am." Beth knelt and tucked her card into an inner pocket. As she stood, she drained her coffee cup and chucked it into a nearby trash can. John adjusted his pack and helped drape Beth's pack over her shoulders. The group was waiting for them at the trailhead. Pastor Phil took a head count. "I recommend the buddy system, so let's pair off."

John tapped Beth's shoulder. "Wanna be my buddy?"

She chuckled. "Sure, why not?"

Phil made a list. Rod and Mindy, Len and Penny, Beth and John, Marla and Sylvia, Phil, and Jack. After everyone had a partner, Phil pointed out a large wooden sign.

STICK TO THE TRAIL
RESPECT VEGETATION
YOU PACK IT IN, YOU PACK IT OUT.
LEAVE NO SIGN OF YOUR VISIT.

"Our map leads to the picnic site," Phil said. "After lunch, we'll continue on. If you decide to return to the lodge, we'll meet you there at four. Any questions?" After a period of silence, he continued. "Okay, let's synchronize our time."

A trail through evergreens beckoned them. Beth stopped to watch a bushy-tailed squirrel scamper up a tree. John wasn't sure if his amusement came from watching the squirrel or watching her. Though Marla was Sylvia's hiking partner, she stuck close to John, gazing into his eyes as he tried to answer her questions. She edged closer, drawing out the conversation.

Irritated, Beth kept going, talking to others along the way. Eventually, John caught up with her. "Hey, you're a fast hiker."

She faced him. "It must be my long legs."

He nodded, "I know what you mean. How tall are you?"

"Five-nine. How about you?"

He ducked behind a low-hanging branch. "Six three. How come you didn't wait for me? You're supposed to be my buddy." He adjusted his pack and drew a breath of fresh air.

"I figured you'd catch up once Marla let you go," Beth said.

John rolled his eyes, and his jaw tightened. "I hate to say it, but she tries my patience sometimes. Before I knew it, she took a selfie of us with her phone."

Beth laughed, "She didn't ask first?"

John shook his head, "Nope." He changed the subject. "Where's Janet today?"

Beth sidestepped a huge tree root. "Her boss called her at the last minute. There's such a nursing shortage these days."

"You're a nurse too, right?"

"Yeah, I work at Evergreen Hospital."

He kicked a stone out of the pathway. "The next time I'm sick, I hope you're *my* nurse."

"I don't know about that, John. You'd have to be pretty sick to be in the hospital."

He stretched out his arm. "I'm feeling a little dizzy, maybe you should take my pulse."

She narrowed her eyes as she held his wrist and felt for a pulse. She feigned shock as she dropped the arm covered with fine blond hair. "It's racing awfully fast."

He stared at his wrist. "Can't you do something about it?"

She shook her head. "I might have to amputate."

He frowned and backed up. "I think I'll get a second opinion."

"That's not a bad idea," Beth quipped.

They passed others along the trail as mountain peaks dared them to come closer. Twenty minutes later, they were well ahead of the group. Beth froze in her tracks. She reached for John's arm to stop him. "Look," she whispered. In a nearby thicket, a doe and two spotted fawns stood nibbling brush. The couple silently watched the deer family until John sneezed, and they scampered away. "Oh, weren't they adorable?"

John sneezed again and nodded.

"I'm guessing you have allergies," Beth said.

"Good diagnosis." They continued until the trail split. John consulted his map. "To the right." The trail narrowed considerably but they could still walk side-by-side. John faced her. "When I realized that you signed up for the hike, I made sure to take the day off."

Beth tensed. His T-shirt revealed his incredible build. He was everything she'd ever dreamed of in a man. Tall, handsome, smart, and spiritual. It just never dawned on her that he might have the slightest interest in her. As she studied his handsome features, she thought maybe the woman at the restaurant was only a date.

Three

John was elated to be with the woman he'd secretly admired for so long. She had a natural, classic beauty. He felt like he knew her well from the things shared in class over the past few months. John sensed her need for time and space to heal from the grief of losing her mother. He'd seen the sadness in her eyes that spurred his prayers for her.

He was quite sure she wasn't dating anyone. Many women he met flaunted their charms and played the aggressor, but Beth was merely polite—which intrigued him even more. Spending so much time at her side made his day. He could no longer deny his feelings for her, at least not to himself.

John inhaled the clean scent of pine and cedar. There was another part of the forest bouquet he couldn't quite pinpoint; a peppery, minty blend. The gentle flow of the river and the sun on their backs was invigorating.

"I'm thirsty," Beth said as she crouched down to remove her pack. She sighed as it left her shoulders. She found her water and offered some to John.

"I'm good," he said as he took water from his pack. He downed it quickly and put the bottle back where he found it.

She unzipped her jacket and tied it around her waist. John helped her reattach her pack.

The rest of the gang caught up with them at a picnic area, complete with restrooms and water faucets. The boisterous hikers settled around cedar tables.

John and Beth sat across from Len and Mindy. The others settled nearby. Len snapped pictures of the groups. John asked him to take a photo of him with Beth.

Everyone agreed that it was a perfect day for a hike as they ate their lunch. Greedy crows watched from fir boughs, waiting for them to finish so they could swoop down and gobble up any remains.

After lunch, John and Beth lingered behind the rest of the group. As the sun rose even higher, Beth took sunscreen from her pack. "We'd better use more of this." She squeezed lotion into John's palm and a generous amount into her hands. Beth watched as he slathered his arms and face. She spread lotion on herself, then reached up and spread lotion on the back of John's neck. "You missed a spot."

Little did she realize how her gentle touch affected him. He longed to take her in his arms, but he didn't dare. He knew the timing had to be right before he made his move. "We'd better try to catch up with the rest of them."

The dirt and pine needle trail led to groves of virgin timber. Vine maples arched over their path, dripping moss curtains. Alongside the trail, nurse logs and old stumps provided loam for struggling seedlings. The couple marveled at the size of the massive trunks of old-growth trees. "Five people could stand in front of that one trunk!" Beth exclaimed as she snapped a picture of John leaning against the bark of a majestic tree. Butterflies flitted back and forth among colorful wildflowers. Soaring birds chirped a spring song known only to their creator. Further up the trail, Beth stopped to pick up a pinecone. "Do you know that certain pinecones hold seeds only released by the intense heat of a forest fire?" She handed it to John.

"Yes," he said as he studied it. "Isn't God's provision amazing?"

Before long, they joined the rest of the group. Some were struggling as the trail grew steeper. They exchanged greetings before passing them on the incline. Since John and Beth were both in great physical shape, they forged on well ahead of their peers. Shafts of sunlight illuminated parts of their path. John took a snapshot of Beth as she posed in one of the brilliant circles of light. Certainly, she must be an angel in disguise.

John led as they trudged single file up a steep trail. It brought them to a series of small waterfalls cascading down rock cliffs. The couple stopped to watch people below them on the winding trail. They leaned against a cedar fence, watching falls that made spectacular backdrops for their photos. One's spray produced an amazing rainbow. John and Beth became acutely aware of one another while admiring the rainbow. They locked eyes. He stared transfixed by her warm hazel eyes and thick lashes. The ardent look in John's eyes completely unnerved Beth. Her heartbeat quickened to a frantic pace. The next step became obvious. She quickly looked away and focused on traces of melting snow etching the trail. She ran ahead and scooped up a sloppy handful. She made a snowball and playfully tossed it at him. In turn he grabbed a bit of snow and chased her as she tried to outrun him. He overtook her and threatened to put the icy crystals down the back of her neck. Though she was laughing, her eyes begged for mercy. "Don't you dare!"

He dropped his snow and put the pinecone down the back of her shirt. She shrieked as he took off running. They were both laughing as they reached a suspension bridge over a bubbling stream. They tightly grasped the ropes of the wobbly bridge that led them further into the woods.

John remarked that the walk of faith was much like crossing a suspension bridge. "It's best to keep your eyes on the goal. Looking down can be scary."

Beth frowned. "I'll try to remember that in the future."

As their trail descended, they stumbled upon an open meadow surrounded by Douglas fir and Sitka spruce trees. Clumps of sword ferns flourished along with the ever-present mossy groundcover. A bald eagle soared overhead. It was paradise.

John crouched down to pick up a discarded Pepsi can. He crushed it in his fist before stuffing it in his pack. "Listen, I hear running water."

"I hear it too." They walked faster until they discovered a babbling creek. Beth sighed, "I need to rest a minute." A layer of perspiration dotted her brow. "Let's sit on a rock and soak our feet."

"Sounds good to me," John said. They removed their packs, jackets, shoes, and socks. John offered his arm as they crossed flat rocks in the middle of the gently bubbling creek. They settled next to each other and rolled up the hems of their jeans.

"Oh, this feels good," Beth exclaimed as she splashed her tired feet in the icy water.

"Oh yeah," John agreed. "This really hits the spot."

Beth playfully kicked water on John's ankles. In turn, he splashed her too. A noisy crow loudly scolded them. "Look!" Beth exclaimed as she reached for a floating twig. She leaned a bit too far and splashed into the water. John slid into the creek to help her. Just as he caught her waist, his foot slipped on a mossy rock beneath him. He fell sideways, taking her with him. They were cheek-to-cheek. They yelped as frigid water took their breath away. John was the first to regain his footing. He helped her up, eyes full of concern. "Are you okay?"

"Other than my dignity? I'm fine." Her hair dripped, and she was still clutching the unusual twig in her hand. "What about you?"

He rubbed his backside. "I'll feel this tomorrow." He gently guided her across slippery stones to shore. "I hope that twig was worth it."

"It's more than a twig; look, it's a cross."

John fingered the odd-shaped branch and smiled. "So it is."

John picked a wisp of moss from her dripping ponytail. "Now what?"

Her teeth chattered as she squeezed water from the hem of her shirt. "I have two towels and extra clothing in my pack. Wait here while I change." She tossed him a towel before disappearing behind a clump of bushes. A few minutes later she emerged in Capri's, a blue shirt, and her dry sweatshirt jacket. John had removed his shirt and was wringing it out. She tried not to stare. She put her pack by his and withdrew a wide-toothed comb. Her long, wavy hair gently cascaded as she combed it. "Do you have anything to change into?"

John shook his head. "Just my sweatshirt."

She began twisting her hair back into a ponytail. "I'm really sorry."

"No apology needed, can't remember when I've had a more enjoyable swim." He stuffed his wet shirt into the outer pocket of his pack. He donned his sweatshirt and ran a comb through his hair. He caught her watching him.

She quickly turned to other things, like trying to twist her wet jeans.

"Let me help with that," John said, reaching for them. His strong hands did a much better job than she was doing. Before long, they heard the rest of the gang approaching.

"Whoa!" Len said as he observed his friends wet hair and jeans. "What happened to you guys?"

"We fell in the creek," Beth said. The hikers crowded around as they shared their adventures. The group stayed together on the trek back. John and Beth lagged behind as the trail descended. He offered her a candy bar. Beth grinned, "I love chocolate, thanks!"

"Don't most women?" he teased.

Beth arched her brows. "Are you an expert on women?"

John's dimples appeared again. "Hardly!"

Beth handed him a packet of raw almonds. "These are good for your heart."

"That's not the only thing good for my heart," he muttered under his breath.

When they returned to the lodge, Len offered John a dry pair of jeans.

Beth took one last look around the lodge. She found Marla and Sylvia sitting by the fireplace. "Too tiring for me," Sylvia said as she put her book aside. Marla scowled with disgust; she had blisters on her feet and insect bites that itched like crazy. Apparently, she was desperately trying to get cell service.

"Time to hit the road," Pastor Phil announced. The three women left the lodge and joined the others waiting to board the van. Beth saved the seat next to her with her pack. She picked it up when John appeared, wearing jeans a couple of inches too short. He tucked their packs on the rack above the seats.

She smiled, "At least you're dry now."

A mischievous wink accompanied his smile. "It's all good." Beth couldn't help but laugh.

Once the van got underway, they relived the day's adventures. "In all my thirty years, I've never fallen into a creek before," John muttered.

"Nor have I," Beth said.

A half hour later, Pastor Phil parked in front of a rustic café. "Okay guys, I know you're starving." Inside the restaurant, they settled around a huge oak table. A radio blared music in the background as the couple studied their menus. "I'm famished, how about you?"

Beth quipped, "I'm so hungry I could eat a horse!"

"Me too, but I think I'll settle for a burger, it's easier to digest."

"A deluxe cheeseburger sounds good, along with a chocolate milkshake."

A gum-chewing server worked her way around the table, taking orders. When she came to John he nodded towards Beth. "Put her on my ticket; we'll have an iced tea and a chocolate milkshake." The waitress scribbled on her pad and moved on.

Beth frowned. "You didn't have to do that; I have my wallet now."

John shrugged. "When a lady is with me, I pay. That's just the way it is."

Beth frowned. *For goodness's sake, does he consider this a date?*

After the waitress served a round of drinks, the group placed their orders while Michael Bolton belted out: *"When a Man Loves a Woman."*

The animated group discussed their day. Most everyone agreed that it had been an awesome day. Marla and Silvia kept quiet. After their meal, the group boarded the van again. Beth closed her eyes and leaned back, feeling wonderful. John shut his eyes too. Before long they were both asleep. John awoke later to find Beth's head resting on his shoulder. It was all he could do to keep from wrapping his arm around her. Ten miles later Beth awoke and looked up into his blue eyes. He smiled. "Good evening, Miss Delaney."

Her cheeks flushed as she quickly sat up. "I guess I drifted off."

"So did I." John suppressed a smile as she stared out the window.

A full moon followed the van back to the church parking lot.

The midnight sky blazed with dazzling stars as John walked Beth to her car. "Will I see you in the morning?"

She met his gaze in the moonlight. "You just might."

Beth pondered her day as she drove home. John was easy to talk to and fun to be around, but he awoke feelings she wasn't ready for. She didn't want to get hurt again by falling for the wrong guy. John must have a woman in his life. After all, she had seen him with a blonde not long ago. Who was she?

The next morning, the video was playing when she quietly slipped into the darkened classroom. Later, when the drapes opened and the discussion began, John smiled from across the room. Beth returned his smile and gave a slight wave. After class, John was busy with some of the class members. Beth headed for the foyer with Janet, and the two discussed yesterday's hike. Beth told her she'd had a wonderful time with John most of the day.

"Oh, I'd better call later for a full report," Janet teased. "I need to be at work by eleven." They hugged before Janet left.

Beth made her way to the fellowship hall. She was trying to balance her cup while pouring coffee when a masculine hand reached out to her, "Let me help." She gazed into familiar blue eyes and smiled.

"Thanks." John looked as if he had just stepped out of a menswear magazine in his chic outfit. He followed Beth to a table and put her cup in front of her. "Would you like a donut?"

"Sure."

A friend greeted him in passing, "Hey, John. I saw you on Facebook this morning!"

John grimaced. He placed the donut in front of Beth and sat next to her. "Marla posted the selfie she took of us on the hike."

"You're kidding."

"The caption read, 'Hiking with my buddy, John.'"

Beth laughed. "She has more nerve than a burglar."

John rolled his eyes, "You can say that again."

Beth took a bite of the fresh donut. John did the same thing. "Man, these are good."

Beth nodded. "They sure are."

"You were late this morning. Is everything okay?"

Beth sighed. "My car was on fumes, so I stopped for gas. The pump was out of order. Then I waited behind a long line of cars for another pump. To make matters worse, gas splashed on my hands, and I had to clean up. Anyway, time just got away from me."

John leaned back in his chair. "Sounds pretty frustrating!"

"One thing I detest is pumping gas."

He changed the subject. "I sure enjoyed our hike yesterday."

"Me too. It was such a fun day. I was afraid you might be limping this morning."

"Limping?"

"I assumed you'd be miserable after our fall in the creek." John glanced across the room and back at her. "Just between you and me, I do have a couple bruises."

Beth stared at the floor. "I'm sorry."

He bent down so he could see her face. "Sorry about what? It was worth every minute."

She smiled as she lifted her head. "You looked sharp in Len's jeans."

"Yeah, right. At least I was dry." John shifted as his eyes met hers. "It looks like you're all alone today."

Beth finished her donut and blotted her lips with a napkin. "As a matter of fact, I am."

"Do you have plans for lunch?"

She tilted her head slightly. "No, not really."

John asked if she'd like to join him for lunch. Beth stared at the man who looked so hopeful. "Well, I suppose—but what about church?"

"After church, of course. Would you sit with me?"

"Sure."

The pianist played a familiar hymn as they walked down the aisle of the crowded sanctuary. John stepped aside so Beth could enter a pew. She scooted next to an elderly woman and greeted her. Beth glanced sideways as she opened her bulletin. John was, without a doubt, the best-looking man in the church. His scent reminded her of cedars and their hike in the forest. He held the hymnbook as they stood to sing, *"Morning Has Broken."* She hoped she didn't smell like gasoline.

Four

J ohn watched Beth from the corner of his eye. Her dark hair accentuated her flawless complexion. He studied her slender fingers, noticing a blue sapphire ring. He was surprised by the richness of her voice as they sang hymns together. Her closeness was a great distraction, just like yesterday. He thought of their adventure in the creek and the wonderful day. When the service was over, John didn't remember much of anything Pastor Sorensen said. They were about to leave when the couple in front of them turned around. The woman smiled. "We so enjoyed hearing you two sing."

Her husband concurred, "We certainly did."

"Thank you," John said. Beth also thanked them, before leaving the sanctuary. Marla made her way over to John and wrapped her arms around him. He flushed as he backed away as graciously as possible. From the look on his face, Beth felt that he didn't appreciate forward women. Marla dashed off to greet another friend.

John turned to Beth. "Shall we go now?" The color in his face had almost returned to normal.

"Yes," she said softly.

"Where would you like to have lunch?"

Beth thought for a minute. "I don't care."

"Well, how about the Lighthouse?"

"I love that place."

"Your car or mine?" he asked.

"Let's drive separately; the restaurant isn't far from my house."

"I'll meet you there." He held the door for her as they left the building.

As she drove, Beth asked herself, *What's wrong with me? I could be sitting next to him right now, and he would have to take me back to the church.*

When they arrived, the restaurant was busy, so John went to the host to give his name. "I'm afraid we have a thirty-minute wait."

"Let's wait in my car." Beth suggested.

Beth sat behind the steering wheel of her Avalon and opened the windows for fresh air. John settled into the passenger seat and stretched out his legs. "I like your car."

"Thank you. It was a gift from my father."

"Nice gift! He must be quite a guy."

"He's a great guy, but the car was really my mother's idea. She didn't want to worry about me having car trouble." Beth sighed. "She was ill for a long time before she died."

John's eyes held compassion. "I remember you shared that in class."

"Oh, I guess I did, didn't I?"

"I could see you were grieving. I've been praying for you."

Her features softened. "You have?"

"I'm sure others in our class were praying, too."

"That's such a comfort." She stared at an elderly couple heading towards the restaurant. "And what about your parents, John?"

"They're both alive and well in North Seattle. My dad's semi-retired, and my mom keeps busy with her charities."

The couple spent the remainder of their time getting better acquainted. Beth knew John worked at a furniture store, but she didn't know he had a master's degree in business from the University of Washington, her alma mater. John said, "It's too bad we didn't meet in college."

Beth sighed. "That was such a busy time in my life. I worked part-time at the university hospital while studying. Then I helped take care of my mom at home."

John glanced at his watch. "It's been twenty-five minutes we'd better head back inside." They left the comfort of her car and entered the busy restaurant. A young host showed them to a booth overlooking the marina. The table had two place settings and a vase of daylilies.

After their server took their orders, Beth noticed John staring at her. "Can I ask you a personal question?"

"I guess so."

"Well . . . I've been wondering . . . "

"Wondering what?"

He wrinkled his brow. "Are your eyelashes real?"

"Excuse me?"

"You have the prettiest eyelashes. Are they real?"

"Of course, they're real! Fake lashes would have come off in the creek yesterday."

He chuckled. "I promise I'll behave myself the rest of the day."

Beth arched her brows. "Are we spending the day together again?"

"I sure hope so."

Beth grew serious. "Do you mind if I ask *you* a personal question?"

"Not at all."

She tilted her head. "Is your blond hair real? Or is that a toupee?"

John laughed. "Touché! Give me five."

A few minutes later their server arrived balancing two platters of halibut and fries. She placed them on the table. "Enjoy!"

The two prayed silently before beginning their meal.

"I'm starved," John said as he dug in. "I didn't eat breakfast."

Beth shot him a disapproving glance. "Donuts don't count?"

The couple bantered back and forth for the next half hour. John asked where she lived. Beth answered, "I used to live a mile from here, but I moved back home when my mother was sick. After she passed, I just couldn't leave my dad to grieve all alone." John nodded.

After lunch they strolled along the waterfront, passing various docked yachts and sailboats. Beth stopped suddenly and looked at her watch. "I should call my dad; he might be worried." She picked up her phone and pushed a button. There was no answer. "I'd better check on him; he's been having some dizzy spells lately." John looked disappointed.

"Would you like to come with me?" she asked.

"Sure."

The pair found Beth's father in his recliner watching television. "I'm sorry I forgot to call." Beth said as they entered. "I hope you didn't worry."

The silver-haired gentleman muted the ball game he was watching. "I wasn't worried, sweetheart."

"Daddy, I'd like you to meet my friend, John Beaumont. John, meet my father, Grant Delaney."

Beth's father stood to shake John's hand. "Welcome to our home."

"It's nice to meet you, sir."

Mr. Delaney smiled. "It's nice to meet you too, John." He motioned towards the sofa. "Please have a seat." Beth excused herself to make a pot of tea.

John silently admired the home Beth shared with her father. The classic architecture reminded him of his parents' home. He appreciated the furnishings and décor. Near the lake shore, branches of a weeping willow tree gently swayed. "That's quite a view you have," John said.

Mr. Delaney nodded. "Yes, we've had many good times on that lake." He settled back into his chair. "Do you work at the hospital?"

"No. I manage my family's stores, Beaumont Home Furnishings."

Mr. Delaney nodded. "Aw, yes, we've shopped in those stores over the years. They have genuinely nice things. Is your father's name Ray, by any chance?"

"Yes! Do you know him?"

Grant's eyes grew serious. "I met him several years ago."

"Where?"

"In court, while defending a client."

"You're an attorney?" John asked.

"He's retired now," Beth interrupted as she brought a tray into the living room and placed it on the coffee table. She settled next to John and began pouring tea. She handed a cup to her father.

"Thank you, dear," he said.

Beth offered a cup to John. "Would you like sugar or lemon?"

Beth's father spoke up. "John tells me his family owns the Beaumont Home Furnishing stores."

"Oh, I didn't know that," Beth said. "I knew he worked in a furniture store, but—"

Mr. Delaney looked puzzled. "How long have you known each other?"

She squeezed a slice of lemon into her cup. "About five months or so."

"Five months?"

"We're just friends, Dad; we go to the same Bible study."

"I see." He shrugged and reached for his remote control. "Let's catch the rest of this game—it's the last of the ninth and they're tied."

The three of them sipped tea while watching the game. It went into an extra inning with the Mariners losing to Arizona. "Not again!" John moaned.

Grant muttered something as he turned off the television. John's phone rang. He reached inside his jacket and withdrew his cell. "Please, excuse me; I need to take this call." He stood and left the room. Beth's father winked at his daughter. "Just a friend, huh?"

Beth smiled. "Just a friend."

John was gone for several minutes. When he returned, he stopped by a grand piano. "Wow, what a beauty. Do you play, Beth?"

"A little," she said.

"Why don't you play something for us?"

"Nah, I know that you play; I've heard you in class."

"Mind if I give it a whirl?"

"Be my guest."

John sat down and adjusted the bench. He smiled as his fingers found the keys. In seconds they produced the most beautiful sounds that old Steinway had ever made. He effortlessly played a sonata from memory. Beth recognized it as Beethoven's "Fur Elise," one of her favorites. John was enjoying himself very much. When he finished, Beth's father burst into applause. "Encore, encore!"

Beth joined her father's clapping. "That was wonderful."

John grinned. "I love this piano; the tone is superb."

"Please, play something else for us," Beth said.

"If you insist." He broke out with *"Ode to Joy"* and began singing, "Joyful, joyful we adore Thee, God of glory, Lord of love." His fingers tickled the keys as his beautiful tenor voice rang out. "Hearts unfold like flowers before Thee, opening to the sun above . . . " His fingers fairly flew over the keys as he played his own arrangement.

Beth couldn't stand it any longer. She headed for the piano. "Move over, Beethoven." John slid over as she sat next to him. "Keep playing," she said as she joined him in two-part harmony. "Melt the clouds of sin and sadness; Drive the dark of doubt away; Giver of immortal gladness; Fill us with the light of day." He glanced at her in wonder and back at the keyboard. When they'd finished the hymn, she lunged into a lively rendition of *Chopsticks*. John picked up the accompaniment, and they filled the house with jovial harmony.

John laughed. "I thought you said you played a little!"

She glanced at him. "I do." She then charged into the *"William Tell Overture."*

This was too much fun. John's spontaneous accompaniment followed as the pair entertained Mr. Delaney for the next half hour. They ended their impromptu concert by playing and singing *"This Land Is Your Land."*

Beth's father stood and applauded. "You two sound marvelous together!"

John stared at his musical companion. "You're something else, Beth. I had no idea you were so talented."

"Look who's talking," she said.

Beth invited John to stay for supper. "It's just leftovers," she warned. John offered to help as she began preparing a salad. "Sure, any guy willing to help wins points with me."

"I hope to score lots of points with you," John confessed.

"Well, you can start by slicing these tomatoes." She handed him a serrated knife. John washed his hands and began slicing the tomatoes on a cutting board. Tomato juice and seeds squirted back onto his shirt. "Oops!" he said. "Guess I'm not very good at this."

Beth grabbed a dish towel and began wiping the spot vigorously. She was so close she could smell his fragrance. "Hang on a sec." She returned a minute later with some Oxy-Clean. After a few more dabs, the spot was completely gone. "There!" She smiled in triumph."

John grinned and carefully continued slicing.

Over dinner, John learned that Mr. Delaney founded the firm, Delaney, Jones, and Davis, before he met his wife. They were married ten years before Beth came along. Their only child was born 26 years ago on Valentine's Day.

"Everyone said she was the cutest baby in the nursery with her long eyelashes," Mr. Delaney bragged.

"I bet she was," John said.

"Did she ever tell you about the time she cut off her eyelashes?"

John's eyes grew wide. "No, she didn't."

"Her mother was horrified. Beth could have put her eyes out."

Beth winced. "Well, since everybody said how long they were, I decided they must need trimming."

John stared at her eyes. "I'm glad they grew back. Did you ever do that again?"

Beth smiled. "No, my mother threatened to punish me if I did."

"She's the spitting image of her mother," Grant said wistfully.

Beth and her dad learned that John had his hands full managing five stores. With the sagging economy and stagnant housing market, furniture wasn't selling as it had in the past. John was challenged to produce some creative marketing. "We take advantage of every holiday for special sales. There are customer appreciation days, summer's end sales, anniversary sales, winter holiday sales, no interest sales, and on it goes." He further explained that much of today's imported furniture is not of the quality of former years. "Even some of the North Carolina manufacturers have moved their factories overseas."

Beth talked about her travels with her parents. She and John had visited many of the same places.

When John raved about the lasagna, Beth's father smiled. "She's taken several gourmet cooking classes."

Beth flushed. "It sounds like you're trying to auction me off."

John smiled. "Don't worry, Beth. I'm already sold on you."

Beth's father discreetly disappeared after dinner, leaving the couple alone as they tidied up the kitchen.

John looked at his watch, "It's eight o'clock. I better get going. I hope I haven't overstayed my welcome."

Beth looked into his captivating eyes. "On the contrary, I can't remember when I've had such a good time." She paused. "Except for yesterday."

"My sentiments exactly," John said as she walked him to the door. He reached out and took her hands in his. "When can I see you again?"

She wasn't sure how to answer him. She wanted to say *Let's have breakfast.* But she didn't think he appreciated forward women. "Next week?"

John gasped. "Next week? How about dinner tomorrow night?"

"I can't," she sighed. I work swing-shift. We could have lunch again."

Disappointment clouded his eyes. "I'll be tied up all day in staff meetings. How about Tuesday?" Beth shook her head. "Tuesday won't work for me. I'm covering for a coworker. What about Wednesday? I have a swimming class that morning at the community center. I'm free at 10:30."

John checked his phone calendar. "Works for me. It's a date!

I'll meet you there." He looked deep into her eyes. "Goodnight, Beth—thanks for another wonderful day."

She hated to see him go. "Goodnight. See you Wednesday."

Beth leaned against the door as she watched him walk to his car and drive away. He'd held her hands in his and said, "It's a date!"

Beth went upstairs and called her friend Carlene. After all, she had urged her to join the singles' class. Beth brought her up to date on things.

"So, you really like this guy, don't you?"

"We're just friends."

"I haven't heard you this excited about a 'friend' in ages." Carlene laughed. "When are you going to see him again?"

"We have a lunch date on Wednesday."

"I'll expect a full report."

Beth was still awake at midnight. She hoped things weren't moving too fast. But she couldn't wait to see John again. It wasn't as if she knew nothing about him. She knew where he stood on spiritual matters, and she respected his perspectives and most of his political viewpoints.

Yes, Carlene thought the Bible class might help her get over her mother's death. And as she'd said, "There's always the chance of meeting a good man."

Beth had been careful to guard her heart from intruders. She still wasn't sure if John had someone else or not. But one thing she did know, she wanted to see him again.

John found Beth waiting in front of the community center as he arrived Wednesday morning. "Don't you look pretty this morning."

Beth opened the door and slid into the passenger seat. "You're not so bad yourself," she said. He looked sharp in tan slacks, and a crisp blue shirt. His masculine scent mingled with the leather interior. The sunshine illuminated his profile. She stared at him—his blond eyelashes were as long as hers.

He squinted back at her. "Your eyes!"

"What about them?"

"They're green."

"So?"

"But . . . I thought they were light brown."

She batted her lashes. "My hazel eyes often turn color if I'm wearing green."

He glanced at her green shirt. "Fascinating! You're full of surprises."

"I like to keep you guessing."

"You're rather good at that. How long do we have?" Beth glanced at her watch. "I have to be at the hospital by two for a staff meeting."

"That gives us two and a half hours before I bring you back here."

"No need to come back, my car is at the hospital, Daddy gave me a ride." She fastened her seatbelt. "How much time do you have?"

"As long as we need." He started his engine. "I can play catch-up tonight." He eased the car into traffic and reached over to squeeze her hand. Twenty minutes later he parked in front of Antonio's restaurant. "I hope this is okay. I know you like Italian food."

Beth squirmed. The last time she'd been here was with Reid Harper. Her mind flashed back to the day he slipped a diamond ring on her finger and asked her to marry him. She shook the image from her mind.

"Beth?"

"It's nothing." She gave him a reassuring smile.

He got out and opened her door. As she stepped out, he offered his arm. She joyfully looped her arm through his.

Inside, they sat at a table with a checkered tablecloth. A wine bottle, dripping candle wax, graced the middle of the table. The owner approached. "Aw, Mr. Beaumont. So nice to see you today."

"You too, Antonio. I'd like you to meet my friend, Beth Delaney."

Beth smiled and extended her hand. Antonio grasped it firmly. "I remember you; I haven't seen you for a while." He turned to John, "A man doesn't forget a pretty girl like her."

John arched his brow. Beth blushed. "It's been far too long."

Antonio reeled off the lunch specials and sent a waiter over to get their orders. When he was out of sight, John smiled at her. "Apparently, you've made quite an impression on Antonio."

Beth shrugged. "I don't know why."

"I do," John said. "I wish we had all day like we did last weekend."

"We had fun, didn't we?"

"We sure did. You blew me away when you played the piano with me."

She giggled. "Well, I couldn't let you have all the attention. Anyway, Daddy enjoyed hearing us play."

"We'll have to entertain him again one of these days."

The couple sipped lemon water while discussing the weather, their jobs, and music. John set his glass aside. "Who's your favorite composer?"

"Living or dead?" she asked.

"Either."

She thought for a moment. "Well, living would be Andrew Lloyd Webber. Deceased, hmm, not sure."

"So, what's your favorite song?"

"That's easy, *Love Changes Everything* by Michael Ball."

"It sure does," John teased.

Beth smiled. "I have a beautiful arrangement of that song."

"I'd like to hear it sometime."

"Next time you're over I'll play it for you. So, what's your favorite song?"

He leaned back. "I have many, but I guess it would be, *You Raise Me Up* by Josh Groban."

"I love that, too." The waiter brought a basket of warm breadsticks to the table along with their salads. Beth looked up at him, "I always enjoy the salads here. They're so crisp and fresh."

John agreed. "And the bread is to die for."

After providing fresh ground pepper, the waiter left them alone. John reached for Beth's hand. "Do you mind?"

"Not at all," she said softly. They joined hands and bowed heads while he offered thanks for their meal. John didn't know it, but that impressed her more than a dozen roses. As he released her hands, he noticed a tender look in her eyes.

Beth dipped her breadstick in a mixture of olive oil and red wine vinegar. "Who's *your* favorite composer, John?"

"Boy, it's hard to choose just one," he said. "I'd have to go with Beethoven, or maybe Handel. And then again, there's always Chopin."

Beth laughed aloud. "It's not easy to narrow it down, is it?"

John shook his head. "Not when there's such a wealth of great music out there. I can't rule out Bill Gaither for his contemporary music."

Beth agreed. "He is such a gift to Christian singers and musicians."

Their waiter brought their orders. Beth eyed her eggplant parmesan rich with marinara sauce and bubbling cheese. John's ravioli looked just as tantalizing as he stuck his fork into a square and cut it in half. "Since we both love music, why don't we go to a concert together?"

"I'd like that. Did you know Josh Groban is coming to town?"

John swallowed. "Would you like to go?"

Her green eyes sparkled. "Would I? I'd love it!"

"I'll go online later and see if I can get tickets. Have you ever heard David Garrett play the violin?" John asked.

"I'm not familiar with him?" She laid her fork down and reached for her water glass.

"He's the best! He can play thirteen notes a second."

"Is that even possible?"

"That's what they say. I heard about him last summer in Europe. He mixes classical with rock. He's amazing. If he ever gets to Seattle, we must see him."

Beth nodded. "Okay, you're on!" She took a sip of water. "The church is having a talent show at the end of August."

John wiped his mouth with a napkin. "I heard something about it."

Beth got an impish gleam in her eyes. "We should do a duet."

"I'd have to think about that."

"It would be fun."

He looked dubious. "That means we'd have to practice."

"Yes, every day. Practice makes perfect." Beth surprised herself. *It's so easy to flirt with this guy.* They continued bantering back and forth, thoroughly enjoying one another's company. The food was delicious, the service excellent, and the companionship priceless.

They lingered over dessert and finished off with cappuccinos. Beth placed her hand on her stomach. "I'm afraid I've overdone it."

"Me too, with all these carbs I'll probably fall asleep at my desk." He reached for the check. "I'd better get you to the hospital."

Beth couldn't explain the joyful feelings she had in John's presence. "Thanks for a wonderful time," she said as he pulled up to the hospital.

"I hate to let you go." He reached for her hand and brought

it to his lips. A current shot through her fingers as he kissed them. He released her hand and exited the car. He walked to the other side and opened her door. They exchanged a brief hug. The kind they gave their Bible class members. "Bye, John."

He watched her walk away. When she reached the entrance, she turned and waved. He didn't drive off until she disappeared behind the glass doors, taking most of his heart with her.

Five

Beth entered the hospital locker room and kicked off her sandals. She changed into a uniform, slipped into sensible shoes, and pinned her ID badge to her smock. Still daydreaming about John, she hummed to herself on the way to the staff meeting. As she entered the meeting room, she bumped into her ex-fiancé, Reid Harper. He still had the same smile as he stared at her. "Beth, you look amazing! How've you been?"

"Fine, Reid, and you?" Beth sat at the conference table. Reid plopped down beside her.

"I can't complain." Before Reid could say anything else, the meeting began. Russell, the hospital administrator, led a discussion on budget cuts and impending layoffs. The head nurse, a no-nonsense woman in her fifties, gave a report on patient care and treatment procedures. She was desperate for more nurses. Russell promised to investigate. Beth knew it would be last on his to-do list.

On and on it droned for almost an hour, and Beth was the first to rise from her seat when they were released. Reid tried to grab her arm, but she quickly ushered herself out the door.

"Sorry, gotta run." She barely noticed the scowl on his face as she walked away.

Beth thought of John throughout the day. Their time together had flown by much too quickly. She had admired him for months, never dreaming he was interested in her. After her broken engagement she'd given up on men. Reid had broken more than her heart; he'd broken her spirit too. All she wanted was to avoid him.

Beth was tired when her shift ended. She dropped paperwork at the main desk and bid the clerk goodnight. She'd almost reached the exit when she heard someone call her name. "Beth, wait a minute!"

Her heart sank as Reid jogged up to her. "What are you doing here at this hour?" she asked.

"I worked a double shift," he said breezily. "Have coffee with me, please? We can go to the all-night diner." He had a determined look in his eyes that she knew all too well.

Beth sighed. There was no way she'd go anywhere with him outside the hospital. "Let's go to the cafeteria." She'd listen to what he had to say and send him packing. The cafeteria was deserted at this time of night. They each filled a cup of coffee and found seats at a corner table. Reid's dark eyes pleaded. "Beth, I can't get you out of my mind. I was such an idiot!"

Yes, you were! She thought.

He reached into his shirt pocket and removed a stack of photos, fanning them out on the table. Beth stared at smiling images of herself showing off her engagement ring, Reid with his arm around her, Reid kissing her. "We were great together," Reid said. "Just look how happy we were."

Thinly veiled anger flashed in Beth's eyes. "Until you cheated on me."

"I did not," he scoffed. "I was just being friendly."

Beth rolled her eyes. "I caught you kissing Susan red-handed!"

"It meant nothing; I swear."

"It was more than that, and you know it. Everyone knew about you and Susan but me."

Reid stared into her eyes. "Well, you certainly weren't giving me the time of day."

"And you refused to set a date for our wedding."

Beth sighed and rubbed her temples. "Look, there's no point in going over this again." Reid leaned forward. "I told you I had to get established financially."

"And in the meantime, fool around with another woman."

"A guy has needs, you know. Susan was only temporary."

"Isn't she still living with you?" Beth couldn't figure this guy out. Did he think she'd jump at the chance to get back together?

"Like I said, she's only temporary," Reid said.

Beth felt her cheeks flush. "In other words, you're just using her." She pushed the pictures towards him. "You know what I think?"

His dark eyes blazed. "What?"

"I think you only want what you can't have!" Beth was furious with herself for being drawn into his web again. Something she'd promised herself would never happen.

Reid's gaze intensified. "Give me another chance. I'll never let you down again."

Beth felt nothing but disgust. "Reid, I've moved on. Try to be happy with the woman you have."

"I don't want any other woman." Reid grabbed her hand. I'd marry you tomorrow if that's what you want."

Beth pulled away and stood up. "I need to go; I'm tired."

Reid's glazed eyes traveled over her body. Beth tried to get around him, but Reid edged his way between her and the doorway. He grabbed her wrist and pulled her into his arms. "Baby, you're so hot!"

Anger boiled over as Beth struggled. "Let go of me!"

His grip tightened as he planted a bruising kiss on her lips.

Beth furiously shoved him, and he fell against the wall, hitting his head.

Beth's eyes narrowed. "If you *ever* lay a hand on me or call me again, I'll file a harassment suit so fast it will make your head spin."

He rubbed the back of his head. "Spoken like a true lawyer's daughter."

She pushed the cafeteria door open and ran down the hallway. At the main desk, she cried, "Call security!" Minutes later, a former wrestler escorted Beth outside and waited until her car disappeared. Reid was nowhere to be seen.

Beth vigorously rubbed her lips with a tissue. She'd been ready to break it off when he surprised her with an engagement ring. The ring was pretty, and she'd always dreamed of being married and having a family. That's when his demands began to take the relationship to the next level, a step she was saving for marriage. The more she resisted, the more determined he became. Then his calls stopped altogether. Three days later, she found Reid and Susan locked in an embrace. One of her nursing friends informed her that Susan had moved in with Reid.

She trembled as she recalled how he stalked her after their broken engagement. He'd called at all hours of the night and day and even showed up at her apartment. She'd changed her cell phone number and began working swing shift to avoid him. It was only after she moved back home and threatened to get a restraining order that he finally left her alone. Beth prayed he wouldn't begin stalking her again.

The next day, John was buried in paperwork following a board meeting. It was official; they'd agreed to close one or two of their stores. Furniture sales were plummeting, and the overhead was killing them. John had hoped to prevent any closures, but even the productive stores were in a slump. The only things selling were mattress sets and recliners. Blowout sales with deferred payments and no-interest loans helped, but sales were nothing compared to the housing boom era. New houses meant new furniture.

John hated to be the bearer of bad news. Giving loyal employees pink slips was something he dreaded. He'd prayed for wisdom and direction, but couldn't put it off any longer. He had hoped to find some of the employees other opportunities within the company, but the truth was that most would simply be out of a job.

The only bright spot in his day was the thought of seeing Beth again. But that was next to impossible, as she was working double shifts to cover for a coworker. He hoped, at least, that things were going better for her.

In the following days, Beth's encounter with Reid left her emotions in turmoil. She avoided him at work until the day she spotted him in the corridor. When he saw her, he abruptly ducked into the nearest room. Beth hoped he'd finally gotten the message.

Reid had been so charming at first, though intensely serious. After their engagement, he said things that scared her. Once they'd argued while he was driving, and he floored the gas pedal, causing the car to veer into and out of a shallow ditch. She'd prayed frantically the whole way home. After he dropped her off, she said they should stop seeing each other. The next day, he sent a huge bouquet with a card.

Her mother had been right. Beth thought about one of their last conversations. Her mother's eyes pleaded. "He's not the one, Beth—he'll break your heart. God has someone special for you, honey. But trust me, it's not Reid."

Could it be that God had someone wonderful for her? Beth found herself sorely missing John. They talked on the phone and sent texts. He asked her to go to a Mariners game on Saturday, but she had to work. They couldn't spend Sunday together because she was still covering for her coworker. The following week was just as crazy. Their schedules clashed terribly. Since her coworker would be returning on Saturday, at least she'd have the following Sunday free.

Sunday morning, Beth awoke with John on her mind. She dressed in fitted slacks with a matching jacket and a blouse with a touch of bling. She wore her hair down again, sensing John liked it that way, and used her favorite perfume.

Beth often invited her father to attend church with her, but he insisted that he didn't need church. He was a good man and didn't want some preacher pointing out his shortcomings. He was watching television when the doorbell rang.

"I'll get it!" Beth said. She opened the door and there he stood. John wore gray slacks, a white shirt, and a leather jacket. He handed her a box of chocolates.

Beth's eyes lit up. "Thank you. You surely know the way to a woman's heart."

John matched her smile. "You look beautiful this morning."

She blushed. "So do you. I mean . . . Well, you look nice. Please, come in."

John followed her into the living room. "I'll be right back," she promised as she disappeared down the hallway.

John walked over to greet Beth's father with a handshake. "Please, don't get up."

Grant flashed a bright smile. "Are you taking my girl away for the day again?"

"I certainly hope so," John said.

"I enjoyed hearing you two play the piano the last time you were here. Maybe we can have another performance sometime."

"I'm sure we will," John said. "Beth thinks we should enter the church talent show."

"Well! I might even go to church for something like that," Mr. Delaney said.

Beth returned with her purse and Bible. She kissed her father's cheek. "Bye."

He patted her hand. "Have a nice day, honey."

John held the door as she brushed past him. It was beginning to rain. When they got in the car, she said, "Thanks for picking me up."

"It's my pleasure! This way, I have you all to myself." She was thinking much the same thing. John faced her. "I've sure missed you."

"I've missed you, too. I'm so glad I don't have any more double shifts. How are things with your work?"

"I'm overwhelmed with decisions," John admitted. "The last thing I want to do is tell someone they no longer have a job."

"I'm sorry, it must be tough. I'll be praying for you."

"Thanks, that means a lot." The rain intensified and the windshield wipers sped up. A car skidded in front of them. John slammed on his brakes. Beth lurched forward and he shielded her with his arm and honked his horn. "Crazy idiot!" They spent the rest of the ride discussing the weird drivers out there.

John let Beth out in front of the church before parking his car. She waited just inside the foyer. Beautiful music came from the sanctuary. John was wet when he entered a few minutes later. Pastor Phil greeted them at the fireside room. "We missed you last week, Beth."

"Good morning, Phil. Too much overtime."

"Glad you're back."

Beth headed for the coffee bar, while John put his Bible on

one of the chairs next to him. Marla plunked herself into the seat next to his. "Hi there!"

John politely nodded. "Good morning, Marla." He watched Beth as she returned with her coffee in one hand and her purse over her shoulder. "Sit here beside me," he said as he reached for her coffee cup.

"Sure," Beth smiled. When she settled next to him, he gave her the cup. "You really need an assistant when you get coffee—you know?"

"Are you applying for the job?" she asked before gently blowing on her cup.

"As a matter of fact, I am."

She tipped her head sideways. "You're hired. When can you start?"

He grinned. "Immediately!"

"It doesn't pay much."

John leaned closer. "I'm willing to settle for the perks. No pun intended."

Marla had heard enough. She rolled her eyes and grimaced. Her sigh went unnoticed as she moved to a chair across the room.

The following hour was filled with thought-provoking discussion. After class, Phil cornered John about filling in for him next week.

Janet drew Beth aside. She suppressed a smile. "It looks like I've lost my best friend."

Beth whispered in her ear. "We're going to lunch again."

"I'm happy for both of you." Janet gave her a quick hug. "John's a great guy." Beth promised to call her during the week. John joined Beth's side and greeted Janet. They exchanged pleasantries before she went on her way. John and Beth headed for the sanctuary to find seats before the church filled up.

Mindy and Len were sitting in front of them. They turned around.

"Hi again, you two," Len said.

"I put your jeans in your car," John said. "I'm sorry I didn't get them to you sooner. Thanks for saving my dignity."

"Glad to help out, even if they were a bit short."

Mindy giggled before they turned around.

The congregation stood for the opening hymn. John and Beth shared a hymnal as their voices blended beautifully. John reached for Beth's hand. It felt much cooler and softer than his. He placed his other hand on top of their joined hands. Their eyes locked.

Long after the song ended, John continued holding Beth's hand. They laced fingers as he gently ran his thumb over hers. That simple act sent shivers down her back. After the sermon, they stood to sing the closing hymn, "How Great Thou Art." Their voices soared as they harmonized. Beth brushed tears from her eyes.

Mindy and Len turned around; Len spoke first. "Wow, you two sound awesome together. I sure hope you're registered for the talent show."

"Where do we sign up?" John asked.

"You're talking to the main man. I'll put you down," Len promised.

After the service, Beth noticed Carlene and her husband across the crowd. She turned to John. "Do you know the Ensors?"

"No."

"I didn't think so. Come on, I'll introduce you."

They wove their way across the foyer where Beth made the introductions. Carlene's husband Richard shook John's hand. Carlene looked him over. "So, you're the guy that has Beth so shook-up!"

Beth shot Carlene an eyeroll. Richard looked amused. The couples chatted a few minutes before the Ensor's excused themselves to get their kids from the nursery.

John gently took Beth's elbow and whispered, "Shall we go now?"

When they reached the quiet of John's car, he faced her. "Have you been all shook-up over me?"

She lowered her head. How was she supposed to answer a question like that?

"I'm sorry Beth, it was a stupid question. If the truth be known, I'm the one who's all shook-up."

Beth stared. "You are?"

John glanced at the car ceiling and back at her. "Yes, I can't eat, I can't sleep. All I think about is you."

Beth touched his arm. "I have the same problem. I think of you first thing in the morning and the last thing at night."

He gently placed his hand under her trembling chin and leaned towards her. Beth closed her eyes as his warm lips met hers. Her heart swelled as she wrapped her arms around his neck and returned his kiss. The fragrance of his aftershave was intoxicating as their gentle kiss lingered. She felt a surge of excitement as his arms tightened, and the kiss intensified. She wanted the moment to last for eternity. He stroked her hair while holding her as close as he could over the console. His lips traveled to her cheek. A sigh of contentment followed. "I've wanted to do that for a long time."

She gently caressed his cheek. "I'm glad you finally did."

John's voice grew hoarse. "Beth, I'm falling in love with you." He kissed her again. Her heart was beating so hard she was sure he could hear it. A car's horn honked. They needed to move on. Church members were coming to their cars. He gently released her. "I made brunch reservations for us."

He held her hand as they drove across town to the yacht club. Strains of beautiful piano music filled the car. They stayed silent as the memory of their kiss bridged any gap between them. Just being next to each other was enough for now.

When the couple arrived and were seated at a table facing

the marina, John reached for her hand again. "These past two weeks have been torture. I've missed you so much."

"I feel the same way. No more overtime for me!"

He kissed her hand.

A waiter approached to take their orders. They decided to try the buffet. They were served coffee and juice and told to go through the line. They stood before a counter featuring ham, prime rib, turkey, fish, meatballs, fruit, and assorted salads. Another section featured platters of seafood.

When they returned to the table, John reached for her hand and prayed over their food. After a few minutes, he pointed out boats in the harbor. "Do you ever go sailing?"

"No."

"I'll take you out someday, if you'd like."

"So, you have a boat?"

"No, but I could rent one."

"My dad has a 24-foot ski boat in the garage."

"I love waterskiing," John said. "Let's do it sometime!"

They tasted delicacies until they were stuffed. "If we keep eating like this, I'll need a new wardrobe," Beth said.

"Me too, next week we'll go to a juice bar."

Beth laughed. "Good idea."

John reached inside his jacket. "Look what I have."

Beth clapped her hands as she saw the small slips of paper. "You got tickets to Josh Groban! I'm so excited!"

His blue eyes twinkled. "They're good ones, too, in the third row."

She reached for his hand. "I can hardly wait, thank you so much."

Outside, the air felt cooler. They drove to the park and walked along trails skirting the lake. "I still laugh when I think about our fall in the creek," John said.

Beth smiled. "I love hiking. Weren't those falls beautiful?"

"I wanted to take you in my arms then," he confessed.

She tipped her head shyly. "I wasn't sure what you'd think of me if I let you kiss me."

John laughed as he tilted her chin upwards. "Is that why you threw snow at me?" She looked contrite. He drew her into his arms. "I'd have thought you were wonderful, just like I do right now." He gently kissed her. It started to drizzle again. They joined hands and dashed to the car. John opened the door for her and ran to the other side. Inside the car he gently ran his fingers through her damp curls. "What is it with us and water?" He kissed her forehead. She closed her eyes and quickly raised her head so that his lips met hers again. His kiss awakened longing from deep within. He sighed as he gently released her. "We better get going."

Beth struggled to compose herself. "I think you're right."

"Would you like to see where I live?" John asked. She looked dubious. John cleared his throat. "From the outside, of course."

She thought for a moment. "Well . . . okay."

A flock of seagulls screamed overhead as they approached John's place. He pointed towards the bay, "I live in the condos overlooking the water."

"Which one is yours?"

"It's the far left one on top." Sunlight pierced through clouds, illuminating the green metal roof. He smiled. "If you don't mind, let me show you the library. It's over by the club-house." He ushered her to the common area and up the stairs to a loft overlooking the water. Sofas, loveseats, and snack tables filled the room. John raised his palm. "There's rarely ever anybody up here."

"It's quite nice," Beth said. They settled on a sofa. She glanced at the bookcases behind them. "Look, there's a Bible on the bottom shelf."

John nodded, "That was placed there by Sam Steadman, he's a Gideon."

"They put Bibles in hotel rooms, don't they?" Beth asked.

"Yes. My dad's a Gideon. That's how he found the Lord—in a hotel room."

"Really?"

"Yeah, he was going through a rough time when he was a young man. I don't know the details, but on a business trip he opened the Gideon Bible and turned to Psalms. It blessed him tremendously."

Beth reached for his hand. "What about your faith journey?"

John looked pensive. "I went to church with my family. I was a happy-go-lucky kid with simple faith. I kept busy with music lessons and Little League sports. I knew I belonged to Jesus."

Beth smiled. "There's nothing like the faith of a child."

"That's not the end of the story." He sighed. "I played varsity football in high school, but I got a big head. My teammates and I celebrated our victories with wild parties. If we lost, we'd console ourselves with beer. It was football, girls, and booze. I quit going to church altogether." Sadness clouded his eyes. "On the night of my eighteenth birthday, a bunch of us were out joyriding and got pulled over. The driver had been drinking and the cop found marijuana in the car. To tell the truth, I was stoned. We all ended up in jail for the night. It was a wake-up call."

"You were a prodigal."

"That's one way to put it. My mom was heartbroken, and my dad . . . well, I've never seen him so angry. I was grounded big time. Worst of all, my buddies and I were kicked off the football team."

Beth's eyes held compassion, "That must have been hard."

"Yeah. But thanks to a good lawyer, we got off with no jail time and six months' probation."

Beth gently touched his hand. "That's what lawyers are for."

John continued, "I hate to think what I put my folks through. I was discouraged and belligerent. I didn't care about anything. Mom had the whole church praying for me. My parents insisted

I attend church with them. It was that or no car. So, I tagged along. The youth pastor started bugging me to come to functions. I told him to 'get off my back.'"

"Wow."

"Yeah, I was a jerk. But one Sunday morning, he gave his testimony. It sounded like he was speaking directly to me."

Beth leaned back to stretch her legs. "I know that feeling."

"I decided to give the youth group a try." He raised his index finger. "I fully intended to reject the whole lot of them. But surprisingly, I found a bunch of kids, some confused like me, but others with powerful testimonies. I figured if they could overcome their troubles, maybe I could, too."

"Was that the 'aha' moment?"

"Actually, it was a church mission trip to Mexico to help fix up an orphanage. Those poor kids lived in terrible poverty, yet they had such joy in their faith. Several months later, I dedicated my life to Christ. I can't explain the difference it made. I even thought about becoming a pastor."

Beth interrupted, "You considered going into ministry?"

"Yes. I felt a call on my life that I still can't shake." He paused. "Anyway, I buckled down in school and made it into college by the skin of my teeth. I hit the books and surprised everyone, including myself, by making the Dean's List my first quarter. I majored in business and minored in philosophy and music. I even played piano for a worship team."

Beth squeezed his hand. John placed his other hand over hers. "I've rambled on long enough. What about you?" Three women entered the library and sat at a game table. One opened her laptop computer.

"Let's go to your car," Beth suggested.

John fed a vending machine, and two bottles of water dropped down. He handed one to Beth. Outside, it felt fresh and clean, and the ground was wet. Safely inside the interior of John's car, she began. "My parents didn't attend church. Our

Sundays were spent reading the papers, going to brunch with friends, and enjoying boating on the lake. That's about the only time we ever saw Daddy. He worked such long hours during the week."

"Sounds like my dad, but we did go to church on Sunday," John said.

Beth took a sip of water. "I enjoyed school and taking piano lessons. One summer, a neighbor invited me to Bible school. At first, I didn't want to go—I thought it would be boring. But I must tell you, John, I loved it! We had so much fun, and I learned about God's love for me. I started going to Sunday school, too. But it was sporadic until our teacher showed a movie that blew me away. As a result, I became rather zealous."

John interrupted. "What movie?"

"China Cry."

"Great film!"

"Anyway, I began playing the piano and directing a youth choir. My parents came to watch me, but never joined the church. Daddy didn't feel the need to make it a habit."

John held her hand as she continued. "When I was a teenager, we traveled abroad and toured art museums and old churches. I was fascinated by religious art and considered majoring in art history in college. But my lifelong dream was to be a nurse. I was thrilled when I was accepted to nursing school." Beth drew a deep breath. "After graduation, I worked in emergency rooms and saw things that blew my mind. I had so many questions about life and death. As I studied my Bible, it struck me how deeply God loves me and how there's nothing I need to do to earn that love. The greatest surprise was that I came to love Him, too." She searched John's eyes. "He's never let me down. He's given me strength when I was weak and direction when I didn't know which way to turn."

John squeezed her hand. "He's been there for me too, and I want to be there for Him. I'm still praying about ministry. I just can't shake this call. That's one of the reasons I joined the Bible study. Phil asked me to fill in for him on a regular basis."

Beth smiled. "I love it when you teach. You have a way of making things easy to understand."

"Thank you for the encouragement. I enjoy playing the piano, too. Music has always been a great comfort to me.'

"I know what you mean."

"You're a gifted pianist, Beth."

She stroked his hand and looked him in the eyes. "We're good together."

He laughed. "In more ways than one!"

"So why didn't you go into ministry?"

John leaned back. "Like my father and grandfather, I'm expected to take over the family business. I've worked for my dad since I was nine, doing everything from sweeping the warehouse to signing paychecks. After graduation, I focused on my career and did my best to upgrade the whole operation. I was trying to prove something." John took a sip of his water. "But God had a different call on my life. I was trying to find a way to convince my family when I met Alice." He paused. "You probably don't want to hear all this."

"Oh, but I do." Beth's eyes widened with curiosity.

"We met at a wedding, I was a groomsman, and she was a bridesmaid. I was infatuated with her even though we had nothing in common. She said she was a Christian, but we certainly didn't see eye-to-eye. Still, I fell for her, and we even discussed marriage. But she made it clear that she wanted nothing to do with being a pastor's wife. She thought it was ridiculous to consider giving up a lucrative career for the church. She eventually even resented my going to church."

"That must have been hard."

John sighed. "The thing is, I compromised. I moved in with Alice and we shared expenses. Before long, it became too much of an effort to attend church. The bottom line is that I knew as long as she was in my life, I'd never be free to serve God. Breaking up was a painful decision, but I knew it was the right one."

Beth felt his remorse. "It takes a lot of courage to walk away."

He stared into her eyes. "I begged God to help me, and He did. I've known greater peace since then and grown closer to the Lord."

"How long ago was that?"

"A little over three years, just before I bought my condo. I haven't dated for a long time."

Beth raised her brows. "Oh really?"

His eyes met her eyes. "Don't you believe me?"

"I'm not sure."

"Why wouldn't you?"

Color flooded her cheeks. *Had she caught him in a lie?* "Well," she stared at her lap.

He tipped her chin upwards. "Tell me."

Beth was losing patience as she struggled to answer his question. "I've seen you with the same woman more than once."

"Where?"

She blushed. "Once in a grocery store, and another time at Mary's Family Restaurant."

He frowned as he studied her unyielding face. "What did she look like?"

Beth was losing patience. "She was a beautiful blonde."

John reached into his jacket pocket for his phone and scrolled through various photos. He held one in front of her. "Is this the woman you saw?"

Beth studied the photo. "Yes, that looks just like her."

John chuckled. "This is Tiffany!"

"And just who is Tiffany?"

"I confess, she's a woman I love." A grin brought out his dimple. "She's my sister."

Now the color in Beth's cheeks flushed with embarrassment. "Your sister!"

"Yes, she was visiting from Oregon. We were planning our parents' 40th wedding anniversary surprise."

Beth shook her head. "I'm sorry. You must think I'm terrible."

"I don't think any such thing. I might have come to the same conclusion if I'd seen you with another guy."

"Your sister is very pretty."

"True. But so are you."

"Can you forgive me?"

He kissed her hand. "Of course."

"So, you haven't dated since Alice?"

"No. I've been seeking God's will for my life. I've considered remaining single if that's what He wants."

Beth sighed. "I've been doing the same thing."

John smiled. "I thought so."

"I was engaged before my mother died, but Reid was all wrong for me. He sometimes went to church to placate me, but afterwards he'd belittle it. I kept hoping he'd change, but he didn't."

"He sounds a bit like Alice," John said.

Beth wrung her hands. "He pressured me to move in with him, which I refused to do." She looked directly into John's eyes. "I don't believe in fooling around before marriage."

John's gaze held. "I respect that."

"Anyway, to make a long story short, I caught him cheating on me and ended our relationship."

John gently squeezed her hand. "He must have been an idiot."

"At the time I was devastated, but I think he actually did me a big favor."

"Did he work at the hospital?" John asked.

"Yes, he still does."

"Is he a doctor?"

"No, he's studying nursing."

"Man, I'm glad you didn't marry him."

"Me too. After Mom's death, Daddy was lost without her. I helped sort out her estate. Even though he's a lawyer, things were complicated." A tear ran down her cheek.

John squeezed her hand. "I'm so glad we found each other." He smiled. "Look, the sun's coming out."

They spent the remainder of the day getting better acquainted and enjoying each other's company. They finally parked in her driveway around 8 p.m. "I hate to let you go." John said. "I feel so complete when I'm with you."

Beth sighed. "I feel the same way. It stays light so long this time of the year. It seems way too early to call it a day."

He walked her to the covered porch. At her door, he turned and drew her close. His lips found hers in an impassioned kiss. Warmth spread throughout her being like liquid gold. She clung to him as he tenderly stroked her hair. They stood locked in one another's arms, not wanting to break the embrace. "You belong in my arms," he whispered.

She snuggled closer. "I think you're right."

The front door opened. Beth's father poked his head out. "I thought I heard voices out here. Come on in, you two."

John's fair skin flushed. "Good evening, Mr. Delaney. I was just leaving."

"Nonsense, I won't hear of it! It's still early, come in and visit awhile."

Beth tugged at his hand. "Sure, John, come on in."

The couple played the piano and shared cups of tea. Grant challenged them to a game of cards. John was apologetic. "I really do have to get going; I have an early morning meeting. Maybe next time."

Beth walked him to the door, and they stepped outside. "Shall we say goodnight again?"

John's eyes softened. "Like we did before?"

Beth smiled, "Mm hm . . . "

He drew her into his arms. Again, his woodsy scent and the taste of his warm kisses sent her head spinning. His lips moved to her cheeks in a trail of baby kisses. She felt the coarseness of the day's growth of beard and forgot to breathe. When he finally released her, he sighed. "I could really get used to this."

Beth caressed his cheek. "So could I." She pulled away, an idea forming in her head. "How would you feel about a picnic? For lunch tomorrow?"

John's smile widened. "That sounds amazing." He traced the outline of her face with his finger. "Goodnight, beautiful." She hugged his neck one more time. "Goodnight."

Beth wrapped her arms around herself as she watched him go to his car and drive away.

She entered the house and smiled at her dad as he walked towards her. "He's a nice guy, Beth. I like him."

"Me too, Daddy." She blushed.

He ruffled her hair. "No kidding!"

Beth picked up their teacups and took them to the kitchen before going upstairs and climbing into bed. The memory of John's kisses still lingered on her lips.

Six

In Beth's dream, she couldn't find the furniture store. She'd forgotten the lunch and was trying to read a map. When she finally got there, Marla stood next to John on the street corner.

It was a relief when her phone buzzed and jolted her awake. Her supervisor asked if she'd come to work early to cover for a coworker who called in sick. Beth had never turned her boss down before, but she did today. "I'm sorry, Kay, but I have an appointment."

She looked out the window at overcast skies. A cool breeze ruffled the curtains. She told herself that surely the sun would break through any minute. Before breakfast, Beth chopped a variety of vegetables for a chef's salad complete with thin slices of broiled rib steak and gourmet dressing. A jug of iced tea and two generous slices of lemon cake went into the picnic basket.

After showering and dressing, she admired her figure in the mirror. Though she was slender, she filled out a sweater nicely. She sprayed perfume into the air and walked through the mist.

Downstairs, Beth grabbed her jacket and kissed her father

goodbye. "There's salad and lemon cake in the refrigerator for lunch."

"Better take an umbrella; we're supposed to get rain," Grant warned.

Beth located the furniture store with no problems. A pleasant aroma of leather, fragrant wood, and fabric greeted her. She walked past a luxurious sofa and a matching loveseat with mahogany end tables. A nice-looking gentleman approached. "Can I help you find something?"

"The way to John's office would be nice."

He grinned. "You must be Beth; I'm John's cousin, Bill."

Beth smiled and extended her hand. "Yes, I'm Beth. It's nice to meet you." He ushered her into John's office and shut the door. John stood by a large desk talking on the phone. He smiled and motioned for her to take a seat. She removed her jacket and settled into a burgundy leather chair. John's desk was covered with catalogs and various papers, along with a laptop computer.

A series of portraits dominated one wall. Five handsome men smiled from silver frames, John grinning from the last one. Another wall displayed an assortment of framed certificates and awards.

She watched a robin sitting on the window ledge as John finished his conversation. "I know, Roger, but there's not much I can do about it. I'll try, but I can't promise anything. Check back tomorrow, okay?" After he hung up, John walked over to her chair. "I'm sorry I wasn't out front to meet you."

"That's okay. This way I get to see your office."

He stepped back. "You look ravishing, and your eyes . . . they're green again."

"And yours are still blue." A clap of thunder startled Beth, and she grasped his shoulder. He drew her close and stroked her hair, gently kissing the top of her fragrant head. "I love you, Beth."

She searched his eyes. "I love you, too." He kissed her again, slowly savoring the moment. Beth kissed his cheeks, his lips, and his cheeks again. "I really do love you, John."

He held her tightly. "I'm crazy about you." They clung to one another while lightning flashed around them. John tightened his grip as another clap of thunder roared. She snuggled closer, feeling safe in his embrace.

"So, what are we going to do about it?"

She stiffened. "Do about what?"

His husky voice trembled with passion. "Marry me, Beth."

Logic told Beth to wait, but her heart spurred her to action. She caressed his cheek. "I'd love to marry you."

"Did I just hear you agree to marry me?"

"Yes, I think you did."

He flushed. "I'd better do this properly." He dropped to one knee. "Beth Delaney, will you do me the honor of becoming my wife?"

She knelt to face him. "Yes, yes, yes. Absolutely yes!" She wrapped her arms around his neck.

He drew her closer, and they both toppled to the floor. Amidst peals of laughter, he drew her into his lap and held her while countless thoughts swirled in his brain. "Do you realize what we've just done?"

"We're engaged," Beth said, giggling with disbelief.

John threw up his hands. "I don't even have a ring."

She kissed his cheek. "I don't care; you can give me a wedding band."

"I didn't plan on proposing quite so soon." He ran his fingers through her silky hair. "You green-eyed temptress, you beguiled me!"

Beth laughed. "And we haven't had our picnic yet. I thought we could go to the lake, but . . . " They gazed out the window as angry torrents of rain pelted the glass.

"We'll have our picnic here," John said. "Let's get the food." He grabbed an umbrella near the entrance before they dashed out into the pouring rain. John carried the basket over his arm. As they entered the store, he reached for her hand and faced the staff. "I'd like you to meet my fiancée, Beth Delaney."

Bill looked surprised. "Your fiancée?"

John nodded. "That's what I said."

Bill smiled and shook John's hand. "Congratulations, you sly old fox! Where have you been hiding this delightful lady, anyway?"

"Far away from you—that's for sure. We're having lunch in my office, so please hold any calls."

Behind closed doors, they removed their coats and John gave her another hug. He shut his computer and placed it on a nearby shelf. Beth noticed a small, framed picture on his desk. She picked it up. "This is so cute."

John put his arm around her. "That's the one Len took of us at the picnic table. On the hike, remember?"

She handed it to him. "I'd like a copy." John nodded, and Beth removed a tablecloth from the basket and spread it across the desk. The overhead lights flickered. John opened the basket and looked inside. "Something smells good!" He rubbed his hands together in anticipation.

The lights dimmed again while Beth began setting out paper plates and cups. After the third flicker, the lights went out completely, leaving the room in dim shadows. Dark clouds poured forth their wrath outside the windows.

"Wait here," John said as he left the office. He dismissed the staff and told them to lock up. Beth stared out rain-streaked windows. She watched puddles morph into small lakes. John returned minutes later bearing a silver candelabra. He placed it on the desk and lit the candles. "This should help." The soft glow of candlelight magically transformed their corner of the world.

Beth clasped her hands. "How romantic!"

Thunder cracked off in the distance as Beth placed silverware on the desk. John walked up behind her and wrapped his arms around her. He kissed the side of her cheek. Beth turned her flushed face towards him. "Honey, we'd better eat our lunch."

John sighed and let her go. She dished up plates of salad and added strips of rare beef before drizzling the dressing. Next, she set out crunchy rolls with butter and two cloth napkins. "Everything is ready."

John placed another chair by the desk, and they sat down. He reached for her hands, "I'd like to ask the blessing."

She nodded. "Of course."

He began. "Dear Lord, thank you for this wonderful day, this delicious lunch, and for my beautiful fiancée. Please bless our food and our lives, and guide and direct our path. Help us to follow you all the days of our journey together. In Jesus' name, amen."

Beth squeezed his hands. "And Lord, thank you for bringing John into my life. Help me to bring him much happiness and love. Show us Your will for our future as we follow You, step by step. Amen."

John kissed her hand. They leisurely enjoyed their candle-light picnic, exchanging smiles and longing looks while savoring their meal. John raved about her salad. "You are a great cook."

"Technically, I didn't cook the salad."

He cupped her face in his hands. "Well, you're a great salad chef then. And I'm a blessed man to have you."

The candles proved to be a special touch as they enjoyed their first meal as an engaged couple. They were safe together while the storm raged outside.

When they finished their dessert, John helped her clear the desk. Beth sighed. "I'd better get going."

John insisted upon driving Beth to the hospital in the rainstorm, and she didn't protest. She felt that he would always be protective of her. His actions made her feel secure and cherished. He parked at the entrance and opened the door for her.

He drew her close as he tenderly kissed her goodbye. "I'll see you later, sweetheart. I love you."

"I love you, too. Drive carefully." As she walked away, she turned and blew kisses at him. He pretended to catch each one with his fist and place them on his lips.

Beth could barely concentrate at work. She felt John's arms around her as the memory of his kisses lingered. She was going to become his wife!

By the time they met after work, the storm had let up considerably. He found her waiting in the lobby, still in her uniform. He stepped back to read her badge. "Elizabeth C. Delaney, RN." John smiled, "What does your middle initial stand for?"

"Christina, after my mother."

"That's a beautiful name, Elizabeth Christina Delaney, soon to be Beaumont." She stared at him. John tipped his head. "You do intend to take my last name, don't you?"

She reached for his hand. "Yes, honey, I shall be known by everyone as Beth Beaumont."

When Beth arrived home her father was asleep in his recliner. She covered him with a blanket and turned off the television. She went upstairs and called John. They agreed to tell her dad their news in the morning before they went shopping for a ring.

Beth answered the doorbell bright and early. Her beloved stood there holding a bouquet of red roses. She welcomed him with open arms and a kiss. "Where on earth did you find roses at this time of day?"

John winked. "I have my sources." Something about his winks made her weak in the knees. She took the flowers and put them in a vase. Her father was enjoying a bagel and a cup of coffee at the breakfast table. "Good morning, John. It's kind of early for a date, isn't it?"

Beth interrupted. "Daddy, we have some exciting news to share."

Grant Delaney set his mug down. "What is it?"

Beth slid her arm across John's back. "John asked me to marry him, and I said yes."

Beth's father furrowed his brows. "How long did you say you've known each other?"

Beth looked adoringly at John. "Six months now."

John spoke up. "Perhaps I should have consulted you first. But things all happened so fast."

Grant rose from his chair and came towards them. He stared long and hard at the man standing before him. "John, promise me one thing."

"Anything."

"That you'll always be good to my baby girl."

"You've got my word. I'll treasure her."

Grant hugged his daughter and kissed her cheek. He turned to his future son-in-law. "I guess congratulations are in order." They shook hands and Grant patted John's back. "You're one lucky fellow!"

"Oh, I'm well aware of that," John said as he wrapped his arm around Beth's shoulder. "And another thing. We'll keep you entertained on the piano."

"I'll look forward to that! And maybe some grandchildren?"

"There will be plenty of time for that later," Beth said as they made their way towards the door.

After breakfast at a local café, the couple headed for Redick's Jewelers, a store with a longstanding reputation for high-quality jewelry. An elderly gentleman offered to help them. John smiled. "We're here to find an engagement ring. I want something special for my fiancée."

The clerk said he'd worked there for years and knew

diamonds well. The couple spent the next half hour trying sparkling rings on Beth's finger. Eventually, they narrowed it down to two. Beth couldn't make up her mind. She wandered to another counter where her breath caught at the sight of a spectacular solitaire in an anniversary collection. Never one to miss a cue, the jeweler asked, "Would the lady like to try this one?" He reached inside the case, withdrew a velvet box, and placed it on the glass countertop. Beth couldn't find her voice.

John reached for the ring. "Yes, the lady *would* like to try this one." He examined the round diamond set in platinum before placing the ring on Beth's finger. She stared at it, turning her hand from side to side to admire the way the diamond reflected light. Her smile said it all. John studied her expression. "Is this the one?"

She fought tears and nodded. As she turned the ring back and forth on her finger, she spotted the price tag. She blushed as she gently removed the ring and handed it to the jeweler. "Maybe not."

John frowned. "What's the matter? I thought you love it."

"Oh, I do! But John, it's far too expensive."

"Says who?"

"Well—I'd never expect . . . No, it's not practical."

John placed his hands on her shoulders and looked her in the eyes. "Sweetheart, listen to me. This isn't the time to be practical. I plan on buying one engagement ring in my life, and it's going to be a good one."

The jeweler stood by quietly holding the ring in his open palm. John reached for it, removed the price tag, and placed it back on her finger. "I love you, Beth."

Her huge hazel eyes glistened as she stared up at him. He turned to the jeweler. "We'll take it." Since the ring fit perfectly, it didn't need to be sized.

The jeweler wrote a receipt with a lifetime warranty. John signed the slip while Beth stared at the stunning diamond on her finger. She turned to the jeweler, "Please show us the groom's band." He graciously handed the platinum band to Beth. She took John's left hand in hers. The ring went about halfway up his finger. "It will definitely have to be sized."

John agreed. "Put this on the bill too," he said as he handed the ring to the jeweler.

Beth crossed her arms. "This goes on my credit card."

John's frown told her otherwise. "No, it doesn't. I'll pay for it."

The jeweler patiently stood there letting them work things out. Beth eyes pleaded. "Please, John, I really want to do this."

"But honey, it's too . . . "

"Says who?" She had an expression that let him know he'd better comply; a look he would come to know well in the future.

The jeweler measured John's finger and wrote up the order. Beth slid her credit card across the counter. After signing the receipt and thanking the jeweler, the happy couple left the store arm in arm. They walked to a coffee shop where they visited until it was time for Beth to go to work. John drove her to the hospital and promised he'd return later to take her home. They kissed goodbye before she exited the car. "I'll see you later, sweetheart."

News spread quickly as Beth proudly showed off her beautiful ring. Most of her coworkers were happy for her, but not everyone rejoiced at the news. Reid watched her from a distance.

Beth spent the rest of the day in a state of bliss, passing her happiness to all she met. Near the end of her shift, she still felt energetic. When John came to get her, Beth took him by the hand. "Come and meet my co-workers." John cheerfully greeted each one, trying to remember names. After the introductions, he draped his arm across Beth's shoulders as they walked out the door. "Are you hungry?"

"I'm starved. I haven't eaten since breakfast."

"What sounds good to you?"

Beth didn't hesitate. "Chinese food."

"I know just the place. It's a hole in the wall, but the best food you've ever tasted."

So, they ate Chow Mein with chopsticks close to midnight. Beth sipped tea while admiring her ring. "I love it, and the wonderful guy who gave it to me." She cracked open a fortune cookie and read the slip of paper. "You will have a long and prosperous life." She showed it to John. "Do you think God speaks through fortune cookies?"

He smiled, "God speaks to us any way He can get our attention. What do you think?"

"I'm not sure. It's just fun to read them. What does yours say?"

He pretended to read. "You are in love with a beautiful woman."

Beth reached for it. "Let me see that." She shook her head. "Time is on your side."

John drove Beth home and walked her to the door. Their bodies meshed as their eager lips connected. Flames of desire flickered as they clung to one another. John was breathless. "Beth?"

"Yes."

"We better set a date for our wedding. I don't want to wait a long time."

"Neither do I. Let's call Pastor Sorensen this week."

John and Beth sat across from their senior pastor. He leaned back in his chair and folded his fingers together. "So, you two want to get married?"

"Yes, as soon as possible," John said.

The pastor looked from one to the other. "Before I marry a

couple, I strongly recommend a series of premarital counseling sessions."

John shifted uncomfortably. "We don't need counseling, do we? I mean—it's not like we're a couple of teenagers."

Pastor Sorensen pursed his lips. "John, right now you and Beth are all starry-eyed. But there's more to marriage than moonlight and roses. Marriage is a serious lifelong covenant that goes down an uncertain path. A path where you will know much joy, but there will be misunderstandings, heartaches, sorrows, trials, and testing. With God's grace he will guide you on this journey." He paused to let his words sink in. "Have you considered how you will handle money matters, resolve disagreements, and raise children?"

Beth and John locked eyes.

Their pastor continued. "Not to mention illness, career decisions, problem solving, intimacy expectations, and so forth. The classes address all these issues and much more. They last six weeks, and there's homework too."

Beth looked pensive. "I think we need these classes."

"I suppose you're right." John looked to their pastor. "When can we start?"

They agreed on Thursday mornings at ten. The wedding date was set for mid-October, four months later. The pastor gave them the name of the wedding coordinator. Beth and John left the church arm in arm. As they drove away, he reached for her hand. "I want you to meet my parents after I tell them the good news."

Seven

"Are you crazy? You plan to marry as soon as possible?" John stood in his parents' kitchen as his father paced back and forth. He braced himself. His father's anger had always intimidated him. "Yes, Dad—I do."

"But why the rush? You barely know this woman!"

"I know it appears that way, but actually, I've known her for six months."

His mother interrupted. "I don't understand how you could get engaged to someone we've never even met. Someone you hardly know yourself!"

John threw up his hands. "I just said I've known her for six months."

"Then why haven't you introduced her to us?"

He rubbed his chin. "Well, we haven't been dating that long."

"My point exactly!" Pamela wrung her hands. "John, this isn't like you, rushing into something as serious as marriage." She arched one of her brows. "You're not in trouble, are you?"

John took a deep breath. "No, of course not!" He tried

another tactic. "Once you meet Beth, you'll love her as much as I do."

"I don't know about that, John." Pamela sighed. "What makes her so special? I mean—you've had lots of girlfriends before, but nothing that's lasted."

"I never found the right woman before. Beth is different from any woman I've ever known. Not only is she beautiful and intelligent, but she's also gifted. You should hear her play the piano."

"She's a musician?"

"An exceptional one. And she sings like an angel."

"It takes more than singing to make a marriage." Pamela was losing ground. "Does she have a job?"

"She's a registered nurse."

"Where did you meet your girlfriend anyway?"

"My fiancée!" John corrected. "I met her at church. In a Bible study."

Pamela had no comeback to that one.

Ray Beaumont could see that John was smitten. He'd always hoped his son would find a good woman, but the string of girls John brought home in the past hadn't impressed him much. He put his hand on John's shoulder. "I'd like to meet her."

Pamela watched her beloved son chatting with her husband. John was so animated when he talked of his girl. She would invite Beth to dinner next weekend. She'd see for herself if this woman were as good as John said.

Beth was as nervous as a kid at her first recital to meet John's parents. The weather had warmed considerably, so she chose a sleeveless navy-blue sheath with a V-neck. The skirt had a small slit on the back, and the hemline just met her knees. She wore a simple cross around her neck. Beth stood before the mirror, taking special pains with her makeup. She applied her lipstick and stood back to inspect the overall effect. For the final touch, Beth sparingly applied perfume, John's favorite. She stepped into navy heels and placed blue sapphire earrings in her earlobes. *Okay, Lord, here we go.*

Her father closed his newspaper and whistled as she walked into the living room. "You'll knock 'em dead, sweetheart!"

When John arrived, he had much the same reaction. "Wow! You're gorgeous."

"And you look adorable."

"Adorable?"

"Absolutely adorable." His light blue shirt made his eyes dreamier than ever. She kissed him and left an imprint on his cheek. "Whoops, I branded you with my seal."

John looked in the mirror above the fireplace, "You little minx!"

Beth laughed as she rubbed the lipstick off with a tissue. "There, now you look perfectly respectable."

Mr. Delaney chuckled to himself.

"We both wore blue. How about that?" John said. They joined hands and walked to his car. "You should wear a dress more often. You have beautiful legs."

She winked at him. "I just might do that." They were both silent as John drove.

He glanced her way, "Are you nervous?"

Beth shifted uncomfortably. "Yeah."

He squeezed her hand. "Don't be, honey. My mom and dad are nice people."

When they reached the Beaumont's driveway, Beth gasped. The sprawling home sat on a bluff overlooking a view of Seattle's distant harbor with the Space Needle off to the right.

John parked in front of a four-car garage. Manicured lawns and shrubbery resembled a miniature park. They passed potted flowers on the stone steps leading to the entrance. John opened the massive door and stood aside so Beth could enter.

An attractive blonde woman appeared and gave John a quick hug.

He smiled. "Mom, I'd like you to meet my fiancée, Beth Delaney; Beth, meet my mother, Mrs. Beaumont."

Pamela's eyes were serious as she extended her hand. "How do you do?"

Beth glowed. "I'm so happy to meet you Mrs. Beaumont. John has told me so much about you."

"Please call me Pamila." She eyed Beth carefully, noticing the ring on her finger. "How lovely, may I see it closer?" Beth held out her hand.

Ray Beaumont entered the hallway. Beth stared at an older version of John with silver hair. He smiled at her. "So, you're John's girl."

Beth extended her hand and smiled. "It's nice to meet you Mr. Beaumont. I can't get over how much John resembles you."

John's father replied. "He's a chip off the old block for sure. Let's go into the living room and have something to drink."

John followed him. "Do you have any of those Italian sodas?"

"Coming right up," he said before disappearing into the kitchen. John and Beth settled on a white brocade sofa. Beth observed her surroundings: polished hardwood floors, a striking oriental rug, and two armchairs by a bay window. Gauzy drapes hung at the windows. A large painting of ocean waves graced the stone fireplace. Beth's eyes settled on a white, grand piano she would love to play.

Pamela took a nearby chair. "I hear you two met at church."

"Yes, we did."

"John tells me you're a musician."

Beth smiled. "I play the piano. I understand that you play, too."

Pamela folded her hands in her lap. "Yes, I did, but not so much anymore."

Beth noticed her gnarled fingers. "John said you played with the Seattle Symphony."

Pamela had a faraway look in her blue eyes. "For fifteen years."

"So that's where John gets his talent."

"I gave all of my children lessons, but John was the only one who showed any lasting interest."

Ray returned with their drinks. "Here you go."

John reached for his glass. "Thanks, Dad. Beth's father says he knows you."

Ray arched his brows. "Is that so? What's his name?"

"Grant Delaney. He's an attorney."

John's father looked as though he'd been kicked in the stomach. "Grant Delaney! Are you kidding?" He faced Beth. "You're *that* Delaney?" Though Beth detected hostility, she proudly looked him in the eye. "Yes sir. Grant is my father."

John stared at his dad. *What's the matter with him anyway?*

A stout brunette woman entered the room. "Dinner is ready to be served." John introduced Beth to their cook, Martha. She shook Beth's hand. "It's nice to meet you, dear."

Ray and Pamela ushered the couple into the dining room. An elegant table, draped in white linen and set with fine China and crystal goblets, awaited them. A bowl of pink and white blossoms graced the center of the table. Pamela lit two silver candles with a taper. Ray pulled out a chair for his wife. John did the same for Beth and then settled next to her.

Martha brought shrimp cocktails to the table for starters. They joined hands and bowed their heads as John's dad said grace. After John's mother began eating, Beth reached for the cocktail fork. "How nice, did John tell you how much I love shrimp?"

Pamela glanced at John. "No, he didn't. I guess that's something we all have in common."

John attempted to keep the conversation going as the meal

progressed. A coleslaw was followed by grilled salmon, creamed asparagus tips, and wild rice pilaf. Beth complimented the cook on the delightful meal.

"Beth is a gourmet cook," John said.

Pamela faced Beth. "You are?"

"I've taken several classes over the years. I do enjoy cooking."

"She made the best quiche the other day," John bragged.

Ray saw the way those two looked adoringly at one another. His hatred for the lawyer who nearly ruined him so long ago kept kicking at his soul. *How did John get mixed up with Delaney's daughter anyway?* He stared at the rock on her finger, thinking how much it must have set John back financially. He tried to be hospitable, but he'd never been good at hiding his feelings.

Pamela nudged her husband. "You're awfully quiet."

He shook his head. "I was thinking." She frowned and kicked him under the table.

He whispered in her ear, "Lawsuit."

Pamela suddenly connected the dots. *Grant Delaney.* He caused them a season of grief and financial hardship years ago.

John was perplexed by his parents' behavior. They seemed distant and cool towards Beth. He tried to steer the conversation by reminiscing about the European countries they'd both visited. Beth said her favorite art museum was the d'Orsay in Paris. John said his was the Rijksmuseum in Amsterdam. Beth agreed that it was a fabulous museum as she fondly recalled Rembrandt's masterpiece, *The Night Watch*. "I've never seen such a huge painting in my life."

John's mother agreed. "Nor have I."

Beth got teary-eyed while relating a memory of her mother in London. They were sightseeing when her mother suffered her first stroke. John reached for her hand. "Beth was very close to her mother."

Pamela battled mixed emotions. Though she was upset by

the fact that Grant Delaney was Beth's father, it was obvious that Beth was crazy about her son. And John seemed happier than he had in ages.

Martha came to clear away their plates before serving strawberry shortcake for dessert. The foursome managed to struggle through more small talk.

After dinner, they retired to the living room for coffee and tea. Beth excused herself to the restroom. On her way back, she noticed a series of family photos in the hallway. She stared at a blond, blue-eyed baby on his mother's lap while two girls sat on their daddy's knees. Other photos depicted the children as they grew. *What a beautiful family.*

John walked up behind her. He pointed to his sisters. "That's Tiffany and this is Rochelle."

"They look close in age," Beth remarked.

"They're 18 months apart. Tiffany is the oldest."

"You were an adorable little boy, and what a cute teenager."

"Aren't I still cute?"

She tickled his chin. "Kind of." He stole a quick kiss before they rejoined his parents in the living room.

Pamela refilled Beth's teacup. "John tells me that you sing."

"Well, yeah . . . I mean . . . yes." Her vision was starting to blur.

Pamela glanced at her son. "John sang before he learned to talk. When he was a toddler, he would sing and dance around the room when I played the piano."

Beth giggled. "How cute is that?!" John rolled his eyes.

When Beth finished her tea, John suggested they play the piece they'd been practicing for the talent show. "Maybe another time. I'm getting a migraine aura; half of my vision is scrambled." She knew a headache and nausea would soon follow. "I'm sorry, but I really need to go home and get my medication."

John stood up. "Thanks for dinner, Mom."

Pamela took Beth's hand. "It was nice meeting you. I hope you feel better soon."

Ray was cordial. "Goodnight, Beth, I'm sorry you aren't feeling well."

Though she felt something was bothering her hosts, Beth bid them both a pleasant goodnight. When they entered John's car, he faced her. "Are you okay? You don't look well at all."

Beth sighed. "I've got a splitting headache."

John frowned. "Let's get you home."

John's parents settled by the fireplace to discuss the strange turn of events. "She seems like a nice girl. To think that Grant Delaney is her father!"

Pamela stared at her husband. "We've got to talk John out of marrying her."

"As if that would do any good. Your father's disdain for me didn't stop you from marrying me. No, Pam, I think if we protest, it will only drive John away from us."

Pamela eventually drifted off to sleep in their four-poster bed. Ray stared at the moonlit ceiling. He considered himself a spiritual man. He attended church and was active in various charitable organizations. He belonged to the Rotary, Chamber of Commerce, and the Gideons. *But could he ever forgive Grant Delaney?*

Ray's mind wandered back to the worst year of his life. At thirty-five, Ray was idealistic and confident. He and Pamela had just celebrated their tenth wedding anniversary. Their little girls were four and five years old, while John was just a baby. The summer day started just like any other. Ray showered, shaved, ate breakfast, and headed to work. As usual, he arrived early to begin his duties of running the stores. A van loaded with furniture stood ready to go. Unfortunately, one of the delivery guys called in sick while another was away on vacation. Another employee was with his wife, who was in labor. Dave, the only available driver, needed someone to help deliver the load.

The customer, Lisa Boardman, threatened to cancel the entire order if it wasn't delivered on the promised date. Though Ray didn't particularly relish delivering furniture, he didn't mind helping out in a pinch. He agreed to help Dave. After they arrived at the stately farmhouse, Ms. Boardman greeted them and directed them to begin the delivery. She disappeared into the house to answer a ringing phone.

Dave and Ray struggled hauling a heavy hide-a-bed sofa up the stairs. They had just reached the porch landing when two small Chihuahua dogs raced out of an open door. They circled underfoot, yapping and nipping at Ray and Dave's pant legs. Ray gently shoved the smaller dog aside with his foot to avoid stepping on him or dropping the massive sofa. Then the two dogs attacked Dave's legs. He lost his balance and dropped his end of the sofa smack on the back of the smaller dog. Horror flashed in Dave's eyes when he realized what he'd done. Ray shouted, "Lift it up!" Beads of sweat dotted Dave's brow as he raised the sofa from the dog. Together, they set the sofa aside. The poor dog yelping in pain lay motionless. The other dog jumped up on Ray's legs, barking incessantly. That's when Lisa Boardman returned. "What's all this ruckus?" She dropped to her knees and scooped up the injured dog. "What have you done to my poor Misty?" Tears streamed down her cheeks as she cradled the limp dog and sobbed brokenly. Ray offered to escort her to the veterinarian for emergency care. Her eyes narrowed. "Get off my property before I call the police. And take your furniture with you!"

She grabbed a crate from the house and placed the lifeless animal inside. She ran to her car and put the crate on the passenger seat. She slid behind the steering wheel while the other dog jumped onto her lap. Lisa slammed her door and leaned out the window. "Misty is a rare show dog, and she's expecting puppies any day."

Ray wanted to ask if the dogs were so important to her, why she hadn't kept them out of their way, but he'd held his tongue. A day later, he learned that Misty had died along with her puppies. Ms. Boardman cancelled the entire ten-thousand-dollar order.

Before long, the Beaumonts were facing a huge lawsuit. Lisa Boardman's attorney, Grant Delaney, sued Beaumont's Home Furnishings, citing carelessness, neglect, and the death of Misty, as well as potential loss of income for each of her dead puppies. Delaney was ruthless, and Ray's lawyer paled in comparison. Though he charged a fortune in legal fees, the Beaumonts eventually lost their court battle.

Ray didn't know where to turn. He wrestled with feelings of anger, guilt, and hostility. He worried constantly and started drinking heavily. His nervous wife harped at him, and they argued about everything. They'd even considered going their separate ways. If it weren't for the kids, they might have split up.

Anger pulsed through Ray's veins at the memory of his worst nightmare. No, Grant Delaney wasn't someone Ray ever wanted to spend time with. And he certainly didn't relish the thought of having Delaney as an in-law. Ray had harbored his grudge for years. How John ever got mixed up with his daughter was a mystery. What did John say? They met in a Bible study. How bizarre was that? Ray stumbled out of bed and headed for the medicine cabinet. He faced a bitter man in the mirror. He opened the cabinet door and rummaged through various bottles. He desperately needed a sleeping pill.

Eight

Ray addressed Pamela at the breakfast table. "What are we going to do about John?"

"I don't know, Ray. You tell me."

His eyes revealed his anguish. "He can't marry her!"

"You said yourself, if we try to discourage John, it will only drive him away."

Ray glared at his wife. "I'm surprised at you. You're usually the one who wants him to break up." How many times had they gone round and round over his choice of women? No one was ever good enough in Pamala's eyes. She toyed with her napkin. "Well, he's already given her a ring, an expensive one too, by the looks of it!"

"Get him on the phone. Invite him to lunch."

John arrived at his parents' kitchen around noon. His mom gave him a peck on his cheek and asked him to sit down. His dad sat across from him. She put a plate of chicken salad sandwiches on the table and poured iced tea into glasses. John felt tension in the air. His father looked like he'd swallowed a lemon. "What's the matter? Does this have anything to do with Beth?"

Ray massaged his temples. "As a matter of fact, it does."

John stared at his dad. "Well?"

Ray cleared his throat. "She seems like a lovely woman, John, but unfortunately, she's not going to fit into our family."

John frowned. "Why on earth not?"

"It has to do with her father."

"Mr. Delaney?"

Ray tossed his sandwich down. "Yes. Grant Delaney is a terrible person!"

John's brows furrowed. "Dad, you're dead wrong. I've met him several times and he's a really nice guy. He loves Beth and wants only the best for her."

"I'm sure he does," Pamela said. "But your father has every reason to disagree with you. He nearly ruined us once, years ago."

"How?"

Ray leaned forward. "John, I've never told you about this, but we were once involved in a horrendous lawsuit. It was one of the worst years of our lives."

John listened while his father and mother poured out the whole dreary story in detail.

John couldn't believe his ears. "That's awful, Dad."

John raked his memory. Mr. Delany hadn't said anything about a feud. Then he remembered. "He did mention something about facing you in court years ago, but that's all he said."

Ray scowled. "Do you suppose he thinks we've forgotten all about it?"

"I have no idea what he thinks." John looked from his father's angry expression to his mother's tense face.

Pamela stood up. "So now you know why this marriage would never work."

John gave a halfhearted laugh. "So, you want me to jilt Beth?"

Pamela wrung her hands. "Oh, don't put it that way."

John felt his emotions swimming against waves of anger. "Hey! I'm sorry for any pain Mr. Delaney caused you. I can only imagine what you went through, but it was a long, long time ago."

Ray sighed. "Don't you see what you're getting into?"

John shook his head. "Tell me, Dad. What am I getting into? The man is a lawyer. The dog breeder was his client! He was doing his job."

Ray's neck veins bulged as his anger surfaced. "The man's a devil!"

Pamela reached for Ray's hand. "Remember your blood pressure."

John stood up, feeling nauseous. "I've lost my appetite."

"Don't act that way."

"What way, Mom? You've found something wrong with every woman I've ever brought home. Why can't you see how wonderful Beth is?"

"It's not her so much, John. It's her father!"

"Well, I'm not marrying her father! I'm marrying Beth. And no one is going to stop me." With that, he stood up. "Thanks for lunch." He slammed the door on his way out.

Ray Beaumont shoved his chair away from the table. "I knew it wouldn't do any good. Love is blind!"

Pamela felt tears stinging her eyes. "Poor John, he's like a lamb being led to slaughter."

Ray snorted. "It's not that bad, is it?"

John fumed on his way back to the office. His parents despised

Beth's father for how long? He pondered his father's words. *"The man's a devil!"*

John gripped the steering wheel as he sped a good ten miles over the speed limit. He tried to understand his father's line of reasoning. It must have been terrible, but he could hardly blame Beth. She wasn't even born yet. And Grant was a kind man. John vowed not to let his father's hatred color his thinking. Would his parents come to his wedding? Things could be very tense from now on. John had a lot of praying to do.

Nine

It had been two weeks since Ray and Pamela heard from John. He'd missed their annual Fourth of July picnic. Even that morning, at a director's meeting, John only briefly acknowledged his father. Ray felt terrible. He and John had always been close. He considered John's words. *"He's a lawyer, she was his client. He was only doing his job."*

Ray knew it was wrong to hate anyone. The lawsuit happened long ago. He'd turned to alcohol for comfort back then. So why did he still feel like he needed a drink when he hadn't had one in years? Why couldn't he sleep at night without pills? And now the friction between him and John further affected his peace of mind. It didn't help his relationship with Pamela either. John was planning his wedding with or without his blessing. Ray didn't want to be one of those dads who distanced himself from his child. He'd always looked forward to the day John would find a good woman and settle down. He hoped to have grandchildren someday. Pamela wanted grandchildren, too. Would his hatred for Grant Delaney put a wedge between him and his son forever?

John debated whether to tell Beth about his dad's hatred for her father. The more he thought about it, the less he liked the idea. Why bring Beth pain over something that happened so long ago? He decided to simply avoid his parents, even missing their annual Fourth of July picnic. Nothing they did or said could ever persuade him to leave Beth. She was going to become his wife no matter what, the sooner the better. Their plans with the wedding coordinator were going smoothly. He saw Beth's father from time to time, but Grant gave no hint of his past experiences with John's father. And John had no intention of making it an issue.

Pamela could no longer stand by while John made the biggest mistake of his life. Missing their Fourth of July picnic was the last straw. The family always gathered for the holiday. She found Grant Delaney's telephone number in the phone book and placed a call. She had to do it before she lost her nerve. Let John hate her for a while. It was in his best interests. An answering machine picked up. "You've reached the Delany residence; please leave your name and number, and we will return your call as soon as possible."

"Beth, this is John's mother, Pamela. Will you please call me? I need to talk to you."

Beth didn't hear the message until the following day. Since she used her cell phone most of the time, she rarely checked the family's answering machine.

Her father informed her of Pamela's message. Beth sat alone in her room as she returned the call to John's mother. She heard Pamela's voice, "Hello."

"Mrs. Beaumont?"

"Yes, is this Beth?"

"Yes, I'm sorry I didn't get back to you sooner, I just heard your message this morning."

"Oh, that's quite all right. Could we meet for lunch sometime soon? It's rather important."

Beth looked at her watch. "I can't today, but I'm free tomorrow. Would that work for you?"

"Tomorrow will be fine. Let's meet at The Fish Grotto at noon."

"Okay. Do you want me to make reservations?"

"No, I'll take care of it. You'll be my guest, and one more thing, Beth. I'd appreciate it if you didn't mention this to John."

Beth didn't relish the idea of hiding things from him. But maybe she was planning a surprise party or something. "Okay."

"Good. I'll see you tomorrow. Bye now."

Beth wrinkled her nose as she hung up the receiver. Why did she feel like a kid about to go to the principal's office? And why couldn't she tell John?

Beth arrived ten minutes early for her luncheon date with Pamela Beaumont. She waited on a bench next to the lobster tank. She watched the spiny creatures with pincers bound by orange bands. The lobsters appeared to be crawling over each other to escape their final fate. Did they know what was coming?

Pamela swished through the main entrance wearing a black pantsuit and a red silk blouse. Her blonde hair was perfectly coiffed. "Hello, Beth. I hope you haven't been waiting too long. I just had my nails done. The woman was incredibly slow!"

Beth smiled. "Not long."

Pamela approached the hostess and asked her to seat them. She led them to a quiet section.

"Thank you for coming," Pamela said sweetly.

"You're welcome."

"Does John know you're here?"

"No, you asked me not to mention it to him."

"Good. We'll keep this just between us girls."

Silence hung like a curtain as they read their menus. When the server returned with their beverages, they ordered. After she left, Pamela began. "I suppose you're wondering what this is all about."

Beth blinked. "Yes, I have to admit—I am curious."

Pamela stretched out her hands, admiring her freshly mani-cured nails. "I thought we should get better acquainted."

Beth glanced at her plain nails and folded her hands. "That's a good idea."

Pamela leaned forward. "Yes, well . . . John is very special, being my only son."

A soft light filled Beth's eyes. "John is very special to me, too."

Pamela tilted her head. "I'd like to learn more about you."

"What would you like to know?"

"Oh, I thought we might discuss your expectations."

"Expectations?" Beth asked. *Was this a trick question?*

"You know, like family traditions, holidays, and such." She gave Beth a detailed report on how she and Ray place great importance on their family holiday gatherings. Beth took mental notes, as if there might be a quiz afterwards. Pamela droned on, painting a colorful picture of their festive family get-togethers.

The server arrived with their orders. She slid a seafood salad towards Beth. Next, she placed Pamela's chowder and salad in front of her. Pamela raised her brows. "I said no croutons." The waitress apologized and returned to the kitchen with her salad. Beth wondered why Pamela hadn't simply pushed the croutons to one side of her plate.

The silence between them grew awkward. Beth sipped iced tea. The waitress returned with Pamela's salad, minus the croutons, and placed it in front of her. "Here you go, I'm sorry about the mix-up."

"Thank you," Pamela said.

Beth squeezed a slice of lemon over her shrimp and crab.

Pamela asked, "What did you do for the Fourth of July?"

Beth blotted her lips with a napkin. "John and I hosted a barbecue for our Bible study friends. They wanted to have an engagement party for us."

Pamela's head shot up. "Hosted! Where?"

"At my house."

"All day?" Pamela asked, trying to hide her anger.

"Most of the day. We swam, waterskied, and played volleyball. Later, we went to Gasworks Park to watch the fireworks."

Pamela frowned. "Why would you go where it's so crowded? The view of fireworks from our place is spectacular! We expected John at the house."

Beth's brows furrowed. "John didn't mention anything about going to your house."

Pamela bristled. "He usually spends the Fourth with us for our annual barbecue and picnic."

"Ah . . . well . . . "

Pamela interrupted. "Tell me Beth, how do you celebrate the holidays?"

Beth looked up. "I'm not quite sure what you mean."

"You know—your traditions; take Christmas for example."

Beth put her fork down. "Well, Daddy and I put up a tree, decorate the house, buy each other presents, and enjoy a feast on Christmas Day." *That should cover it,* Beth thought.

"Do you get together with relatives?"

Beth shook her head no. "When my mother was alive, we usually celebrated with friends. My grandparents are no longer living."

"What about aunts, uncles, and cousins?"

"They're scattered throughout the United States."

"So, you pretty much spend the holidays alone?"

"Now that my mother is gone, it's just Daddy and me. Last Christmas was our first without her."

"I'm sure that must have been hard. It sounds like you and your mother were close. Tell me about your father."

"Daddy?"

Pamela pursed her lips. "I find it interesting that you still call him Daddy."

Beth shrugged. "I've always called him that."

Pamela laughed nervously as she twisted her napkin. "John called Ray that too, when he was a child." Beth felt utterly foolish. Pamela continued, "John loves his family."

Beth nodded. "He's told me how close you all are."

"Let me ask you a question. Where do you intend to spend Thanksgiving and Christmas if you marry John?"

Beth studied Pamela's expression. *What an odd question.* "With John of course."

"What about your father?"

Beth knit her brows. "He will always be part of our lives."

"So, he would be present during the holidays?"

Beth stared at her future mother-in-law. "I suppose we'll spend time with him and your family as well."

"Hopefully, you and John will spend Thanksgiving and Christmas Day with our family." She grimaced. "I don't know how to say this without hurting your feelings, but I'm afraid your father won't be welcome in our home."

Beth froze. "Why not?"

"Our family has every reason to despise your father."

Waves of anger lodged in Beth's soul. "Excuse me?"

Pamela tried to soften the blow a bit. "John loves you, Beth. Anyone can see that. But if you love him, you need to think about what's best for him. He values our family traditions. And your father could never be a guest in our home."

"If that's the case, I wouldn't come either."

"That's just my point! If you wouldn't come, you'd deprive John of his family."

Beth felt nauseous. "Why do you hate my father?"

Pamela furrowed her brows. "You mean you don't know?"

"No, I don't." Beth pinned her down with her eyes.

For the next ten minutes, Pamela poured out the story of the lawsuit that nearly ruined her marriage so long ago. Beth leaned back in her chair. Tears stung her eyes, but she swallowed them. She would not give this woman the satisfaction of seeing her cry.

"So, you see Beth, your marriage to John would never work. It would be best to let him go now before you devastate him later."

"You're serious?" Beth felt like she'd been stabbed in the heart.

"Of course, I am. It would be best for everyone, all the way around."

"You mean best for you! Because it wouldn't be best for John or me."

"I'm sure, if you think about it, you'll realize this is the only solution that makes *any* sense."

Beth couldn't take it anymore. She slid out of the booth and stood up. She opened her purse and pulled out a twenty-dollar bill. She dropped it on the table. "I have to go to work."

Pamela grabbed her wrist. "I'd appreciate it if you didn't say anything to John about our lunch today, okay?"

Beth jerked her hand away. "Goodbye, Mrs. Beaumont." She restrained her tears until she reached her car. She cried for herself, and she cried for her father, but most of all, she cried for John. She voiced a silent prayer. *Help us, Lord.*

Beth prayed about her predicament that evening as she worked. Would it really be best for John to let him go? As much as it broke her heart to think so, she had to pray until she got an answer. Did God bring them together only to break them up?

Would her future relatives' hatred of her father cause them only pain? Would John find love again? Would she?

She was confused and needed time to think. She called John and cancelled their counselling session for the following day. John sounded upset. "Is everything okay?"

"I think I'm coming down with something." That fib worked for one day. When John couldn't reach Beth on her phone, he called her father to see how she was feeling. Mr. Delaney told him that she wasn't sick; she was at work. It didn't sit well with John. Beth had never lied to him that he knew of. He tried calling her again, but she wasn't returning his calls.

Grant couldn't help but notice the sadness in his daughter's eyes. "What's the matter honey?"

She sighed. "I'm not ready to discuss it yet."

"Is everything okay between you and John?"

A tear slid down her cheek. "Not really."

He put his arm around her. "Let me know when you're ready to talk."

Beth couldn't put John off any longer. His text messages indicated how upset he was with her for not returning his calls. She finally called him to break their Sunday morning church date. John wouldn't listen. "I don't know what's going on with you, but I'll be there at 8:30 sharp. Be ready!"

The next morning Beth prayed for the right words to break their engagement. As she opened the door the sight of him standing there erased any doubt of her love for him.

"Hey," he said. His eyes held confusion, sadness, and a glimmer of anger.

"Hey yourself."

"Are you ready?" She nodded and stepped out onto the porch. They were silent as they walked to his car. Inside the car, he turned to face her. "Why haven't you returned my calls? Have I done something to upset you?"

She looked down at her lap. "No."

"Then for heaven's sake tell me what's wrong."

"Can we talk about it later?"

"No."

She sighed. "Okay, let's go to the park, and we'll talk. But we'll be too late for class."

"I don't feel like going to class anyway. There's no way I'd be able to concentrate."

She looked into his troubled eyes. "I'm sorry . . . it's just that . . . "

When she didn't finish her thought, John started the car and headed for the nearest Starbucks. He swung through the drive-through and ordered two cappuccinos. He then drove to the park and pulled into a lot by the lake. The area was deserted except for a few early morning joggers. Off in the distance, a lone water skier followed a boat. Beth turned towards him. "Let's walk."

It was a beautiful morning. Songbirds chirped in the over-head trees. They strolled along a trail next to the lake. Before long, they spotted a bench near a clump of bushes. "Let's sit here," John suggested.

They finished their drinks in silence while watching the lake. A fish jumped, leaving circles in its wake. John turned towards Beth and looked directly into her sad eyes. "What is it, Beth?"

She looked towards the lake. "I don't know where to begin." She twisted her diamond ring back and forth on her finger. "Maybe we should call off our engagement."

Her words sliced John's heart like a razor blade. "You can't mean that!"

She thought about removing the ring, but she just couldn't do it. Her eyes sought his. "I'm not sure I'm the right woman for you, John."

He couldn't believe his ears. "Are you trying to break up with me?" She didn't answer. He crooked his finger and lifted her chin. His beautiful blue eyes glistened. "Is there someone else?"

His question shocked her. "No, of course not."

"Then look me in the eyes and tell me you don't love me."

She stared at the lake, struggling to keep from crying. Once again, he turned her face towards him. "Tell me you don't love me."

She sniffed. "I can't do that."

He wiped an errant tear from her cheek. "Then I won't let you go."

She leaned against him. "I do love you, with all my heart."

His arm tightened around her. "Then please . . . tell me what I've done so I can make things right."

She shook her head. "You haven't done anything. It concerns my father."

Suddenly, he understood. "Your father?" He squinted his eyes. "Has my mother or father contacted you?" Her silence told him the answer. John's face flushed. "Who contacted you?"

Beth sighed. "Your mother invited me to lunch."

Frustration clouded his eyes. "Why didn't you tell me?"

"I couldn't. She asked me not to."

John leaned against the bench. "Did she talk about your father?"

"Yes."

"So, you know about the lawsuit?"

"You know?"

"I should have told you myself, but I didn't want to bring you any pain."

"Well, your mother is probably right, John. They hate my father. And she's worried about the holidays and where we'll spend them. Daddy wouldn't be welcome at your parents' home."

John's anger boiled over. "I'll spend the holidays with my wife, not with them!"

She looked sad. "You'd resent me eventually, John."

"Never! You mean everything to me. What I *would* resent is losing you." He drew her close and kissed her tears away. Their eyes met with longing and pain.

John stroked her hair. "Let's pray about this. God will show us what to do. But breaking up will never be an option for me."

She wrapped her arms around his neck. "I love you so much." They held one another tenderly for the next few minutes. Gentle kisses made their world seem almost right again.

John sighed. "You're so beautiful, Beth. Not only outwardly, but inside."

She caressed his cheek. "I see that same goodness in you."

John glanced at his watch. "We can still make church. Do you want to go with me?"

She leaned against him. "For the rest of my life."

Ten

Saturday morning dawned bright, clear, and warm. Beth rinsed her father's breakfast dishes and placed them in the dishwasher. He'd gone to play golf with his cronies. She wiped the counters down and dried her hands on a towel. John was due to pick her up for breakfast and a morning of choosing gifts for their bridal registry. She was especially excited because tonight they were going to see Josh Groban. A new outfit lay on her bed.

She looked at her watch while checking the driveway for the third time. Where was he? It wasn't like him to be late. She heard her phone and answered on the first ring. "Hi honey, where are you? I thought you'd be here by now."

"I'm sick."

Beth frowned. "What's the matter?"

"I've been miserable all night. At first, I thought it was indigestion, but now I have a terrible pain in my side. I tried to get ready, but I couldn't." She heard him groaning.

"Do you have a fever?"

"I don't know." His voice was barely audible.

"Lie down. I'll be right over."

Beth grabbed her purse and headed for the front door. She prayed all the way to John's condo. *Lord, please watch over him.* Since it was Saturday, morning traffic was light, and she made good time. She parked her car and headed for the elevator. After pushing the button and waiting for what seemed like ages, it finally opened so she could enter. On the top floor, she hurried to John's door and rang the bell. There was no answer. She tried the knob, but it was locked. She rapped loudly. "John, it's me, Beth!"

The door slowly opened. John's ghastly appearance startled her. Dressed in gray sweats, his pasty skin flushed as he clutched his side. He was shivering as she gave him a gentle hug and felt his forehead. "You're burning up! Come; sit on the sofa while I take your pulse." He leaned against her shoulder while she felt his wrist and timed the beats with her watch. "It's racing. Who's your doctor?"

John shook his head. "I haven't seen a doctor in years. I don't have one."

Beth rolled her eyes. "Let me feel your abdomen."

"You sure about that?"

"Come on, don't be silly." She gently placed her hand over his right side.

"Ouch!" He recoiled.

She stood up. "We're going to the hospital!"

John shook his head. "No baby, we're not."

Frustration clouded her eyes. "You need to see a doctor."

"You take care of me."

"Don't argue with me John. It could be appendicitis! Where's your wallet?"

"It should be on my nightstand." He doubled over.

She headed towards his bedroom. John's covers looked like he'd been in a fight with them. She grabbed his wallet from the nightstand and a jacket from his closet. Her heart was racing as she returned to his side. "Here, let's put this on."

John waved her away. "I'm not going anywhere."

She placed her hands on her hips. "Don't give me a hard time." She took his arm and tried pulling him up. He resisted. She stood back and glared.

"I don't like hospitals," he whined.

"Well, I do! So, give me your arm."

He continued to shiver. "I told you, I'm not going to any hospital!"

Anger flashed in her eyes. "Then I'll call 911 and have the paramedics deal with you." She reached for her cell phone.

"No, don't do that!" He grabbed her hand. "I'll go with you." She kept her arm around him on their way to the elevator. As they neared her car, he doubled over and leaned across the hood. She helped him stand upright. He leaned against her as she helped him into the passenger seat. His breathing became ragged and shallow. "Try to breathe slowly and deeply," she said in her most professional voice.

Beth called the hospital as she backed out. She told the receptionist they were on their way and what John's symptoms were. She kept praying as she drove. His color worried her. She ignored her fear as her medical training kicked in. *Stay calm.*

John moaned as she zipped through traffic. When they arrived at the emergency entrance, an orderly met them with a wheelchair. Beth took charge. "Charly, please take him back right away, while I take care of his admittance." Charly's brown eyes twinkled as he gave her a salute. "Yes, ma'am." The huge, jovial man settled John into the wheelchair against his protests and wheeled him off.

At the admission desk, Beth opened John's wallet for his insurance card. Josh Groban concert tickets caught her eye. She fought tears. After explaining the circumstances and getting the paperwork started, she went to find John. He was lying on a gurney while nurses hovered over him taking vital signs. A nurse inserted an IV in his arm and a phlebotomist began drawing blood. Beth reached for his free hand as his fear-filled eyes sought hers. "Don't leave me."

"I won't darling. Hang in there."

The ER doctor confirmed Beth's diagnosis of appendicitis. His white blood count was soaring, and an ultrasound showed a grossly inflamed appendix. Dr. Conrad, a surgeon, was called in. When he arrived, he greeted her. "Hello, Beth, what have we got here?"

"This is my fiancé, John Beaumont. He has appendicitis."

"Your fiancé!" He shook John's hand. "Well, sir, you're in good hands. You have one of our finest nurses looking after you." John's smile disappeared with his next groan. "Have you eaten anything today?" The surgeon asked as he gently pressed on John's side.

John grimaced, "No, just some orange juice."

"We need to remove your appendix before you get any sicker. Any questions?" The doctor asked.

John grimaced. "Will it hurt?"

"You won't feel a thing, we'll put you to sleep. You'll be sore afterwards for a while."

John moaned. "What choice do I have?"

The doctor read the ultrasound report. "The risk of doing nothing is far more serious than the risk of surgery. We'll open you up and remove the inflamed appendix. Then we'll examine the surrounding organs. Following surgery, we'll watch you closely for any complications."

"Like what?"

"Fever, bleeding, infection, redness, or swelling; I'll have the nurse go over the consent forms with you, detailing the risks. Then you can sign them." He turned to the nurse on duty. "Who's the anesthesiologist on call?"

"Dr. Miller."

"Good. Let's get him in here STAT. Prepare John for surgery."

Beth turned John over to the nurses and promised to return shortly. She took the surgeon aside. "What do you think?"

"From the looks of the ultrasound, he's in bad shape. It's too risky for laparoscopy. I'll open him up and hope the appendix doesn't rupture in the meantime. It's a good thing he got here when he did. What about his family? Have they been notified?"

Beth sighed. "No, I'll call them right away."

She returned to John's side. "I've got to call your parents; I have your mom's number."

John flinched. "Do you have to call them?"

"They deserve to know. Wouldn't you want to know if one of them were in the hospital?"

"I guess so." She brushed his hair back with her fingers and kissed his forehead. "I'll be right back."

Beth stepped outside into the sunshine and placed the call. A gentle breeze caressed her body as she drew a deep breath. The Beaumont's answering machine clicked on. She told them John was in the hospital and left her cell number. When she returned to the ER, the anesthesiologist was checking John's medical history. He explained that he would give John something to help him relax. Then a breathing tube would be inserted down his throat. John shuddered.

Beth went to his side and held his clammy hand next to her cheek. His head moved from side to side as he winced in pain. His nurse put medicine into his IV and before long John visibly relaxed. Two aides pushed his gurney out of the emergency room and down the hall. Beth walked beside him, holding his hand and praying silently. His eyes never left hers as he was wheeled towards the operating room. Before he went through the double doors, she kissed his cheek. "I love you, John."

He squeezed her hand. "I love you too, baby. Pray for me."

"You know I will." She watched the man she loved disappear behind the operating room doors. *Please take care of him, Lord.*

She went to the waiting room and tried calling John's

parents again. She hadn't spoken to Pamela since the day they went to lunch. She wasn't sure just what she would say if Pamela answered. Since there was still no answer, she left another message. "This is Beth. John has just been taken to surgery for an appendectomy. I'm here at the hospital with him."

Next, she called her father to let him know. Since he wasn't home either, she left another message. She called the church to add John's name to the prayer chain. Afterwards, she headed to the hospital chapel. She quietly entered the dimly lit room. The fragrance of a lily permeated the small space. She knelt to pray. A simple altar held an open Bible, a cross, and two candles. Her tears flowed freely now as she interceded for John. The possibility of losing him filled her with tremendous sorrow. She thought of how she'd almost let him go for Pamela's sake. She sobbed at the memory of his sad eyes. "I can't let you go," he'd said. Well, she couldn't let him go either.

Beth moved to a wooden bench and relaxed in a peaceful atmosphere. She felt confident that her beloved was in God's hands, the safest place in the universe.

Eventually, she left the chapel and returned to the waiting room. Her nursing supervisor, Kay, entered the room. "Beth, what are you doing here? Isn't this your day off?"

The look in Beth's eyes made Kay realize that she wasn't there for work. She took Beth's hand and asked what the matter was.

"It's my fiancé, John. He has appendicitis."

"Who's his surgeon?"

"Dr. Conrad."

"He's exceptionally good. I'm confident your guy will come through fine."

"I sure hope so."

Kay squeezed her shoulder. "I'll see if I can find out anything."

Beth gave her a grateful nod. Kay left with a promise to return soon. Beth paced the floor and studied her watch. He'd been in the operating room for nearly an hour.

She heard her name. "Beth." She turned to see her father walking towards her. She went into his open arms. "How is he?"

"I don't know. He's still in surgery."

He released her. "Tell me what's going on." They settled on a sofa while she explained.

"How are you holding up?" he asked.

She gave him a weak smile. "The best I can."

His brown eyes held compassion. "Can I get you anything?"

"I could sure use a cup of coffee."

"There's an espresso cart just down the hall."

Beth gave a half-hearted laugh. "I guess I forgot." She followed him along the corridor towards the cart. The aroma of freshly brewed espresso permeated the area. The barista recognized her. "Hi Beth, what'll it be? The usual?"

"Yes." She turned towards her father. "What would you like?"

"A small latte is fine, no flavoring." He withdrew a twenty from his wallet and laid it on the counter. The barista tamped her coffee and turned the machine knobs. She attached a metal pitcher and started frothing milk. Before long, rich dark espresso shot into two small shot glasses. Beth savored the tantalizing aroma.

Kay walked up. "There you are. The doctor is almost finished."

"It shouldn't take this long, should it?"

"It depends on what they found when they opened him up."

Beth threw up her hands. "I should be with him."

Kay touched her shoulder. "No, Beth, that's not a good idea."

Beth knew she was right. She'd only be in the way. She didn't think she could bear seeing John on the operating table. What was taking so long anyway? She ran fingers through her hair. Her father took her by the arm. "Let's go back to the waiting room." Beth sipped her drink as they walked the hospital corridor.

They met Pamela and Ray in the hallway. Pamela no longer looked like a sophisticated woman. She appeared scared and desperate. "Beth, we just got your message! How is he?"

"He's still in surgery."

Pamela put her hand over her mouth.

Beth tried to reassure her. "He has an excellent surgeon," she said as she fell into a familiar role of reassuring distraught parents.

Ray Beaumont and Grant Delaney stared at one another, but their faces showed no emotion. Grant put his coffee down and extended his hand. "I'm sorry about your son."

Ray studied Grant's face. The silver-haired gentleman was nothing like the man he remembered. Grant's soft brown eyes held deep concern. Ray hesitantly shook his hand. As he did so, a measure of peace flooded his way. He wasn't ready to befriend Grant, but at that moment, he no longer felt hatred for him.

A short time later, Dr. Conrad walked out in green scrubs with his face mask looping around his neck. He wore a cap on his head. Beth introduced him to John's parents. "Your son came through surgery fine, but we had some complications. His appendix ruptured just as we entered. We contained most of the infection, but a small amount entered his abdomen. We rinsed it with saline and vacuumed out the residue. We'll keep him on antibiotics. He's in the recovery room, still groggy."

Pamela grew pale. "When can we see him?"

The doctor looked from her to Beth and back again. "When he's fully conscious, then you can see him." He faced Beth. "It's a good thing you got him here when you did. Another hour and we might have lost him."

Beth sank into the nearest chair. "Thank you, Jesus."

Pamela started to cry. Ray took her in his arms. "It's going to be okay, honey."

Beth couldn't stop her tears either. Grant put his arm around his daughter. The two men's eyes met. They were both comforting women who loved John. Beth's stomach growled. She hadn't eaten all day. Grant heard it too. "Let's get you something to eat."

They excused themselves and headed for the cafeteria, where they found a good selection of sandwiches and snacks. Beth faced her father, "I hope they let me see John first."

"His mother probably feels the same way."

She wiped away tears. "Daddy, I didn't know I could love anyone as much as I love John."

He reached out and patted her hand. "That's how I felt about your mother."

"I miss her so much."

"Me too."

They were silent for a few minutes; each lost in their own world. Grant reached for her hand. "I'm sorry for the pain my past involvement with the Beaumonts has caused you and John."

"It's all so bizarre," she said. "And so long ago."

"Frankly, I'm glad those litigation days are behind me." Grant shook his head. "It's no wonder there are so many bad lawyer jokes."

"But you're a fine lawyer. Look at all the good your foundation has done."

He shrugged. "I wish I'd started it a lot sooner." Grant finished his sandwich and pie and wiped his face with a napkin. "You ready to go back?"

She wrapped her half-eaten sandwich in a napkin and put it in her purse. "Let's go."

They found John's parents pacing the waiting room. "Is he awake yet?" Beth asked.

Pamela's eyes met hers. "Not yet. I'm going crazy."

Beth sighed. "I'm going to check on him." Pamela began to follow her. Ray pulled her arm back and shook his head. She started to protest but thought better of it.

Beth decided to use her hospital privileges to her advantage. She washed her hands and arms and quietly entered the recovery room. She went to John's side and took his free hand in hers. His cheeks were nearly as pale as his sheet. Beth stroked his forehead as she prayed over him. She could tell he was still running a fever. The IV pumped fluids into his system. Other machines and wires monitored his blood pressure and heart rate.

A young nurse named Sara came to his side and bent over him. "Wake up, John. Come on now. It's time to rock!" He moaned but did not open his eyes. She turned to Beth. "What are you doing here? Are you on call?"

Beth managed a weak smile. "John is my fiancé."

"Lucky you. What a hunk!" She studied Beth's worried face. "He should rally again any minute now."

"Rally again?"

"Yeah, he was awake a few minutes ago, so we removed the tube. Keep an eye on him for me, will you? Sonya's on break. I'll be right back."

Beth frowned. *What a hunk! How unprofessional.* She heard John mumble something. She bent close to his lips. "What is it?"

"Beth."

"I'm right here, darling." She stroked his forehead.

"I feel sick." John moaned as he turned towards her. She grabbed an emesis basin and put it in front of his mouth just as he heaved. Brackish orange vomit splashed out of the basin onto Beth's shirt. She gently wiped John's face with a cool cloth. Next, she cleaned vomit from her shirt and arms before emptying and rinsing the basin.

Sara returned. "Hey John, you're awake! Welcome back." She rolled up the head of his bed and stuffed a pillow behind his head. "I need you to cough for me."

He shook his head. "I can't—it hurts."

"I know it hurts, but do it anyway. We've got to clear your lungs."

He looked at Beth; she nodded. He grimaced and made a feeble attempt to cough. Sara crossed her arms. "Come on big guy, you can do better than that!" He coughed harder and clutched his side. Beth squeezed his hand.

Sarah typed something on the computer. "Take some deep breaths now." He did as she instructed. "Good job!"

He moaned. "Where am I?"

Beth stroked his forehead. "You're in the recovery room. You've just had your appendix removed." John gave her a blank stare. Beth noticed that he was shivering. She walked to the blanket warming cabinet, brought him two toasty blankets, and lovingly tucked them around him. "How's that?"

His grateful eyes sought hers. "Thank you."

Dr. Conrad entered the room. "Mr. Beaumont, you came through just fine."

"I feel terrible."

"You'll feel rocky for a while. We'll take you to a room as soon as you stabilize. Your parents are waiting to see you."

Beth was ashamed she'd forgotten all about them. "I'll go get them."

John grabbed her arm. "Please, don't leave me."

Sara smiled. "Stay here, Beth. I'll find them for you."

Shortly after Sara left, John vomited again. Beth was ready this time. Afterward, he squeezed her arm. "I guess you didn't sign up for this, did you?"

She bathed his forehead and face with a cold cloth. "All in a day's work." She held a glass of cool water to his lips. "Here, honey, rinse your mouth." He did so, spitting the water into the basin. She wiped his lips with a tissue. He sank back onto the pillow and groaned. Beth continued gently stroking his forehead. "Hang in there."

Sara returned to John's side. "Your parents are outside the door."

Beth asked, "Does John have an order for nausea meds?"

Sara checked the computer. "Sure does. I'll get right on it."

John's parents entered the room. Pamela rushed to John's side. Beth stepped back so she could embrace her son. Her arms opened wide. "My poor baby!" She suddenly drew back. The stench of vomit permeated the air. Disapproval distorted her features. "There's vomit on his gown and blanket!"

"He's very nauseated," Beth said.

John grimaced. "She's being polite. I puked on her."

Beth wiped the remaining vomit with a damp towel. "We'll get him bathed and into a clean gown right away."

Pamela looked shocked. *"You're* not going to bathe him, are you?"

Beth suppressed a giggle. "No, his nurse will do it."

John grinned. "I like Mom's idea better."

"John!" Pamela chided. Ray snickered.

"Just kidding, Mom. Oh . . . no." Beth placed the basin in front of him again. He gagged, but nothing came up. Beth hoped he'd stop retching before his incision suffered any more trauma.

Pamela fought nausea herself. Ray took his son's hand. "Let's pray."

After John finally stabilized, his gurney was wheeled to a hospital room. With pain meds and nausea relief, he was sleeping peacefully. Pamela hovered in a chair next to him. Beth decided to leave her alone with her son. All she wanted was a hot shower, shampoo, and clean clothes. Besides, she needed to pack a bag. Next time, she would be better prepared. For now, she planned on getting a good night's rest so she could return in the morning. She offered up prayers of thanksgiving as she drove home.

Eleven

Grant Delaney faced Ray Beaumont over a cup of coffee in the cafeteria. "Thank you for coming. We really need to talk."

Ray sighed as his eyes met Grant's. "I suppose we do, since our children plan on marrying each other."

Grant didn't believe in beating around the bush. "Beth was heartbroken when your wife asked her to break up with John."

Ray flinched. "What are you talking about?"

Grant gave him a sideways glance. "You don't know?"

"She asked Beth to break up with him?"

"She certainly did."

Ray clenched his jaw. "She *shouldn't* have done that."

Grant exhaled and massaged his temples. "It seems that our past dealings have wounded your family greatly."

Ray leaned forward. "That's putting it mildly, Delaney. I've despised you for a long time."

"I suppose you're not the only one. Honestly, Beaumont, I'd forgotten all about that lawsuit. In those days, I had a terrible caseload. I jumped from courtroom to courtroom. Ms. Boardman was just another client. I represented her interests to the best of my ability. I don't regret that, but I am sorry for any grief it caused you personally." He looked down at the table and back at Ray's eyes. "I'd like to ask for your forgiveness."

Ray leaned back in his chair. Now the ball was in his court. "Let me mull this over."

Grant sighed. "We must make peace for our children's sake. They're crazy about each other. And I don't want any feud to ruin their lives."

Ray slowly shook his head. "I don't either. Beth's a lovely young woman. She's good for John. I haven't seen him so happy in ages."

"Beth adores him. I'm fond of him, too."

"The doctor said if Beth hadn't acted so quickly, we might have lost him." Ray closed his eyes. "I don't think I'd ever forgive myself if anything happened to John."

"It would devastate all of us, especially Beth." Grant's brown eyes mirrored sorrow. "I'm truly sorry for any pain I've caused you."

Ray looked across the room. "That pain brought me to my knees. Now, as I look back, I see a lot of good came from that miserable time. I was a changed man by the time it was all over."

Grant's eyes softened. "I'm not the man I used to be either. When I was younger, work consumed twelve hours a day, six days a week. My family suffered as a result. Eventually, I chucked it all to start a charitable foundation."

Ray looked surprised. "Yeah?"

Grant explained his nonprofit corporation to help first-time offenders, "Fresh Start."

Ray brightened. "I've heard of Fresh Start. They do splendid work. *You* founded that?"

"Fifteen years ago, this month."

Ray stared at the back of his hand. "That program helped a young man who worked for us. It literally turned his life around." He looked Grant in the eyes. "So, what caused the change of heart, Delaney?"

Grant chuckled. "Life! I saw too many bright kids headed in the wrong direction. After one heartbreaking court case, I asked myself, 'What if someone helped these kids rather than sold them down the river?'"

Ray leaned forward. "Interesting concept."

"It's been rewarding. Many of our clients have gone on to become upstanding citizens."

"What all does your program offer?"

"Besides free legal counsel, we supply tutors, life coaches, financial planners, and tuition vouchers. We even have clothing stores donate outfits for job interviews."

Ray looked around the room and back at Grant. "Do you know Rich Matthews?"

"I remember him, a nice lad."

"He's my nephew. That program saved his life. Are you the attorney who worked with him?"

Grant folded his hands. "One of my colleagues represented him. We have a large staff of volunteers. I help from time to time, when needed."

"Rich is now a gifted mechanic. He even runs his own shop."

Grant looked Ray in the eyes. "It's a small world, isn't it? The way our lives have intertwined. Rich reminds me a little of John."

"He does, doesn't he? Speaking of John, I'd better see how he's doing."

Grant cleared his throat. "He's in my thoughts."

Ray felt lighter as he entered John's room. Pamela was sitting next to John's bed. "How's he doing?"

"He's been calling her name."

"Beth's?"

"Who else?"

"He's in love." Ray went to his son's side. His brow was covered with beads of sweat. He placed his hand on John's forehead. "He feels cooler."

John rolled his head back and forth. "Beth . . . Beth."

"It's me . . . Dad. Mom's here too."

"Where's Beth?" he whispered.

Pamela stroked his hair. "She went home to get some rest."

In a raspy voice he said, "My throat hurts."

John's nurse walked into the room and checked his monitors. "How are you doing?"

He moaned. "I've been better."

Pamela pulled her aside, "I think his fever's broken, but his throat hurts."

The elderly nurse took his temperature. "Good, it's almost normal." She brought him some ice chips to suck on. "You're most likely sore from the tube that went down your throat. It may affect your voice for a while."

"My stomach feels like it's on fire!"

She checked his incision. "I'll up your pain meds. I need you to sit up now."

Pamela looked horrified. John groaned as the nurse rolled up his bed. She pulled the curtain around his bed for privacy.

"Let's get those legs over the side of the bed." She pulled back his covers and adjusted his gown. "Do you think you can stand for me?"

"I'll try." John leaned on her as he stood on wobbly feet. He took a couple of steps before the room began spinning. He backed up and sank onto the bed. "I'm pretty dizzy."

The nurse patted his arm. "You did fine Mr. Beaumont. Dangle those legs for a while.

She smoothed his sheets and fluffed his pillow. "You can get under the covers now." She opened the curtain and faced Pamela. "Try not to worry, we're watching him closely."

"Does he really have to stand up?"

"Yes. We'll have him walking in the morning. Don't want him getting blood clots or pneumonia."

Pamela shifted nervously. John sank back and closed his eyes. "I want to call Beth." John's mother handed him the phone next to the bed. John sighed. "Would you mind giving me a few minutes alone?"

Ray glanced at his watch. "It's getting late. We should get going anyway."

Pamela kissed his cheek. "We'll come back tomorrow."

Ray touched his shoulder. "See you tomorrow."

"Bye, Mom. Bye, Dad. Thanks for coming."

John looked at the clock on the wall. It was nearly eleven. He reconsidered calling Beth. She was most likely asleep. Though he longed to talk to her, he decided to wait until morning. He sucked on ice chips and tried to get comfortable. The phone rang. He startled, then reached for the receiver. "Hello?

"John, it's me."

"Beth! I wanted to call you, but I thought it was too late. You read my mind."

She laughed. "No, honey, I'm not a mind reader. I asked the nurse to call when you were awake enough to have a conversation."

"How come you're not sleeping?" he asked in a raspy voice.

"I dozed off a while ago."

"So, you were asleep?"

"Maude's call woke me."

John smiled. "Thanks for everything, even though I gave you a hard time."

"You sure did! You can be a stubborn guy."

"I've heard that before."

"How do you feel?"

"Like I've been hit by a truck."

"That's normal, honey. Have you walked yet?"

"The nurse got me up for a few minutes, but I'm pretty woozy."

"The sooner you walk the better."

"I thought the nurse was a tyrant for making me stand up."

"Trust me, I'd be worse."

"No mercy at all, huh?"

"Nope."

John suddenly remembered what day it was. "Honey, I'm so sorry about missing the concert. I know how much you wanted to go."

"I'm sorry too but this couldn't be helped."

John sighed. "I guess it's true. Life is what happens while you're making other plans."

"It seems that way. You just concentrate on recovering."

"Will you come and see me tomorrow?"

"Right after church. I'll spend the day with you, how's that?"

"Sounds like heaven."

"Is there anything I can bring you?"

"One of your hugs would be nice."

"Seriously, John."

"Maybe some throat lozenges. And some clean sweats. I hate this hospital gown."

She chuckled. "I'll check with the doctor. Good night, sweetheart. I love you very much."

"I love you, too, baby. See you tomorrow."

Beth attended the early service after alerting the singles class to pray. Pastor Phil promised to keep the prayers going and sent his best wishes to John. Pastor Sorensen also asked the congregation to pray. Beth drew strength from the scripture lessons and her pastor's sermon. A trio's rendition of "Amazing Love"

ministered to her troubled spirit. She didn't stick around long after the service. Her heart was elsewhere.

John was sitting up when she entered his room. A gravelly voice greeted her. "Hello, Beautiful."

She set her packages on a chair and walked to his side. She bent to give him a gentle kiss on the cheek. "How's my favorite patient?"

"Better, now that you're here. I need a hug." She bent down and held him as gently as she could with the IV still in his arm. He clung to her and kissed her cheeks.

She studied him. "Your color is better this morning, but you're running a fever again."

"My throat's really sore."

Beth reached into her pocket. "I have lozenges. I checked with the doc." She unwrapped one and popped it in his mouth. He fixed his eyes on her as she settled next to him. "I brought my Bible."

He nodded. "How was church?"

"Good. The pastor asked everybody to pray for you."

"That's good to know."

Her warm hazel eyes softened. "Let me share something with you." She opened her Bible to Isaiah 40 and began reading:

> Even the youths shall faint and be weary, and the
> young men shall utterly fall:
> But they that wait upon the LORD shall renew
> their strength; they shall mount up with wings
> as eagles; they shall run, and not be weary; and
> they shall walk, and not faint.*i*

She patted his shoulder. "We'll claim that promise just for you."

He squeezed her hand. "What would I do without you?"

She put the Bible aside and rose to hug him again. "I love you."

He looked deep into her eyes. "You must love me if you can say that after I barfed on you."

She stroked his hair. "Would you stop loving me if I barfed on you?"

"Of course not. I'd be worried sick."

"Well, there you go." She settled in the chair next to his bed and continued reading aloud until he fell asleep. She watched his chest rise and fall. His handsome head faced her. She closed the Bible and stood to straighten his blankets. He looked so vulnerable lying there. She felt a deeper dimension of love than ever before. She leaned over him and gently kissed his prickly cheek.

Beth heard the door open and turned to see who it was. Pamela entered the room carrying a bouquet of flowers. Beth put her finger on her lips. "He just dozed off."

Pamela stood next to John's bed watching him sleep. A tear spilled from the corner of her eye. She turned to Beth. "Is there somewhere we can talk in private?"

Beth headed for the door. "There's a lounge down the hall."

Pamela followed as Beth led her to a small room. They settled in chairs across from one another. *She probably wants an update on his medical condition.*

Pamela spoke first. "I want to thank you."

Beth was surprised. "Oh?"

"For taking such good care of John." She sighed. "From what the doctor told us, it's likely you saved his life."

Beth felt tears stinging her eyelids. "He refused to come with me at first. I literally had to drag him."

Pamela nodded knowingly. "John's a lot like his father. He can be awfully stubborn. I'm so glad you made him come with you."

"I'd do just about anything for him."

116

"I was out of line when I asked you to break up with him."

Beth shifted uncomfortably. "I couldn't do it. I tried, but John was just as heartbroken as I was."

Pamela looked down. "I know. He barely spoke to us after that. Ray was furious with me when he found out I'd talked to you."

Beth became defensive. "I didn't tell him."

"I know you didn't. Your father told him last night."

"My father?"

"Yes. He and Ray had a talk. It seems they came to an understanding."

Beth frowned. "What kind of understanding?"

"Let's just say they're willing to let bygones be bygones."

Beth tilted her head. "Really?"

Pamela continued. "As Christians, we know hatred is wrong. And frankly, we've nursed this grudge far too long. Last night the men agreed to bury the hatchet, and I plan to do the same." Pamela took Beth's hands in hers. "I'm so sorry for the way I acted. Can we just start over? The bottom line is we both love John and want him to be happy."

Beth squeezed Pamela's hands as tears of forgiveness escaped her eyes. "Okay."

Twelve

Reid Harper learned about John Beaumont on Monday morning. Though John wasn't his patient, gossip traveled fast. "Poor Beth." He'd heard her name linked with John's once too often. He logged on to the computer and pulled up John's chart. "John Michael Beaumont, thirty-year-old, 6'3", 200 lbs., well developed, well nourished, white male, presents with acute abdominal pain, tenderness and guarding, lower right quadrant . . . " Reid scanned through the admit history and physical. "Patient denies illegal drug use, tobacco . . . "

An idea played in Reid's head. What if he could fix things so that Beth would drop John like a hot potato? Within a few seconds he could add something to John's IV that would render him a vegetable for life. He wouldn't kill him; after all, he wasn't a murderer. The plan took root as Reid considered his options. Suddenly, his day brightened. Beth might not be out of reach after all.

Beth visited John before starting her shifts. His appetite improved, and his incision was healing nicely. He reached for her hand and brought it to his lips. "I didn't realize how hard you work." She kissed his unshaven cheek. "If all my patients were like you, my job would be much easier."

"Do you kiss all of them?" he asked, his eyes teasing.

"Absolutely."

"Really?"

"Of course not, just you."

"Too bad for them because I'm convinced your kisses are magic."

"In that case here's another one."

"Mmm." No longer hampered by the IV, he wrapped his arms around her. "I hear you and Mom had a good talk."

Beth fluffed his pillow and handed him a glass of water. "We did, your mom said she's sorry. But the best thing is that our fathers are now on speaking terms."

"That's definitely an answer to prayer," John said.

"It is, isn't it?"

"Promise me you'll never listen to anyone who tells you to break up with me."

"I promise. But that goes for you, too," Beth said.

Dr. Conrad entered the room. "How are you feeling today, John?"

"Much better. I'd like to go home."

Reid had a terrible time finding John alone. There was always someone at his side; his mother, or father, or worst of all, Beth. There were visitors from his church, including pastors and Bible Study friends. The nurses hovered over him, too. Reid shook his head; he'd have to come back in the middle of the night to make his move. It was too late to add something to his IV. John was no longer hooked up. Time was running out.

Reid considered his options. If something happened while he was on duty, he'd never get away with it. He planned to sneak into John's room around three a.m. He'd have no visitors then. Getting past the nurses' station would be his biggest hurdle. He'd have to wear a disguise.

Reid parked his pickup behind a hedge in the field next to the hospital. He glanced at his phone. It was 2:40 in the morning. Wearing coveralls, his plan was to mop the hall when the charge nurse took her break. The night staff wouldn't recognize him with his hair hidden under a ball cap and fake glasses. Twenty minutes later, he slipped through the hospital employee's entrance and headed for the janitor's closet. He kept his head down as he pushed a mop bucket. He was in luck! The nurse on duty was busy reading when he quietly passed the counter. She didn't even look up. In a few minutes, he'd be in room 404.

His heart raced while he fingered the syringe in his pocket. He broke out in a sweat as he entered the darkened room. It took his eyes a few minutes to adjust. Something was wrong. The room was too quiet. He withdrew a small flashlight from his other pocket and aimed it at John's bed. Horror gripped his soul as he focused on the empty bed. The bedding had been stripped, exposing the stark plastic mattress. Reid left the room as quickly as he'd come, still undetected by anyone.

John returned to work three weeks later, only allowed to do light work. He was feeling much better. The only problem was his inability to sing. Try as he might, he couldn't hit the high notes anymore. In fact, his voice sounded more like a foghorn.

He and Beth made this a matter of prayer. They needed to catch up with their premarital counseling classes, too.

John had the newspaper spread before him. An article about Beaumont Home Furnishings dominated the business section. They had recently supplied a homeless shelter with new beds and living room furniture. The article mentioned that the Tukwila store was scheduled to close soon due to the faltering economy. John sighed; he hoped that seeing it in print would make it more of a reality to the Tukwila store's staff.

"What do you mean you want me to stay home after we're married?" Beth demanded. The two had just left their church after a marriage counseling session. Their session had unearthed a new issue.

John cleared his throat. "I can provide for you; there's no reason for you to continue working."

Beth's eyes grew wide. "But I love my job. I don't want to stay home. What would I do all day anyway?"

"I don't know, take care of our place or work with charities."

"Oh, John, be reasonable! What if I asked you to stay home and goof off all day?"

"That's different, Beth. The man is supposed to be the breadwinner."

Beth raised her hands. "I can't believe my ears. You're a male chauvinist!"

John's face flushed. "I certainly am not!"

"Yes, you are!" She opened her car door.

"But what about our lunch?"

"I'll meet you at the Lighthouse! I have an errand to run first." She was irate as she started her car. *Why did he have to be so pigheaded?* She didn't like his caveman ideas about money either. He expected to handle all their finances and leave her in the dark. The nerve of him, telling her not to worry her pretty little head about finances. What planet was he from anyway?

She stopped at the drugstore and sat in the parking lot, grasping the steering wheel. She had to pick up a prescription for her father. Inside the store, she shifted from one foot to the other as she waited in line. How was she going to change John's mind?

John floored the gas pedal on his way to the restaurant. *What's the matter with that woman anyway? She has such liberal ideas. How am I ever going to tame her?* He heard a siren and saw blue lights flashing in his rearview mirror. *Oh, brother, this is all I need.* He pulled to the shoulder of the road and parked. While fumbling for his wallet, he opened the window.

A state trooper approached. "Where are you going in such a big hurry?"

"To meet a difficult woman for lunch!" John sputtered.

After a brief search in the glovebox, he found his documents. The surly officer wrote out a hefty ticket and handed it to John along with his paperwork. "Next time, watch your speed. And good luck with that lunch."

John wasn't the least bit amused. He hadn't had a ticket since he was a teenager. He was in a foul mood when he arrived at the restaurant. Where was Beth anyway? She was really getting on his nerves. One thing he especially valued was punctuality. Half the time she had been tardy lately. As he sat in the lobby staring at his watch, a familiar face entered the restaurant. "John Beaumont! How are you?"

John stood to greet her. "Alice, hello. You look great. How's life treating you?"

"I'm engaged!" She beamed.

"That's wonderful. Who's the lucky guy?"

"I don't think you know him. His name is Ben Hart. Our announcement just came out in today's paper."

John laughed. "Well, guess what? I'm engaged too! Beth should be here any minute. I'd like you to meet her."

"I'd love to! I guess congratulations are due for both of us. How about a hug for old times' sake?"

Beth entered the restaurant and spotted John across the lobby. Her heart stopped; another woman was in his arms. She was everything Beth wasn't. She was short, curvaceous, and had curly red hair.

Beth felt the floor buckle beneath her. She remembered how she'd caught Reid embracing another woman in the hospital cafeteria so long ago.

The woman handed John a card and disappeared into the restroom.

John noticed Beth standing near the door. He walked over to her. "There you are—what took you so long?"

Beth was livid. "As if you cared!"

John looked puzzled. "What's the matter with you?"

"You! That's what!" She fought the urge to slap his face.

John looked around; they had an audience. "Let's get out of here." He placed his hand on Beth's elbow. She jerked her arm away. John followed her to the parking lot.

She unlocked her car, got in and shut the door. She sat there with her lower lip jutted out as John got in on the other side.

"Are you this upset about our session this morning?" he asked. "Because if you are, we need to pray."

Beth rolled her eyes. "Oh, don't act so pious, you two-timer!"

Now John was angry. "Beth, how could you say such a thing?"

"I saw you with that redhead!"

John rolled his eyes. "She's just an old friend."

"Yeah, right. That's what they all say!"

John's eyes widened. "Don't tell me you're jealous!"

"Who wouldn't be when they find their fiancé in the arms of another woman?"

John heaved a sigh. He'd never seen her so angry before. "I can explain."

Fire danced in her eyes. "Just get out. I need to get to work!"

"Beth, be reasonable!"

She raised her voice, "I said get out!"

John exited her car and slammed the door. He walked to his car muttering, "Women, I'll never understand them as long as I live."

Beth headed for work with tears streaming down her cheeks. Her cell phone rang a few minutes later. She saw that it was John's number and turned off her phone. She never wanted to see him again as long as she lived. She ran to the employees' entrance and headed for the nearest restroom. Thankfully, she didn't meet anyone along the way. After splashing her face with cold water and touching up her makeup, she changed into her uniform and began her shift. She busied herself with her patients and snapped at her co-workers.

"What's eating her?" a nurse asked.

John's day didn't go much better at work. The manager of the Tukwila store said an employee was threatening to sue if he was laid off. An entire order of household furniture was cancelled, and one of the delivery trucks broke down. John juggled invoices, cranky customers, and disgruntled employees. On top of that, Beth was mad at him just for hugging an old friend. She wouldn't answer her cell either. He was tired of hearing, "Your call has been forwarded to an automated voicemail. Please leave a message after the tone."

There was a knock at the door. John opened it, surprised to see his father standing there. "Dad?"

Ray stared at John's crestfallen face. "What's the matter? You look like you've lost your best friend."

John let out a sigh. "I may have." He motioned for his father to join him before he sat down.

Ray lowered himself into a chair opposite John's desk. "What's going on?"

John rolled his eyes. "Women."

"How's the wedding plans coming along?"

"At the moment? Not so well!" John tipped a pencil end to end as he told his father about his rotten day, including the speeding ticket and his argument with Beth. "I just don't understand women at all!"

Ray Beaumont chuckled. "Join the club, son. It's best not to try. Half the time you're dealing with hormones."

"But she's so stubborn. How am I ever going to tame her?"

Ray's eyes grew wider. "Tame her?!"

John stood and began pacing. "As I said, she's very stubborn!"

"And you, John? You're not stubborn?"

John frowned. "What do you mean?"

"I've always known you to be hardheaded. That's part of what makes you a good CEO; but—well, it may not be the best way to handle a relationship, or a wife for that matter."

"But you and Mom . . . "

"Mom and I have hashed out many differences over the years. There have been times when I was so mad at her I could spit. I've taken many burdens to the altar in prayer. And so has she." He knit his brows. "I can be irritating, too. But then again, nobody has given me more happiness than your mother, either."

"But Dad, I think I'm right. Beth wants to keep working after we're married."

Ray scratched his head. "Marriage is a compromise, my boy. You can't expect Beth to see everything the way you do. Most likely, her career is just as important to her as yours is to you.

She's worked hard to get where she is. Do you want to strip her of her identity?"

John frowned. "Well, no."

"What if she asked you to choose between her and your career? Could you do it?"

John looked shocked. "I don't know."

"A good marriage requires give and take. It's not fifty/fifty either. It's more like ninety/ten. John, trust me, it's better to be loving than right. That's something I'm working on myself these days." He sighed. "To be perfectly honest, I still have issues with Grant Delaney. I don't expect you to understand or agree with me. But for your sake, I'm trying to move on. I realize that you've found a gem in Beth. She will bring you much happiness, but things won't always be perfect. According to scripture, your spiritual calling is to love her as Christ loved the church."

John studied his hands. "I guess the church can be pretty stubborn, too."

Ray chuckled. "You've got a point there. Let's pray." Ray rested his hand on John's shoulder and prayed for peace, wisdom, and direction. He asked the Lord to help John sort out his problems with the business and his personal life.

John prayed too. He asked for peace for his father as he worked on forgiving Beth's father. When they finished praying and discussing the pressing business issues, they parted with a hug.

Beth twisted her engagement ring back and forth as she sat in the break room reading the paper. She missed John but was too proud to call him. She glanced at a newspaper and turned to the social page. A picture of an engaged couple smiled up at her. The redhead looked familiar. In fact, she looked just like the woman she'd seen earlier in John's arms at the restaurant. "Benjamin Hart and Alice Stewart announce their engagement."

Beth felt like a fool. John had told her all about Alice and how their relationship ended a long time ago. Beth's jealous nature had gotten her in trouble before. But she still didn't understand why John had hugged Alice in the first place, especially when he knew she was due any minute. He wouldn't be that blatant, would he?

Beth scowled. He'd tried to explain, but she'd cut him off. Sometimes her Irish temper got the best of her. She closed her eyes and silently prayed for forgiveness and wisdom. She also asked for God's blessing on John. *Show me how to understand him better, Lord.*

When Beth finished her shift late that evening, she found John waiting for her in the lobby. "John! What are you doing here?"

His troubled eyes pleaded with her. "Beth, we need to talk."

She nodded. "Okay."

They walked to her car. She unlocked the doors, and he got in on the other side. "Beth . . . I don't want anything to come between us. Please hear me out."

"I'm listening."

John explained how excited Alice was about her engagement, and that he'd told her of his engagement too. She'd asked for a celebratory hug for old times' sake. "It was just a friendly hug, darling, nothing more."

"You're sure about that? Weren't you two once lovers?"

John looked away. "Don't go there."

"Well, weren't you?"

"What we had was over a long time ago. So, when I say today's hug didn't mean anything, you have to believe me." His tone was firm yet level.

Beth stared at her hands. "I'm sorry, John; I do have a jealous streak. It's one of my worst faults."

He reached for her hand. "Let's get one thing straight! I'll never give you any reason to be jealous. Trust me; you're the only woman in the world for me." Beth's lashes caught her tears. John continued. "And what's more, I've been behaving like a fool. We'll compromise on how we handle our finances."

"And my job?" Beth's chin quivered. "Must I quit working if I'm your wife? Because if that's what you *really* want, I'll do it." Tears trickled down her cheeks.

He took his handkerchief and dabbed away her tears. "No, darling, your career is just as important to you as mine is to me. I won't ask you to give it up."

A huge sigh escaped her lips. "Oh, John, let's never quarrel again." She leaned into his embrace. His arms tightened around her as he gently kissed her. "I adore you, Beth."

She snuggled into his arms. "I adore you more."

His eyes searched hers. "So, we're good?"

She smiled. "We're good."

A few days later, after church, John and Beth went out to lunch together. Beth squeezed his hands. "Honey, your voice sounded much better this morning."

He shook his head. "I still can't hit the high notes like I used to."

"It's improving, though. We'll keep praying."

They began going over their wedding plans. "Have you decided where you'd like to go on our honeymoon yet?" John asked.

She squirmed. "That's something I need to talk to you about."

John recapped their last conversation. "We talked about Paris or Hawaii or maybe the South Seas."

Beth placed both hands on the table. "There's no easy way to say this, so I'll lay it all out."

John stroked the back of her hand. "What is it?"

"It's my father! He wants to send us on a cruise through the Panama Canal as a wedding gift."

John tilted his head, "Would you like that?"

A weak smile played on her lips. "I'm not sure. I don't want to hurt his feelings. What do you think?"

He leaned back before answering. "That might be a lot of fun. We wouldn't be running from hotel to hotel. I've never taken a cruise before."

"I haven't either. It could be kind of romantic. But I don't want to disappoint you if you'd rather go elsewhere."

His warm smile reassured her. "I don't care where we go as long as we're together. That's a very generous wedding gift."

"So, you don't mind?"

"Not at all. I'd enjoy cruising anywhere with you. What more could a guy want?"

She leaned over and kissed his cheek. "Oh, how I love you."

The following week at their pre-marital classes, they faced another homework question. Pastor Sorensen left them alone after their session on the topic of children. Beth faced John. "I certainly want children, don't you?"

He nodded. "Yes, of course."

"The sooner the better. My biological clock is ticking."

He shot her a reassuring smile. "No problem. I want a family, too."

"Being an only child can be lonely at times. I'd like at least two." She watched his reaction. "Maybe more?"

John slipped his arm around her shoulder. "We'll have as many babies as you like, my dear, God willing."

"I hope they look like you."

"Are you kidding, a big Swede like me? I'm hoping they'll look more like their mother."

"I thought you were French. I mean . . . with a name like Beaumont."

"My father is half French, but my mother is a full-blooded Swede."

"Well, you look just like your dad, so I'd say you're a Frenchman."

John chuckled. "Whatever."

Beth read the next question asked, "What steps will you take if you are unable to have children?"

John frowned. "How do they expect us to figure all this stuff out now?"

She shrugged her shoulders. "We're just supposed to think about these things. Personally, I think it's best to take one day at a time."

"I agree," John said.

"Que sera, sera! — what will be, will be."

After class, John walked Beth to her car. He stopped abruptly with a frown on his face. "You have a flat tire."

Beth stared down at her wheels and panicked. "Oh no! Now what am I going to do?"

John began removing his sports coat. "Calm down, honey, I'll change it for you. Open your trunk so I can get at the spare tire."

Beth popped the trunk, and John retrieved the jack and tire iron along with the spare tire. He knelt and loosened the lug nuts and jacked up the car. He removed the flat tire and mounted the spare. After making sure the lug nuts were secure, he stood up. "This will get you to the garage."

Beth gave him a hug. "Thank you, sweetie. If I had to call the motor club, I'd probably have to wait forever."

John circled her car, examining the rest of her tires. He looked up. "Your tread seems to be wearing unevenly; it might need an alignment. I'll follow you to the dealer. Let's see if they can do it today. If so, I'll take you to work."

"I'm low on gas too," Beth said. John followed her to a service station and pumped the gas for her. Beth appreciated the kind things he did for her. She let him know with a kiss.

When they reached the dealership, Beth put her purse and jacket in John's car before entering the shop with her paperwork. John gave the flat tire to a mechanic and asked him to check out her car's alignment, too. He found Beth inside the lobby going over her papers with the manager.

Beth called to him, "Honey, would you mind getting my purse out of your car?"

"Be right back." When John approached his sports car, he stopped short. A large red gas can was on the hood. He lifted the container only to discover an ugly scratch. Anger loomed as he glanced around. He put the can aside and ran his finger over the blemish. He fumed as he returned to the shop with Beth's purse.

"What's the matter?" She asked as she noticed his brooding eyes. He placed Beth's purse in front of her on the counter and addressed the manager.

"Somebody put a gas can on the hood of my car, and it left a deep scratch."

The manager had no idea what John was talking about. He followed him outside. After examining the scratch, he looked at John and asked. "So, where's the gas can?"

John frowned, "That's strange; it was here a minute ago."

The manager asked the shop mechanics if anyone had seen a red gas can. Nobody knew anything about it. It had simply vanished.

"Maybe someone put it on the wrong car and realized their mistake and took it away," Beth said.

John frowned. "I'm not happy about that scratch, but there's not much I can do about it at this point. We'd better get lunch so you can get to work on time."

After lunch, John dropped Beth at the hospital and kissed

her goodbye. He then went to his office to catch up on work. He was entering figures on his computer when his phone rang. It was the garage mechanic. He said that Beth's tire had been punctured in three places and needed to be replaced. "I'd make a police report if I were you. This looks suspicious."

John shook his head. "Who'd do such a thing, and why?"

"I've never seen tire damage like this before," the mechanic said.

John called Beth, told her the news about the tire, and asked for additional information for the police report. He scratched his head. "First a flat tire, then the scratch on my car. What's going on anyway?"

That afternoon, John's dad drove him to pick up Beth's car, driving it back to the furniture store where he spent the evening working in his office.

Later that evening, John entered the hospital lobby where Beth was waiting for him. She looked worried. John drew her into his arms and kissed her forehead. They left the hospital together. "Who would do such a thing to my tire?"

"That's a million-dollar question. Do you have any enemies?"

"Not that I know of." She was silent for a minute. "Except for maybe Reid, but I don't think he'd stoop that low."

John frowned. "Reid?"

She told John about their chaotic relationship and how he'd cornered her in the cafeteria. John was livid. "Why didn't you tell me about this before?"

"I didn't want to upset you, and besides, we weren't even engaged then."

John felt rage. "The thought of you in that guy's arms drives me crazy. Especially under those circumstances!"

Beth looked him in the eye. "That's how I felt when I saw you with Alice."

"Well, that was different. It didn't mean anything."

"Neither did Reid's. Not to me anyway!"

John sighed. "And I accused you of being jealous."

"Maybe we both need to grow in that area. But back to the tire issue . . . "

"Do you think he did it, Beth?"

She frowned and slowly shook her head. "No, he wouldn't do that. Why should he?"

"It could be a random act of crime."

"Honey, we need to pray about this," Beth said.

John took her hand. "You're absolutely right." Before they left the parking lot, they lifted a prayer request to the Lord. John drove Beth to her car and insisted on following her home. When they were safely in Beth's driveway, John walked her to her door. They sat together on the porch swing. "Don't worry; we'll get to the bottom of this."

Beth took his hand, "I never worry when I'm with you. You make me feel so secure."

He wrapped strong arms around her. "I don't know how I ever got along without you in my life."

She looked into his eyes. "It's funny, but I feel like I've known you all my life."

"I feel the same way. I'll be so glad when we're married, and I won't have to leave you on your father's doorstep every night."

"That will be nice." She touched his cheek. "Kiss me goodnight."

"I'd be happy to."

∼

The next morning John rifled through a pile of mail on his desk. He opened a letter with no return address. It began simply:

To John:

No young punk is going to ruin my life. Not after all the years I've worked for Beaumont Home Furnishings. I managed the warehouse before you learned to walk. Now you're going to toss me aside like a sack of garbage. There's no such thing as loyalty anymore. I've given this place the best years of my life and made your family a bundle of money, a fraction of what you've paid me. My father worked for the company too. He'd never understand this generation, no way. Something must be done and I've a good mind to do it to teach you ungrateful Beaumonts a lesson.

Clem

John rested his head on the desk.

Thirteen

~~~

I t was a beautiful August morning, Beth's day off. Janet and Carlene were taking her shopping for a wedding gown. Beth had mixed emotions. Though she was over-joyed to choose a dress for her wedding, she'd always envisioned sharing this day with her mother. Sadness flooded her heart. After shedding a few tears, she dropped to her knees. "Lord, I miss her so much. How am I going to do this without her?" While praying, John's mother came to mind, and she heard an inner voice. *"Ask Pamela."* Beth opened her eyes. *Ask Pamela? That couldn't have been the Lord's voice. Or could it?* She pondered the notion for the next hour. Her fingers trembled as she made the call. *What if she thinks I'm presuming too much?*

Pamela was stunned at Beth's invitation to go shopping with her. She stammered that she'd check her calendar and get back to her. She tried to think of an excuse not to go, but something tugged at her heart. She realized Beth must be missing her mother, especially at a time like this.

Like her husband, Pamela wrestled with her feelings about Grant Delaney. But the more she prayed about it, the more she knew it all came down to genuine forgiveness. Forgiveness that must be walked out. She agreed to meet Beth at the bridal salon at ten.

Carlene arrived in Beth's driveway at nine and tapped the horn. Beth came running out to meet her. "It's going to be a scorcher today," she said as she entered her friend's car. "It's already seventy-five degrees." Beth buckled her seatbelt.

"Are you excited?" Carlene asked.

Beth smiled, "Yes ma'am, I sure am. John's mother is meeting us at the bridal salon."

Carlene's lips formed a straight line. "Why did you ask her after the way she's treated you?"

"I can't explain it, but I feel led to."

"Really, Beth?

"Really."

Carlene shrugged. "I swear, you don't have a mean bone in your body." She backed out of the driveway. "How's Janet doing anyway?"

"She keeps busy with work but misses David."

"I'm sure it's really hard."

"I don't think I could stand being away from John that long." They stopped at Janet's house fifteen minutes later. She was waiting for them on her porch. She waved and ran towards the car. "This should be a fun day!"

The three women entered *Love's Inspirations Bridal Salon* where they met Pamela in the lobby. She gave her future daughter-in-law a friendly handshake. Beth introduced her to Janet and Carlene. They all politely shook hands.

A smiling bridal consultant ushered the ladies into a private room where they were seated on comfortable sofas. After quizzing the bride-to-be on her budget and looking over pictures from Beth's bridal magazines, the consultant pulled several gowns for Beth to try on.

Beth entered a large dressing room surrounded by mirrors, and the consultant helped Beth into the first gown. She laced up the back and smoothed the skirt. The billowy satin number reminded Beth of something Scarlett O'Hara might have worn in *Gone with the Wind*. The bridal consultant thought it looked lovely. Beth walked out to model the gown for her audience. The women stared at the gown.

"It's beautiful!" Janet said.

Carlene scrutinized the gown before shaking her head. "No, it's all wrong for her."

Pamela stood up and circled Beth to examine it more closely. "Hmm . . ." she said. "I agree, it's not quite right for you, Beth." She frowned, "It's too, too . . ."

Beth finished her sentence, "Ostentatious?"

The women laughed. Janet stood back. "I think you're right. It reminds me of Princess Diana's wedding gown." Beth picked up her skirt and returned to the dressing room. The bridal consultant helped her out of the yards of material and into a gauzy bell-shaped ball gown. Beth frowned at the girl in the mirror. She had absolutely no sense of style. *Oh well*, she thought as she went before the others to get their opinion. They agreed that it wasn't the right one either.

"With her figure, she'd look good in a gunnysack," Carlene said. "But that dress does nothing for her."

The consultant smiled. "I think I know what you're looking for." Minutes later she returned with more dresses. Beth stepped into a white floor-length gown as the consultant helped her zip up the back. Beth's heart quickened at her image in the mirror. The sleeveless scoop-neck bodice featured a trail of tiny seed pearls. The sleek skirt shimmered as she turned from side to side. It was stunning. Beth turned sideways to admire the mini lace train at the back of the skirt. She pictured herself standing before John at the altar as she ran her fingers over the tiny pearls. The gown fit so well that it would only need minor alterations. The consultant fawned over the gown.

Beth left the dressing room to face her panel of judges. She heard gasps as she walked in front of them. "Oh, Beth," Carlene whispered.

Janet walked around her. "It's so shimmery and beautiful. You look gorgeous." Beth put her hands on her chest. "Do you think it shows too much cleavage?"

The consultant spoke up. "We can alter it a bit to help with that."

Pamela gave the gown a critical eye. "I think it's very tasteful the way it is—I love those tiny pearls. I'm sure John would love it too."

Beth said, "This may be the one, but I have more gowns to try on."

Beth modeled more dresses. One of the gowns, a pale ivory number, featured elaborate tucks throughout the lavish skirt. "Oh wow!" Carlene said. The others liked it too, but Beth insisted she needed something simpler and something white.

Several dresses later and after re-combing her hair, Beth returned to the gown with pearls. Once again, she stood in front of the mirror, lost in visions of marrying in that gown. She slowly walked out to face her judges. The consultant pinned a sheer veil on the back of her head. Beth's eyes teared up. Janet handed her a tissue. "It's just lovely."

The consultant smiled. "Is this the one?"

"Definitely!"

After Beth dressed in her regular clothes, she joined her friends. "Now let's look at bridesmaid's dresses."

The consultant served a light lunch in the salon dining room. Over cups of tea, they discussed bridesmaids' gowns and the color scheme of turquoise and silver.

Pamela found a beautifully beaded silver suit that Beth loved. Before the end of their shopping spree, the gowns were ordered. It had been a very profitable day, especially for the bridal salon.

As they were getting ready to leave, Pamela took Beth's hands in hers. "Thank you so much for including me today. I know you must miss your mother terribly."

Beth's eyes misted. "I really do, but I must say you were a big help. Thank you so much for coming."

Pamela drew her aside. "I'd be happy to help with the wedding expenses."

Beth shook her head. "You'd have to fight my father for that. He's adamant about giving me the wedding of my dreams. Believe me, there's no way he'd take your money. John already offered, but Daddy made it clear, this is his treat, period. No ifs, ands, or buts!"

"I know someone else very much like that." Pamela tucked her purse under her arm. "This was so special, being here with you today."

Beth gave her a gracious hug. Pamela held on a little longer than one might think a future mother-in-law would.

Grant Delaney was out for the evening when John arrived at Beth's home. He was taking her downtown for dinner and a musical. He whistled when she greeted him in a sleeveless black and white sheath, black heels, and silver earrings. Her hair was done up on the sides but cascading down the back.

John drew her into his arms. "Hello, my beautiful lady."

"Good evening, sweetheart."

He kissed her lips lightly. "Are you ready to go?"

"Yes, I'll get a sweater for later. It should cool off once the sun goes down."

"That's one thing about Seattle. No matter how hot it gets in the daytime, it cools off at night."

"I've got all the upstairs windows open. My room is like an oven."

"It hit 94 today, almost a record."

Beth reached for her purse. "I'll have to sleep downstairs tonight. I'm looking forward to your car's air conditioning."

"You're welcome to spend the night at my place if you like; it's air-conditioned too."

Beth laughed. "Nice try, John! Tell you what. I'll take a raincheck for some night in November."

He smiled. "Just trying to be helpful."

She tickled his chin. "You're always so thoughtful." They were on the freeway when Beth excitedly recapped her day. "I found my wedding gown today."

"You did? Tell me about it."

She clasped her hands together. "Well . . . I can't tell you too much, but I'm sure you will love it."

"When can I see it?"

She turned towards him. "Oh, honey, not until our wedding day."

"Why not?"

"It's tradition, the groom can't see his bride's dress until she walks down the aisle."

He reached for her hand. "I can hardly wait."

The next day after church, they went to Beth's to practice for the upcoming talent show. Grant sat in his recliner, working on a crossword puzzle, listening as they played. John's voice had improved considerably, but it wasn't perfect.

"I'm still having trouble hitting the high notes."

Beth kissed his cheek. "Let's take it down to a lower key and see if that helps."

John agreed. "What about you?"

"I'm an alto so it shouldn't be a problem."

Fourteen

ᡣᢕᡅᠥ

The church buzzed with excitement as people gathered for the talent show. Beth and John's friends surrounded them in the crowded foyer. Beth's father made his way to their side and greeted Beth with a hug and shook John's hand. John's parents approached from the opposite direction. Ray nodded and extended his hand to Grant Delaney. As they shook hands, Ray noted once again how the silver-haired gentleman was nothing like the fiery lawyer he'd remembered. He was struck by Grant's soft brown eyes, unmistakably tinged with sorrow. As much as Ray used to detest the man, his rancor was slowly fading into the woodwork. Pamela stood by silently.

John's sister, Tiffany, was visiting for the weekend. The statuesque beauty, with eyes like John's, met Grant Delaney for the first time. "I've heard such nice things about your daughter, and I've never seen my brother happier."

Grant smiled. "It's nice to meet you, Tiffany. John mentions you often."

Tiffany gave her brother an affectionate smile. "I do have a soft spot for the guy." Her eyes met Beth's. "I'm happy to finally meet the woman John has been raving about." They shook hands.

"I'm happy to meet you, too," Beth said.

Tiffany glanced at the flyer she'd received at the door. "I'm anxious to hear you two perform."

Just then, an attractive woman with silver hair and blue eyes arrived. Tiffany gave her a warm hug. "Gladys, I heard you might join us today. I'm so happy you could make it."

Gladys smiled. "When your mom told me about the talent show, there's no way I'd miss it."

John introduced Beth to his parents' long-time neighbor, Gladys Taylor. She took Beth's hand. "I've watched John and his sisters grow up, and I can't wait to hear you two."

John scanned the crowded sanctuary. "I'm having second thoughts; I sure hope we know what we're doing."

"You can't back out now," Beth warned.

He winked at her. "Okay."

Tiffany snickered. *He's one lovesick guy.* "I think your outfits are cute."

John grinned. "Beth decided we should both wear red."

Grant, Gladys, and the Beaumonts settled in a pew together. John and Beth bid their families goodbye before leaving to join the other contestants. The quaint church was packed with families and friends of nervous performers. Grant surveyed the traditional sanctuary with stained glass windows. He hadn't been in a church in years. Pastor Sorensen opened with prayer.

A teenage contestant skipped to his place on the platform. The smiling youth, with shoulder-length hair, wore a black T-shirt. He introduced a song he'd composed. While strumming his guitar, he began singing in a clear voice, "Walking Life's Trails." The performance received hearty applause. He bowed to the audience and grinned as the clapping died down. He sauntered off the stage while his friends continued to cheer for him.

The next act featured a mother and daughter performing

"Climb Every Mountain." The mother strummed a harp while her daughter played the violin. The church was alive with the sound of music, and they received enthusiastic applause. The panel of judges had their work cut out for them.

A middle-aged couple took the stage. The woman was as round as her husband was thin. They sang a touching rendition of Gaither's "Because He Lives." The man seemed a bit nervous and got off-key a time or two, but they, too, received hearty applause. They joined hands as they left the platform.

Next, a group of children bounded across the stage and surrounded the lead singer, a young man from the singles' Bible study. They sang a fun rendition of "Any Dream Will Do" from the musical *Joseph and the Amazing Technicolor Dream Coat*. The lively children's voices and movements were well-choreographed. They also received resounding applause. That act was followed by a male quartet singing "I'll Fly Away." The men had the congregation clapping and tapping along with the music. Beth's father, Gladys Taylor, and the Beaumonts appeared to be thoroughly enjoying themselves.

John and Beth joined hands before walking to the grand piano. They sat side-by-side on the piano bench. John announced their number into his microphone. He faced Beth, giving a slight nod. She softly began playing "The Impossible Dream" with her light touch. Strains of beautiful music filled the church. John's accompaniment added richness as they began singing. John carried the melody while Beth harmonized. Their voices intertwined so beautifully that it was difficult to tell where one started or the other left off.

How they coordinated the singing and playing all at once was a mystery to Beth's father. He could have listened to them for hours. He fought tears that threatened to run down his cheeks. *If only her mother could see her. Perhaps she is watching from a window in heaven.*

Tiffany stared at her brother and his fiancée. She'd expected they'd sound good, but this was unbelievable. Their playing intensified as their voices rose. It sent shivers up and down her spine. Ray Beaumont reached for his wife's hand. Throughout the church, people were dabbing their eyes. Gladys was mesmerized.

When John and Beth finished playing, there was complete silence. As if the audience awaited more notes to flow their way. Then the applause began, slowly at first, but before long, people stood. Thunderous applause was interspersed with a few whistles.

Beth and John walked to the front of the stage, bowing ever so slightly towards their audience. *What a beautiful couple,* Pastor Sorensen thought. *God will use them mightily.*

Several acts followed John and Beth's performance, but they couldn't compare.

At the end of the program, the emcee announced the finalists. The children's choir took third place for their performance. The kids skipped across the stage to receive their certificates. They bowed towards the standing applause. One of the boys high-fived the boy standing next to him. When they cleared the stage, the judges announced that second place went to the harp/violin duo, Susan and Mary Chapman. They blushed as the enthusiastic applause rang out. A hush settled over the sanctuary as the women left the stage. The smiling judge stood up. "I'm happy to report that first place goes to Beth Delaney and John Beaumont for their rendition of "The Impossible Dream.'"

Beth and John glowed as they walked together for their certificates. Again, people were on their feet, applauding for an encore. Pastor Sorensen asked John if they could do another number. He turned towards Beth. "We did prepare another piece."

They walked to the piano again and settled next to each other. John began playing a moving rendition of The Lord's Prayer. Beth softly joined him. They sang with such deep emotion and reverence that it brought tears to the listeners' eyes. John's powerful voice soared as Beth harmonized. She silently prayed that he'd be able to hit the high notes. *"For Thine is the kingdom and the power and the glory, forever. Amen."*

Beth fought tears. *He did it!* Lowering the key had done the trick. He had no trouble finishing the song.

The audience, clearly moved, stood as they applauded. Beth's father took out his handkerchief and blotted his eyes. Pamela and Tiffany did the same. Gladys was crying softly.

Pastor Sorensen beamed. This was more than mere talent; they had an anointing on their performances.

Ray Beaumont had an epiphany. *John should be using his talents for ministry.* He'd pushed his son into the furniture business, brushing aside his wishes to go to seminary. He prayed silently, asking the Lord's forgiveness. He'd never been prouder of his son in his life. And John's fiancée, what a blessing she was turning out to be. At the close of the talent show, a crowd of friends surrounded the couple. They were showered with hugs and congratulations. Pastor Sorensen said they had a rare gift that should be used to bless the church. He asked them to sing on Sunday if they were available.

Tiffany hugged her brother and future sister-in-law. "Oh, my goodness! You two are something else. I never dreamed that you were this good."

"Thank you," Beth said.

Grant nudged them. "Come on you two celebrities, it's time to go to the restaurant." He turned to John's parents and Gladys. "Would you folks care to join us for dinner?"

Ray's eyes lit up. He turned to Pamela, and she nodded.

"You must come too, Gladys," Tiffany said.

When they reached the parking lot, John picked Beth up and swung her around. "Have I told you lately that I love you?"

"No, tell me again."

The party of seven settled at a round table in the Lighthouse restaurant. The couple heard repeatedly how proud their parents were of them. Tiffany asked about their wedding plans, and Beth filled her in on the latest details. She took Tiffany's hand. "Would you like to join our wedding party? You could be one of my bridesmaids."

John added, "We'd love it, Tiff."

Tiffany's eyes twinkled. "I'd be honored!" She pinched John's cheek. "I still remember when you were a baby. You were much more fun to play with than my lifeless dolls."

Beth giggled. "I bet he was." John laughed so hard he nearly spilled his water.

During their meal, Beth learned that Tiffany wasn't in love with her job and had recently broken up with a man she'd dated for two years. Ideally, she'd like to return to Seattle to be closer to her family.

"I guess you'd say I'm in transition," Tiffany said wistfully.

The party conversed easily while feasting on steaks and seafood. Surprisingly, they were an amiable bunch, and time flew by quickly. At the end of their meal, Ray removed several bills from his wallet and laid them on the table. Grant pushed the money back at him. "Put that away. You're my guest."

Beth turned towards Ray. "There's no use arguing. Nobody ever talks my dad out of treating."

Ray sputtered, but Grant raised his hand. "It's a small token of thanks for raising such a fine son for my daughter."

Ray smiled as he shook his head. "I'm quite fond of your Beth, too. They make a great couple, don't they?"

Grant agreed. "Indeed, they do!"

Later that evening, John parked his car in Beth's driveway. He walked her to the porch and took her in his arms. She snuggled closely and slipped her arms around his neck. His lips met hers in a slow, tender kiss. He sighed, "I wish I could take you home with me tonight."

Beth clung to him, fighting the urge to take him up on his offer. "Our day will be here soon, honey."

"Not soon enough for me," he whispered.

She sighed. "I hate to let you go."

He ran his fingers through her hair and cupped her face in his hands. "Not half as much as I hate to leave you."

"I wouldn't be so sure of that."

He looked deep into her eyes. "Goodnight, my darling."

Beth ruffled his hair. "Kiss me again, John."

He drew her closer and kissed her with a hunger that left her barely able to stand. His warm, sensual kiss sent wildfires racing throughout her. It took every ounce of willpower to resist him. Beth pulled back, finding it hard to breathe. She gently pushed him away. "You'd better go home. Now!"

His husky voice murmured, "Oh how I hate to leave you. If your father wasn't on the other side of that door . . . ."

Beth drew a deep breath. "Six more weeks, honey, then we'll never have to part again."

"Right now, six weeks sounds like an eternity."

Beth kissed his cheek. "I promise you darling, it will be worth the wait."

He chuckled. "I have no doubt about that."

She turned to open her door. "I'll see you in the morning. The pastor wants us to sing 'The Lord's Prayer' again."

Late Monday morning, Ray Beaumont called John. "I need to talk to you right away."

"Sure, Dad. What is it?" He looked out his office window. A beautiful rainbow caught his attention.

"Not on the phone, John, we need to meet face-to-face. I want to run something by you."

John was curious. "Do you want to come to my office?"

"No, I don't think so. Could you possibly come to the house?"

John balanced the phone on his shoulder while he checked his planner. "I can be there by two; will that work?"

"Yes, two would be fine. I'll see you then."

John leaned back in his chair. His dad sounded evasive. He thought of the time he'd gone there only to receive a lecture about marrying Beth. He picked up a framed engagement photograph of the two of them. He stared at it for the tenth time that morning. She was leaning on his shoulder as they smiled at one another. He set it back on his desk and tried to focus on his computer screen, but he couldn't concentrate.

At two, John parked in his parents' driveway and walked to the front porch. He rang the doorbell. His father greeted him. "Thanks for coming."

"No problem. Is Mom home?"

"No, she went shopping with Tiffany for her bridesmaid gown. I wanted to see you alone."

He motioned for John to follow him. "Come into my study." John entered the masculine room brimming with overcrowded bookshelves. Ray settled in a chair behind his desk. "Please, sit down." John lowered himself into a leather chair facing his father. His dad looked so serious, John wondered if someone was terminally ill. His father's somber eyes met him. "John, I'm afraid I've made a terrible mistake by asking you to run Beaumont Home Furnishings."

John flinched. "Look, Dad, I know business has been slow, but I think with time I can turn things around."

Ray shook his head. "No, no John, that's not what I mean at

all! You've been a terrific manager. You've held things together when others would have thrown in the towel."

John was puzzled. "Then what is it?"

Ray sighed. "John, I need to ask for your forgiveness."

John stared at him. "For?" *Was this about Beth?*

"What I'm trying to say is that I'm sorry I didn't listen to you when you said you wanted to become a minister. I'm afraid I forced you into a career that may not be God's perfect will for you." John didn't know what to say. He just sat there. His father continued: "Your mother and I have decided to release you from the furniture business. You have our blessing to go to seminary if you like. We'll help you and Beth any way we can."

"But . . . what about the stores?"

"I hope you won't be offended, but I've discussed this with Tiffany. She's extremely interested in the possibility of running the stores."

John was taken aback. "I'd like to pray about this. And talk it over with Beth. That's a big step."

"I agree, don't rush into anything. There is plenty of time to make up your mind. Your mom and I just wanted to give you that option." He rubbed his chin. "Son, you're an amazing musician and singer, and a good speaker too. I want you to think about it. Pray about it, and let me know what you decide. Tiffany is willing to take your place, but only if that's what you want."

"Could we pray now?" John asked.

"Certainly." The two men bowed their heads and prayed for direction for John's career. John stood and they embraced.

"Thanks, Dad, you don't know what this means to me."

His father smiled, "Do you have time for a cup of coffee?"

"Sure."

"Oh, by the way, Mom wants Beth and her father to come to dinner next week. What do you think?"

"I think that's a great idea."

John drove back to work feeling like a boulder had tumbled from his shoulders. Joy welled up from deep within his spirit. Could it possibly be that he'd get his heart's desire to enter ministry? With Beth at his side and her prayer support, he knew he could do anything God asked of him. He had no illusions about ministry being easy; on the contrary, it could be an extremely hard climb. He'd observed difficult personalities in churches and how his pastors had to juggle numerous responsibilities. Much of it would depend on Beth. He remembered how Alice had no interest in anything to do with ministry. Would Beth want to be a pastor's wife? He didn't want to lose her. She meant everything to him. He could hardly wait until they were married so he could love her to his heart's content and fall asleep in her arms.

Fifteen

The next morning Beth joined John at a small café. He was drinking coffee. She sat across from him. "Good morning, you look cute."

He raised his brows. "Just cute? Not adorable?"

Beth swatted him with a napkin. "Okay, adorable."

John winked at her. "You look beautiful as usual."

Their waitress appeared with menus. She stared at John. "Would you like some more coffee?"

He nodded, "Yes please." She poured him a cup and walked away.

Beth sputtered. "What about me? I need coffee too."

John tried to catch their server's eye. She soon returned, placed creamers on the table, filled Beth's cup, and took their orders. "Now, where were we?" John asked.

Beth said, "You were about to tell me something."

"Yes." He reached for her hand. "My father called yesterday and asked me to meet with him. He's offered to release me from the furniture business."

Beth arched her brows. "What?"

"He said that after hearing us perform, he realized I should be using my talents for ministry."

Beth squeezed John's hand. "Honey, that's wonderful news."

"Is it?"

She frowned. "Don't you think so?"

"Yes, yes, I do. But I wasn't sure if you'd object."

Beth looked confused. "Why would I object? You'd make a wonderful pastor."

"It might place a lot of demands on you," John pointed out. "I'm not sure if you signed up. for this."

Beth withdrew her hand. "Are you trying to talk me out of marrying you?"

John shifted uncomfortably. "No, of course not! I just want you to know what you're getting into."

Beth was adamant. "Listen to me, John Beaumont! I don't care what you do for a living as long as it's honest. I love you with all my heart. I'll do anything I can to help you succeed in life."

"It might not be very lucrative; I know you like nice things."

"Oh, for goodness's sake! I have a sizable nest egg of my own. It will be yours too."

John took a gulp of coffee. "People might think I'm marrying you for your money."

Beth rolled her eyes. "Are you?"

"Of course not! I won't take your money anyway."

"Why not?"

"Because!"

Beth stiffened. "Because you're the man?"

John frowned. "Something like that!"

Beth leaned back against the booth and crossed her arms. She stuck out her lower lip. "Then I won't take yours either!"

John's eyes narrowed. "Listen, Beth, pouting may work with your father, but it won't fly with me."

She sat there drumming her fingers and staring into space.

The waitress approached with their orders. "Here you go! Eggs Benedict and a mushroom omelet. Can I get you anything else?" John assured her they were fine. After refilling their coffee cups, she went on her way.

Fire danced in Beth's eyes. "So, you think I pout to get my way, huh?"

John nodded and took a bite of his omelet.

Beth chided him. "John! What kind of a pastor eats his eggs without praying first?"

John chuckled. "An ungrateful one." He reached for her hand. "Let's ask the blessing. Lord, things have turned a corner in our lives. Not only do we thank you for our food, but we thank you for each other and your plans for our future. Whatever we do, let us serve you honorably. Amen."

Beth added. "And Lord, please grant us wisdom to know and follow your will for the rest of our lives. And help the transition to be a smooth one. Amen." Before releasing her hand, John kissed it.

A tender look filled her eyes. "I'd be honored to be a pastor's wife, especially if you're the pastor."

He got teary-eyed. "You'll make a wonderful wife, Beth."

"I hope so." John ate a forkful of his omelet. "Did I tell you my groomsmen got their tuxedos?"

"Good! I really like your best man."

John buttered his toast. "We've been friends since grade school."

Beth had a faraway look in her eyes. "Carlene and I go back a long way too. We met in the fourth grade."

John smiled, "Isn't she the one who said you were all shook up over me?"

Beth rolled her eyes. "She was right about that."

John's smile spread across his face. "That's the day we first kissed."

The server arrived to fill their cups and leave the check. John finished his coffee and looked at his watch. "I've got to run, honey; I have a meeting with Tiffany."

"About the business?"

"Yes. But first I wanted to talk to you before I made any career decisions."

"I appreciate that. Tell her hello for me."

"I'll do that. Where's the check?"

"I've got it, it's my treat!"

"Beth, give it to me!"

She hid it behind her. John reached behind her back. She caught him off guard with a kiss.

John frowned. "You're impossible."

"Yes, but you love me anyway, don't you?"

John looked flustered. He left a tip on the table while Beth paid the bill. He walked her to her car and kissed her goodbye. "Oh, I almost forgot, my mom wants you and your dad to come to dinner next week."

"Really?!"

"Really!" John grinned. "At least we know how to entertain them."

John joined his father and Tiffany at the office. They spent the rest of the day going over the furniture business. Tiffany confessed that she'd always hoped to work for her father in some capacity. She'd worked high school and college summers in the showroom and the business office, so she wasn't a novice.

Tiffany knew since childhood that the helm would go to John as family tradition dictated. With her degree in accounting, she'd landed an excellent job with United Airlines. At first, the perks of traveling the world were enough to keep her happy. But with the recent cutbacks and her personal life challenges, she longed for a change. The knowledge she'd gained with the airline provided additional experience. She was excited about moving back to Washington and being near her family. John and his father promised to spend as much time as needed to help her adjust to the demands of running the stores. Besides, it might take John a while to get into seminary.

The more John thought about ministry, the more excited he became.

Invitations for John and Beth to perform came from churches, county fairs, and various community events. The hospital was sponsoring a benefit and asked them to sing. Much of their time was spent preparing for the events.

With planning a wedding, working full time, and performing, the couple kept themselves remarkably busy. Each performance had the same magical quality. The harmony and beauty of their duets left audiences wanting more. An article about them, along with their pictures, appeared in the local newspaper.

Their joy and love grew daily, and their longing intensified with each kiss. They did everything possible to avoid temptation. Beth rarely went to John's condo alone with him.

They both knew they'd be far too vulnerable. However, Beth needed to take some of her belongings to John's place before the wedding, so they'd be there when they returned from their honeymoon. Tiffany volunteered to help.

They lugged suitcases and armloads of clothing up the elevator. Beth carried another bag of shoes and cosmetics. They entered the condo and took her things to John's bedroom. They spent a bit of time hanging up most of Beth's clothes, but she decided to leave unpacking her suitcase for another day. John rolled it into the office next to his desk. She set a small bag of cosmetics on top of the suitcase.

They returned to the living room, where Beth settled on the sofa. She fanned her face with a magazine. "I'm beat." Tiffany headed to the kitchen and filled three glasses with lemonade.

Beth watched her future husband sort through a stack of mail. She surveyed the home that would soon be hers, too. Cathedral ceilings highlighted two skylights. Gleaming hardwood floors ran throughout the condominium. An oriental rug defined the sitting area, rich with leather furniture. Though it seemed masculine, Beth envisioned how all it needed was a woman's touch. She noticed an acoustic guitar leaning against the wall. "Do you play the guitar?"

John put the mail aside and picked up the instrument and strummed a few notes. While looking into her eyes, he began singing, *"I Can't Help Falling in Love with You."*

Beth's eyes glistened as his tender voice wooed her. When he finished singing, she tilted her head. "Is there anything you *can't* do?"

He set the guitar on the floor, and his arms went around her. "I can't get along without you." She sighed as he kissed her lightly on the lips.

A week before their wedding, John's friends surprised him with a bachelor party at the church fireside room. That same weekend, Beth's girlfriends threw her a shower at a local Victorian tea-room. She opened lavish gifts of lacy lingerie as well as a few practical household items. Tiffany gave her an ivory satin nightgown and matching robe. Before the evening was over, Beth was well prepared to be a blushing bride.

Finally, their big day drew near. At the wedding rehearsal, Pastor Sorensen had Beth and her father practice walking down the aisle behind her attendants. They stumbled over their lines a couple of times.

Afterwards, the couple joined their families at a hotel for the rehearsal dinner hosted by John's parents. Beth met John's sister, Rochelle, and her husband Jerrod. Numerous aunts, uncles, and cousins had flown in for the wedding. John's grandmother, Marie, took Beth's hands in hers. "It is so nice to meet you, dear. John raves about how special you are."

Toasts were given as guests reminisced on how they knew John or Beth. The festivities lasted well into the evening. Eventually, John drew Beth aside. "Let's go, honey. We need our beauty sleep." John drove her home and parked in her driveway one last time. "One more day and we'll be husband and wife." He leaned over to the glove compartment and took out a small box. "This is for you."

Beth's eyes lit up. "A present?"

"For my best girl."

She opened the velvet box and stared at a pair of luminous, pearl earrings. "Oh, how beautiful. Thank you, darling, I'll wear them tomorrow."

John beamed. "I was hoping you'd say that."

Beth reached for his hand, "I've never been so happy."

"Neither have I. I'll walk you to your door."

The crisp evening displayed a golden moon suspended in the sky. A million stars winked at them. John's arms found their way around her. Their lips met repeatedly. Beth didn't want to leave the excitement of his arms. Nor did he want to let her go. He yearned for so much more of her. Beth's eyes met his. "Tomorrow, darling, tomorrow." She reached into her purse and withdrew a lacy handkerchief that she'd sprayed with perfume earlier that day. "Put this on your pillow tonight."

He put it into his pocket, then drew her closer. "How about one more kiss for the road?"

Beth had a tough time falling asleep but eventually drifted off. She awoke in the morning, relieved to see blue sky and bright sunshine filtering through the window slats. She sat up and surveyed the room that had been hers since childhood. Her desk held various medical books and nursing journals. Her open luggage was packed for her honeymoon. The ivory satin lingerie lay in folds on top. A picture of John leaning on a huge spruce tree smiled at her from her laptop screensaver. She felt such love for him. She needed to get moving. Beth put on her robe and slippers and went downstairs to the kitchen. Her father sat at the table, reading a newspaper and sipping coffee. "How's the bride to be?"

Beth kissed her father's forehead. "I'm a little nervous. I need coffee."

"Won't coffee make you more nervous?"

"I'm sleepy too." She glanced out the window towards the lake. The sky was as blue as John's eyes. A smattering of red and gold leaves blanketed the lawn. Grant poured her a cup of coffee, and she gratefully took a sip.

"Would you like me to make you breakfast?" she asked.

Grant frowned. "Heaven's no, not on your wedding day. I had a bowl of Cheerios and a banana." He smiled at his only child. "I'm happy for you, honey."

"Oh, Daddy, I'm happy too, more than I ever dreamed possible."

She noticed an envelope lying on the table with her name on it. It looked like her mother's handwriting. She frowned as she stared at her father. "What's this?"

Grant rubbed his chin. "It's a letter from your mother. She wrote it with instructions to give it to you on your wedding day." He looked at the letter. "She made me promise not to give it to you unless you get married."

"Do you know what it says?"

"No, I've never opened it. It's yours; feel free to read it in private." After Beth finished her toast and coffee, she took the letter upstairs to her room. She sat on the edge of her bed and opened the letter. Her hands trembled as she unfolded the stationery and began to read:

My Dearest Beth,

If you are reading this, it's because today is your wedding day. As I write this letter, I know my time on earth is short. There are so many things I'd like to share with you. You've been such a wonderful daughter, bringing your father and me so much pride and joy. I remember the day you were born, my special valentine from God. You were such a beautiful and content baby. I cherished your first smile, your first attempts to crawl and walk. When you were a little girl, you loved dressing up in my clothes and parading around in my high heels. One day, you made me laugh hysterically when you draped a lace tablecloth around your hair and pretended you were a bride. You sang "Here Comes the Bride" as you carried a centerpiece from the dining room table. Maybe that moment was just for me.

I cherished our little tea parties at your small table and enjoyed playing grandmother to your dolls. I am so proud of your achievements. Being on the honor roll in school, your beautiful singing voice, your amazing piano playing ability, and your sweet personality. You are such a gift to this world.

I have been praying for you to find someone incredibly special to spend your life with. Someone who will love and cherish you as you deserve. I know you have a lot of love to give to some blessed man. Men are sensitive creatures who sometimes try to hide their vulnerability. Be his helpmate, listen to his advice, and love him with all your heart; enjoy your husband's love and satisfy his needs as you trust the Lord together. I know that God has wonderful plans for your life. If you are blessed with children, welcome them and cherish them. My spirit will be with you on this special day. I can imagine you in a lovely gown, glowing with joy.

My wedding day was the happiest day of my life. I love Grant more today than I thought possible. He was and still is an exceedingly kind, loving, and handsome man.

Rejoice, my daughter, for this is the day the Lord has made! Know
that I am at peace and with my wonderful Lord.

I love you,
Mom.

Beth folded the letter and placed it inside her Bible. She dabbed away tears and took time to pray. She thanked God for her mother and father and for John. She prayed to be the best wife possible, and that their wedding would be blessed in every way. She asked for safe travel for their wedding guests and for traveling mercies for her and John on their honeymoon. And she prayed for God's will to be done in their lives.

Sixteen

Fragrant flowers permeated the sanctuary while the bride and groom waited at opposite ends of the church. Ray Beaumont presented his son with a pair of diamond cufflinks that he'd worn at his wedding forty years ago. Pamela pinned a white rosebud on her son's lapel and straightened his silver tie. John radiated joy.

In another room, bridesmaids surrounded Beth in her shimmery gown that graced her slender frame. Her dark hair looped back on the sides with curly tendrils trailing down the back of her neck. A sheer fingertip veil fell just below her shoulders. Her earrings complemented the pearls on her gown.

Beth glanced in the mirror. Lush lashes framed hazel eyes that sparkled like the ring on her finger. With a song in her heart, she eased a garter belt onto her shapely leg and slipped her stocking feet into white brocade heels.

Grant Delaney hadn't worn a tuxedo in a long time. Looking quite distinguished with his thick silver hair, he was still a handsome man at the age of seventy. His mind was as sharp as ever. He rejoiced that Beth had found a man like John. He paced nervously in the foyer, waiting for Beth to appear.

Heavenly strains of music filled the sanctuary as the ushers seated guests. The church pianist, along with the harp/violin duo, played Beth's favorite song, "Love Changes Everything."

Elegant bouquets graced the altar area. Silver bows decorated the end of each pew. Two of the ushers served as candlelighters, lighting all the altar candles with a taper except the unity candle. An unusually small twig cross rested at its base. A white candle flickered in honor of Beth's mother.

Beth's friends, colleagues, and relatives filled the bride's section. Her nursing supervisor sat next to Doctor Martin and his wife. Three of her high school teachers and two of her college professors sat waiting. Her cousins came from various states.

John's relatives and friends filled the groom's side. Their Bible study friends took up three more rows.

The handsome groom and his groomsmen entered the altar area with the pastor. They stood side-by-side, waiting for the wedding to begin. John looked elegant in his black tuxedo with the silver vest and tie. His thick blond hair waved ever so slightly. His blue eyes glittered in anticipation of his bride's appearance. Were all grooms this nervous?

The pianist accompanied the harp/violin duo in a moving rendition of Pachelbel's Canon. Tiffany followed Janet as they made their way down the aisle in floor-length turquoise gowns, each carrying a small bouquet. Beth's matron of honor, Carlene, walked down the aisle in her sleek silver gown. Behind her, little four-year-old Kelly stood proudly waiting to walk down the aisle. Her blond curls, tied back with a silver ribbon, bounced. Her frilly dress, a mixture of light and deep turquoise ruffles, complemented her white shoes. The music continued as she shyly began tossing rose petals along the aisle runner. She stopped halfway down the aisle, turned around, and began picking up her petals. As she put them back into her basket, her grandmother appeared from the side and coached her to continue. Kelly turned and headed in the right direction to the amusement of John and the wedding guests. When Kelly reached the front of the church, her grandmother took her hand and guided her to sit in the third row with her daddy.

The organ and piano resounded together for Wagner's wedding march processional. Everyone stood. Beth appeared on the arm of her father. Radiant from head to toe, she was by far the most stunning bride John had ever laid eyes on. A quiver shot through his body as tears spilled down his cheeks. The best man offered him a handkerchief. Beth's shimmery gown drew audible gasps from the guests. She carried a unique bouquet of various flowers. Tears threatened John's eyes as his joy bubbled forth. *Truly, my cup runs over.*

Grant Delaney was as proud as he'd ever been; walking his dazzling daughter down the aisle was the highlight of his life. Beth was so nervous she could barely walk. Now she knew why brides needed their father's arm so desperately. Grant steadied his daughter's steps as they walked together. Her nervousness dissipated at the sight of the handsome groom waiting for her. She fixed her gaze on John. *How could it be that such a man is waiting for me to be his bride?*

When Beth and her father reached the front of the church, Pastor Sorensen stepped forward. "It's with great affection for John and Beth that we've gathered to witness and bless their union in marriage. To this sacred moment, they bring the fullness of their hearts as a treasure and a gift from God to share with one another. They bring the dreams that bind them together in a holy commitment. They bring their gifts and talents, their unique personalities, and spirits, which God will unite into one as they build their lives together. We rejoice with them in thankfulness to the Lord for creating this union of hearts, built on friendship, respect, and love." Pastor Sorensen asked the congregation to be seated. "Who gives this woman to be married to this man?"

"I do." Grant Delaney proudly declared. He released his daughter's arm as she turned to kiss his cheek. John shook Grant's hand and took Beth's hand as they stepped up to the altar. She handed her bouquet to Carlene and turned to face John as they joined hands.

Janet straightened the train of Beth's gown.

Pastor Sorensen began his sermon, and John and Beth got lost in each other's eyes. "John Beaumont, I ask you in the presence of these witnesses, do you intend to enter into holy wedlock with Elizabeth Delaney? If so, answer 'I do.'"

John answered with a resounding, "I do!"

The pastor looked at Beth. "Elizabeth Delaney, do you intend to enter into holy wedlock with John Beaumont?"

Beth fought tears. "I do."

Pastor Sorensen signaled to John. He gently squeezed Beth's hands. "I, John Michael Beaumont, take you, Elizabeth Christina Delaney, for my lawfully wedded wife. I promise to love and cherish you always, for better or worse, for richer, for poorer, in sickness and in health, until death parts us."

Beth smiled as she softly vowed, "I, Elizabeth Christina Delaney, take you, John Michael Beaumont, for my lawfully wedded husband. I promise to love and cherish you always, for better or worse, for richer, for poorer, in sickness and in health, until death parts us." Now John was fighting tears.

Pastor Sorensen asked, "May I have the rings?" The best man, Jeffery, and the matron of honor, Carlene, each handed a wedding band to the pastor. He prayed a blessing over them and handed a ring to John.

He smiled at his bride as he slid the platinum band on her finger. "With this ring, I marry you. I promise to be faithful as long as we both shall live."

Beth glowed as she looked her groom in the eye. She gently placed the band on his finger. "With this ring I marry you. I promise to be faithful as long as we both shall live." He winked at her. She smiled in response. The couple lit the unity candle together.

The pastor said, "For as much as John and Beth have pledged their love in marriage, in the company of these witnesses, and by the power vested in me as a minister of the gospel, I now pronounce them husband and wife." He turned to John. "You may kiss your bride."

John took Beth in his arms and gave her a tender kiss, and she wrapped her arms around his neck and kissed him back. Pastor Sorensen chuckled, "It is now my privilege to present Mr. and Mrs. John Beaumont."

Cheers and applause rang out. The organist began playing the recessional, "Ode to Joy." Beth and John linked arms and walked down the aisle as newlyweds, their faces radiating joy.

The bridal party lined up in the foyer to greet their guests. Their Bible study friends were the first in line. "I guess this means you won't be in the singles group anymore," Mindy said.

John chuckled. "You've got that right!"

After posing for pictures and signing documents, they made their way to the waiting limousine, while guests blew bubbles at them. Their attendants joined them for the ride to the reception. John had Beth in his arms when the limo approached the venue. The driver held the door while the couple and their attendants stepped out. A photographer caught the moments on his camera.

The hotel staff directed guests to the ballroom. A harp and violin duo played softly as guests arrived. Round tables bearing white linen, roses, and silver candles seated eight people. As the bridal couple entered the festive ballroom, they heard, "Ladies and gentlemen, please welcome Mr. and Mrs. Beaumont!" Cheers and applause reached a crescendo.

The wedding party took their place at the head table. The room was alive with music as waiters served a festive four-course meal. Beth was too excited to eat much. John managed better than she did. He coaxed her with a bite of salmon. "Try this, darling, it's delicious." He fed her with his fork.

"Mmm, that is good!"

The best man, Jeffery, stood to offer a toast. "I would like to congratulate the happy couple on their wedding day. Anyone who knows these two finds a loving couple who walk in faith and integrity. Along with all of you, I wish them life's finest blessings as they discover the joys of marriage." He raised his glass as the guests joined in the toast. "To the bride and groom!"

Before long, it was time to cut the cake. Beth and John posed for pictures as they held the cake knife. They sliced a piece of chocolate cake and fed it to each other. Beth whispered in John's ear, "Be sure not to get any on your tux or my dress."

John teased, "We've only been married an hour and you're nagging me already!" She started to protest, but he shushed her with a sticky kiss.

The emcee announced that it was time for their first dance. A small combo band replaced the harp and violin duo. They played a romantic ballad while John waltzed with Beth in his arms. He sang along in her ear. "I will love you forever."

She pressed her cheek against his and sang the next line with him. "Forsaking you never."

"Did I ever tell you how lovely you are?"

"Maybe—once or twice."

John nuzzled her fragrant hair. "I love you very much, Mrs. Beaumont."

"And I love you too, Mr. Beaumont. Do you like my dress?"

He stood back admiring her gown. "I'm crazy about it!"

"Your mother said you'd love it."

He arched his brow. "My mother?"

"Yes, she helped me pick it out."

John smiled as he drew her closer. "I've never seen a lovelier bride."

Beth sighed, "And I've never seen such a handsome groom!"

When the music stopped, Beth's father approached. He tapped John on the shoulder. "Excuse me, John, it's my turn."

John gently released her and kissed her cheek. "Hurry back, honey."

The band played as Grant Delaney took his place. "You're such a stunning bride. I'm immensely proud of you and John. I know your mother would say the same thing."

"Oh, how I wish she were here. Her letter was wonderful. Would you like to read it?"

"Only if you want me to."

"I do. It's in my room on the dresser, tucked inside of my Bible."

"You're a wonderful daughter. I'll miss you terribly."

"You'll always be in my life." Grant spun his daughter around. "I didn't know you were such a good dancer!"

"I was quite dashing in my day."

"You still are. You look so handsome tonight. All the guests are watching you."

Grant tossed his head back and laughed. "No, Beth, they're watching you."

Nearby, Pamela waltzed with John and told him how much she loved him. "I'm happy for you, John. Beth is a gorgeous bride, isn't she?"

John smiled. "That she is, Mom."

At the end of their waltz, he bowed slightly and thanked her for the dance. He couldn't wait to find Beth again. Together, they visited each table to thank their guests for coming. They received many warm wishes for their happiness. One couple invited them to their next gathering of friends. Dr. Martin and his wife stood to dance with each other. A boy about six years old danced with Kelly, the flower girl.

Beth and John began dancing again. "Look, your dad is dancing with Gladys Taylor."

Beth smiled. "I think they like each other."

"How long before we can leave?" His arms tightened around her.

"Aren't you having a good time?"

"Sure, I'm having a good time, but it's been a long day." Beth looked at John's watch. "Why is it only eight o'clock!"

An hour later, women lined up hoping to catch Beth's bouquet. She artfully tossed it over her shoulder. Marla nearly knocked a woman down as she dove for the bouquet. She proudly waved it in the air, "I'm next."

A few minutes later, the bachelors lined up to catch the garter that John had artfully removed from Beth's leg. He flung the garter like a rubber band. Pastor Phil caught the frilly belt. His girlfriend yelled, "Yes!"

At last, it was time to leave the festivities. Beth panicked when she couldn't find the outfit she was going to change into. She told John she must have left it at home. Her suitcases were in the waiting limo. John put his arm around her, "Just wear your gown to the hotel. I'll ask Tiffany to pick it up tomorrow."

The newlyweds hugged their family members goodbye before John helped Beth into the waiting limousine. They were finally alone as the limo driver headed for the freeway. Beth snuggled in John's arms. He nuzzled her ear. "Hello, my lovely wife."

Beth turned and looked deep into his eyes: "Well, hello, my darling husband."

"Can you believe it, Beth? We're actually married!"

She caressed his cheek. "Now you won't have to leave me on my father's doorstep every night."

He took her hand in his and kissed it. "Never again! I have better plans for our evenings now."

She looked into his dreamy eyes. "I'll just bet you do."

John held her face in his hands as he kissed her tenderly. Beth felt dizzy as she rested her head against his shoulder.

John sighed. "I love you so much, Beth."

"I love you more." She whispered.

John muttered under his breath, "I don't think that's possible."

The next morning, Beth woke up first. She quietly slipped out of John's arms and headed for the bathroom. She turned on the water and stepped into the shower. She hummed to herself as she gently soaped her body. The warm spray was invigorating. After drying off and applying fragrant lotion, she put on her satin robe. She brushed her teeth and fixed her hair. She admired herself in the mirror before dabbing on a bit of lipstick. She wanted to look beautiful for her husband when he awoke.

Since he was still sleeping, Beth wandered around the elegant suite. A large bouquet of roses graced a side table. Her wedding dress was draped over a wingback chair. She lovingly ran her fingers over the shimmery fabric.

Beth went to a small kitchenette and looked inside the refrigerator. She discovered an assortment of coffee creamers, juices, and bottled water, a coffee maker, and a bag of coffee. She filled the carafe with tap water and poured it into the pot. After measuring the aromatic grounds into the filtered basket, she pushed a button. Instantly, the rich brew began to seep into the pot.

She returned to the living area and lifted a rose to her nose. John walked up behind her and wrapped his arms around her. "There you are! I woke up and my beautiful bride was gone."

Beth turned to face him. "Good morning, darling. Your bride is right here waiting for you."

His arms tightened around her as he held her close to his heart. "You were right."

She met his eyes. "About what?"

He smiled. "You were definitely worth waiting for."

Her cheeks flushed a deep red. She smiled shyly. "So were you."

He kissed her before releasing her. "Do you like the roses?"

"I love them! They're beautiful. Thank you. This suite is awesome."

"I hoped you'd like it."

She noticed for the first time that his robe was exactly like hers. "Did Tiffany give you that robe?"

He laughed. "I see she matched us up pretty well."

She stroked his cheek. "Darling, your face feels like sandpaper."

"I'm thinking of growing a beard like Amish married men do."

"Really?" Beth ruffled his hair with her fingers. "You'd look good with a beard. Would you like a cup of coffee?"

"I sure would. Then we need to order breakfast and get ready for our flight."

Beth drew her husband close to her. "We still have plenty of time. After breakfast, how 'bout a few more kisses for the road?"

John smiled. "Whatever you say, baby."

Seventeen

B eth and John thoroughly enjoyed the luxurious cruise ship. They posed for pictures with breathtaking sunsets in the background and texted updates and photos to their parents. They used the fitness rooms and swimming pools to help burn off the extra calories of the extravagant meals.

They strolled hand in hand wherever they went. Their cabin opened to a veranda where they had breakfast. They watched ocean waves as they sipped coffee and shared bites of their omelets and crepes.

The veranda was also a good place for prayer. John read from their couple's devotional. In the evenings they sat in the moonlight snuggling under a blanket on a chaise lounge. Nothing hampered their desire now.

When the ship docked in various ports, they explored shops, ate, and talked until they ran out of things to say. In one port they spent the afternoon on a beautiful beach. Beth wiggled her toes in white sand while John rubbed lotion on her back. They splashed in calm, warm water and snorkeled. Several fish of various colors moved swiftly ahead of them. The beautiful couple stole kisses as they sunbathed on beach towels.

On Sunday morning, they attended an onboard church service. A small crowd gathered in one of the entertainment lounges. When the chaplain apologized because their piano player missed the cruise due to illness, John volunteered to help. He and Beth quickly adapted to the songs the minister needed. As a result, the congregation encouraged them to enter the ship's amateur talent contest. After some arm twisting the couple agreed to check it out.

Beth enjoyed being married. John was kind, gentle, and protective of her. She no longer fumed when women stared at him. John only had eyes for his bride. His heart was full of gratitude to God for bringing this jewel into his life. She challenged him to be all that he could be. But there were times when Beth kept John guessing. She did love to tease him. Like the morning they were on their veranda discussing what kind of a house they'd like to build someday. "I'd like a rambler," Beth said.

John gasped. "A rambler! You've got to be kidding."

Beth leaned in closer. "No, I'm not kidding. I think a rambler would be nice."

John scowled, "I'd like something with character. Something with a second floor at least."

Beth studied her nails. "Stairs are a lot of trouble to climb and clean."

John recalled their premarital counseling. "Well . . . maybe we can compromise."

Beth said, "I suppose we could have a rambler with stairs."

John chuckled. "That sounds like a split level. I don't particularly care for those either."

She was trying to be patient. "Well . . . how about a tri-level then?"

John nodded. "That's a possibility. With the right architect."

Beth had an impish gleam in her eye. "Let's talk about furniture!"

"Now that's something I know well. I like classic pieces, don't you?"

Beth crossed her fingers behind her back. "I'm thinking more like early American furniture."

John gave her a sideways glance. "Are we talking real early . . . like antiques?"

"Well . . . I was thinking more like a mid-century early American. You know, like the flowery sofa in the church fireside room."

John gasped. "There's no way I'd put that tacky thing in my house!"

Beth stuck her lower lip out in her famous pout.

John leaned back in his deckchair and put his hands behind his head. "Now listen here, my dear, I've told you before, pouting won't fly with me."

Beth covered her face and pretended to cry.

Flabbergasted, John leaned forward. "Do you really want *that* kind of furniture?"

Beth giggled behind her hands. John pried her fingers open and glared at her. She was now laughing so hard her whole body rocked. John stood up and crossed his arms. It was no use; everything he did struck her funny. She laughed from deep within. The more he glared, the more she hooted.

She stood and ran inside the cabin. John followed and caught her shirttail. "What's the matter with you, anyway?"

Beth doubled over. "The look on your face was priceless." She turned and shook her head. "Truthfully, I don't like early American furniture either."

John glowered. "You did that on purpose." She fell backward on the bed holding her sides. She couldn't stop laughing.

John flopped down beside her. "Are you making fun of me?"

She slipped her arms around his neck. "Sometimes I have a real mischievous streak."

John rolled his eyes: "What am I going to do with you?" She

gave him a look that made him chuckle, too. They clung to each other, laughing until tears rolled down their cheeks.

Mr. Bickel, a tired old talent scout, had been on one too many cruises. They'd stopped being fun years ago. He'd listened to mediocre talent on ship after ship. Sometimes he was lucky and discovered a promising act, but usually he heard amateurs that wouldn't survive a week on a reality talent show. Though bored with his job, he couldn't afford to retire. He'd squandered most of his earnings in casinos. It wasn't such a bad life. At least he got plenty to eat and a roof over his balding head.

Tonight's talent show was sure to be more of the same. He had to give a full report on each act, or he didn't get paid. One of the guys who tried faking a report was fired on the spot. Bickel wasn't dishonest—just bored stiff. A drink or two usually helped him endure the ordeal.

He mentally tried to conjure up interest in the acts lined up for the evening.

The first to take the stage were adults dressed in red silk capes. Mr. Bickel yawned as they performed a magic act as lame as anything he'd ever seen. He rolled his eyes and took a sip of his highball, crafted just the way he liked it. After two or three he'd feel better. Following the magic act, three teenage sisters sang and danced. The girls were cute as they could be, but their harmony was off. Next, a wannabe cowboy sauntered across the stage, hugging his guitar and doing an imitation of Johnny Cash. It was like most of the others he'd heard before. Poor ole Johnny wouldn't like any of them.

A woman who looked at least sixty stood before the crowd. She plunked her guitar and warbled out a sad rendition of "The Rose," but she was certainly no Bette Midler.

Next, a family with teenage boys sang barbershop. They

received hearty applause from the crowd. Bickel scribbled on his pad.

A comedian took the stage with a lot of original jokes, amusing to say the least. He might even make it somewhere, Bickel thought.

Next, a handsome, blond man and a beautiful brunette entered the stage. She wore a black dress and red heels. The striking couple announced that they'd sing and play their own arrangement of "The Impossible Dream." Mr. Bickel frowned as they approached the grand piano and sat next to each other. He reached for his drink as the man signaled to the woman. She began playing with a light and poignant touch. The man joined her playing harmony. And they began to sing! Their voices blended like opera stars. Bickel leaned forward as their moving rendition filled the theater. The performance was fresh and original. He put his drink aside, mesmerized, along with the rest of the crowd. He could have been watching a Broadway musical. He forgot to write on his pad. For the first time that night, the audience was on their feet cheering for the couple even before they'd finished. They chanted "More! More!" Beth and John walked to the front of the stage and bowed while the crowd went wild.

The emcee explained that other acts were waiting to perform, so there could be no encores. It seems everyone had been waiting to see some real talent. As far as the audience was concerned, the talent show was over. Mr. Bickel felt the same way. When the next act started, he went backstage to find the couple seated with the other contestants. Mr. Bickel introduced himself. John stood and shook his hand. "I'm John Beaumont and this is my wife, Beth."

Mr. Bickel smiled. "Are you two really amateurs?"

John answered, "Yes, why?"

Mr. Bickel raised one eyebrow. "Because you sound like pros. Where are you from anyway?"

John put his arm around Beth's shoulder. "Seattle."

"And you don't sing anywhere?"

"We sing in church," Beth said.

"In church," he echoed like a parrot.

Beth nodded. "Yes, and at fairs or benefits."

The talent scout beckoned them with his index finger to a secluded area away from the other contestants. He whispered, "Would you two be interested in a recording contract?"

Beth's eyes widened. "A contract?"

Bickel eyed the rock on her finger. "Yes, dear lady."

John and Beth stared at each other. They could hear the other acts on stage.

"Let's get out of here," Mr. Bickel said.

"We can't leave until the results are in," John said.

"I guess you're right. But I can tell you right now who won."

Mr. Bickel groaned as the ship's entertainment director approached. The dark-eyed man faced the talent scout. "Hey, Bickel, aren't these two amazing?"

"That's one way to put it."

"I suppose you're trying to lure them away, but they can't leave yet, and you know it."

Bickel rolled his eyes. "Okay, okay. I'll play the game."

After several more acts John and Beth were declared the winners. When they took the stage again, the audience became rowdy, demanding an encore. The emcee shrugged and asked them to sing again. John whispered in Beth's ear. They went to the piano and began to play "You Raise Me Up."

There was complete silence as music filled the theater with superlative sounds. Their voices blended with majesty and beauty. This was what old Bickel had lived for, hoped for, and dreamed of. He'd finally found his pot of gold. The radiant couple connected with their audience as they played and sang the powerful song. Once again, the crowd went wild.

Beth and John finished the song and walked to the front of the stage. They joined hands and bowed.

Afterward, people lined up to greet them, seeking autographs. When the crowd thinned out, Mr. Bickel promised he'd have more information the following day.

The Beaumonts signed more autographs before making their way down the long corridor to their cabin. John opened the door, and they entered a spotless room with an elephant towel sitting on the bed. John removed his jacket and hung it in the small closet next to a terrycloth robe.

Beth pondered their evening as she sat on the edge of the bed, removing her shoes. She moved to a counter and began removing her makeup with cleansing cream. After splashing chilly water on her cheeks, she turned towards John. "Can you help me unzip my dress?" John did as she asked. Beth stared into his dreamy eyes. "Do you think he was serious about a recording contract?"

"Maybe." John said as he removed a clip from her hair, letting the curls fall softly around her face. "But right now, I really don't care." He ran his fingers through her curls.

Beth closed her eyes and leaned into his embrace. Nothing else mattered except responding to his kisses.

The next morning, Beth opened her eyes to find John smiling at her. "How's the most beautiful woman on the ship?"

She smoothed his hair with her fingers. "Are you talking to me?"

He chuckled. "Who else?"

She protested. "You still think I'm beautiful with no makeup and messy hair?"

He traced her cheek with his finger. "I do."

She eyed him carefully. "I think you're pretty cute too, even though your hair is almost as bad as mine."

"No thanks to you."

"Happy Birthday, darling!"

Surprise registered in his eyes. "You're right! Today is my birthday. How shall we celebrate?"

She tickled his chin. "I'm sure we'll think of something."

He smiled, "You're the only present I need."

"I do have a gift for you, honey." She adjusted her nightgown before rolling towards the nightstand. She withdrew a card and a small package from the drawer. "Open it."

He sat up and carefully removed a greeting card with a picture of ocean waves crashing upon the seashore. It read:

> *Happy Birthday to My Husband.*
> *I wandered aimlessly along the seashore, searching for treasure.*
> *Then I found you, my precious one, a blessing beyond measure.*
> *You fill my heart with joys untold; your arms mean more than rarest gold.*
> *I wish for you your heart's desire on this, your day of birth.*
> *I thank the Lord for blessing me with the dearest husband on earth.*
>
> *All my love, Beth*

He closed the card and looked deep into her eyes. "Thank you, darling—it's beautiful."

"You're most welcome, now open your present."

He removed the paper to find a small wooden box. He lifted the lid. His eyes beheld a gold cross on a chain. He recognized it as one he'd been admiring in the gift shop. "Hey! How did you know I wanted this cross?"

"I saw you going back and forth to look at it. I was afraid you'd buy it and spoil my surprise."

"Well, I have to admit I was disappointed when I learned it was gone yesterday."

"Then you really do like it, don't you?"

He pulled her close to him. "Yes baby, I really do. You are a most thoughtful wife. Now what do you say we order breakfast?"

"Let's go to the dining room today." She'd secretly arranged with the headwaiter to have a small birthday cake waiting to surprise him.

Beth and John were invited to dine at the captain's table that evening. Since it was a formal night, they dressed to the nines. Beth wore a turquoise and black sleek gown while John dressed in his tuxedo. Heads turned as they entered the dining room.

On the final evening of the cruise, Beth and John were asked to close the evening show with two numbers, "The Impossible Dream" and "You Raise Me Up." The couple insisted that their second number was to be a surprise.

Ship passengers as well as staff members gathered to see the new stars perform. Beth chose a chic white dress with pearl accessories, while John opted for his tux. Beth carefully checked him over, telling him how handsome he looked. They stood before the mirror in their cabin. "Not a bad looking couple," John remarked.

Applause rang out as they entered the stage holding hands. Bickel didn't think it was possible to outdo their original performance, but they did. Once again, they received a standing ovation. There was a hushed expectancy as the crowd awaited their final number. The striking couple took their places at the piano, and Beth began softly playing "You Will Never Walk Alone."

A sacred hush settled over the theater. As John and Beth's incomparable voices soared, people dabbed tears from their eyes. Then a strange thing happened. All over the audience, people began to stand in reverence and awe. There was no applause or whistles, just people reconnecting with their God. The couple's voices rose in perfect harmony and majesty.

Beth felt shivers running over her body. Again, the anointing was upon them. The anointing that breaks the yoke of oppression.

Lives changed that night. Even Mr. Bickel would never be quite the same. By the time the song finished, most people were already standing. The applause came slowly at first and then rose to a crescendo. Beth and John walked to the front of the stage, joined hands, and bowed to their audience. The applause lasted a full three minutes.

Afterwards, John and Beth were offered jobs on the cruise ship, and possible bookings in major cities.

Back in their cabin they knelt in prayer, asking just who they were to play their lives to. Was this their calling or not? They needed direction. Beth searched John's eyes. "I only want God's will for us, John. I don't want anything to sidetrack us or spoil the love we have for each other."

John took her in his arms. "Neither do I, darling; neither do I." He recalled a scripture from Colossians. "'And let the peace of God rule in your heart.ⁱ'" He looked at his wife. "Do you have peace about our lifestyle as it is, Beth?"

"Absolutely."

They agreed to await God's guidance and not rush into anything. After all, they had just begun their lives together. Fame could prove to be a very enticing snare, luring them away from God's best plans for their future. Only time would tell. The following day, they graciously turned down the offers of employment. They promised to consider future opportunities on an individual basis. All they wanted now was to return home to the life that was waiting for them.

John and Beth spent their last night at a lovely Florida hotel before heading to the airport. Their flight home was cancelled due to mechanical problems. After another layover, they finally boarded an overcrowded flight bound to Seattle. John's knees bumped against the seat ahead of him, forcing his legs into the aisle. Beth shot him a sympathetic glance and squeezed his hand. A toddler squirmed while his mother cradled a howling infant in her lap. The baby's screams pierced the air as the mother desperately tried to quiet her. Beth helped the little boy with his snack while the mother jiggled her fussy baby.

Eventually, the baby fell asleep against her mother's shoulder, but the toddler became anxious. He knocked over a carton of chocolate milk which spilled onto Beth's lap. Beth and John helped clean up the mess. Beth asked the flight attendant for some crayons and paper for the kid to play with. Before long, the child was coloring pictures while his mother cradled her sleeping baby.

John whispered in Beth's ear. "You're going to make a wonderful mother someday."

"I sure hope so."

As they finally landed and exited the airport, a blast of frigid air welcomed them home. Dark overhead clouds threatened rain. John hailed a taxi for their ride home. He put his arm around Beth's shoulder, and she leaned into his embrace.

Outside the door of his place, John set the luggage aside. He picked up his bride and carried her across the threshold and into the living room. He carefully put her down. "Welcome home, baby."

John went outside and brought the bags inside, and Beth surveyed the view overlooking the bay. A flock of seagulls swooped down towards a dock. John came to her side. "It's good to be home. Can I get you anything?"

"I'd love a cup of hot tea, but I've got to get out of these dirty clothes."

He agreed. "Good idea."

She grabbed her carry-on bag and excused herself. After shedding her milk-stained clothes, she entered the walk-in shower. Warm soapy water soothed her tired body. After drying off with a fluffy towel, she noticed John's terrycloth robe hanging on the back of the door. She put it on and tied the belt. She would wear it until she unpacked her lingerie. It felt so good to be clean again.

Upon reentering the living room, she tickled the keys of John's Yamaha keyboard. He walked up behind her. She turned to look up at him. "Do you mind my wearing your robe?"

He chuckled. "Of course not. It looks better on you than it does on me."

She shivered. "Honey, I hate to complain, but this place is absolutely freezing."

John took her by the hand. "We can fix that." He drew her close.

"Seriously, darling. I need some heat." He walked her to the fireplace and showed her how to light the gas fireplace with a remote control. "I was about to make the tea when I found a note from Tiffany; she put your wedding gown in the second bedroom with your other stuff and bought a few groceries for the fridge."

Beth smiled, "How very thoughtful."

She suggested he shower while she made the tea. He agreed, but first he put on a selection of piano love songs. He also took a comforter from the closet and placed it on the sofa. "This should keep you warm until I get back."

The leather sofa welcomed her tired body as she snuggled with the comforter and sipped tea. Her body relaxed to the strains of soft music. Darkness had fallen outside while flickering flames cast dancing shadows on the walls.

John returned to her side wearing sweatpants and a T-shirt. She shared the comforter with him. He tucked it around his lap. "Are you warm yet?"

"Warm as toast." He picked up his teacup. "I suppose now we're an old married couple."

"I guess so." Beth leaned against him as they listened to love songs by firelight.

A clap of thunder rumbled off in the distance. "Remember when thunder scared you right into my arms?"

Beth smiled at the memory. "I'll never forget the day you asked me to marry you."

"I was surprised you actually said yes."

She touched his cheek. Her finger traced his dimple. "I'm so glad I did."

They finished their tea and set the cups aside. John drew her close as they cuddled in the firelight. Beth's heartbeat quickened as he kissed and caressed her. Their kisses intensified, igniting their passion for one another. Their blanket slid to the floor. He nuzzled her hair. "I love you, darling."

She kissed him. "I love you more."

Later, Beth lay awake in an unfamiliar bed. Eventually, his rhythmic breathing, along with the heat from his body cradling hers gently, lulled her to sleep.

The following morning, John awoke to an aroma of freshly brewed coffee and bacon. He found his wife in the kitchen beating eggs in a glass bowl. He kissed her cheek. "You're up early."

"That's because I want to make sure you have a decent breakfast before we go to church."

He poured a stream of coffee into a mug. "I think I'm going to like this married life."

She tickled his chin, "You'd better, because you're stuck with me now."

John sighed deeply. "Such a fate."

When Beth and John arrived at church that morning, their friends surrounded them with hugs and comments on how much they had enjoyed their wedding. Pastor Sorensen welcomed them back with warm handshakes. Worshiping as a married couple brought additional joy. They held hands throughout the service as their hearts overflowed with gratitude.

Later that afternoon they joined their parents for a festive welcome home dinner. They had gifts to open and wedding and cruise pictures to share. Grant Delaney brought a bouquet of flowers for Pamela. Beth hugged her father and kissed his cheek. She and John thanked him repeatedly for the wonderful cruise he'd sent them on. Grant said he'd been tempted to go with them but thought better of it. John looked thoughtful, "Yeah, that might have put a damper on things. But you can come the next time we cruise."

"Hey, what about us?" John's dad asked.

"We'd like to go too!" Pamela agreed. They made a pact that the next time they cruised the whole family could come along.

After a tasty spaghetti dinner, they settled in the family room. John downloaded a wedding video on the TV. The family watched a series of photos from which they could order formal prints. They especially loved one of the newlyweds smiling at each other just after the ceremony. The photographer artfully captured expressions of love and joy radiating from their faces.

Beth's favorite was John placing the wedding band on her finger.

They'd also purchased formal night photos on the cruise ship. Their biggest surprise was a video of the talent show. Grant and the Beaumonts took great delight in their children's photos.

The proud parents watched as their kids sat on the floor opening wedding gifts. They were surrounded by dishes, pottery, stemware, silver, linens, and cookware. Beth lovingly handled each item as she noted whom to thank. John placed a large soup pot on his lap. "Where are we going to put all this stuff, honey? My place doesn't have much storage."

"We'll figure it out," Beth said. "I need time to reorganize things."

"Oh boy, here it comes!" John said with mock disgust. "She wants to rearrange my whole place."

"Our place," Beth corrected.

John set the pot aside and crossed his arms. He looked as stern as he dared. "My place!"

Beth was indignant. "Listen, John, if you're not nice to me, I'll go out and fill the whole place with mid-century, early American furniture!"

Ray, Pamela, and Grant stared at one another while their children rolled on the floor laughing hysterically.

John and Beth settled into married life. She made sure John ate nutritious breakfasts in the mornings and took particular care to prepare balanced meals. He loved coming home to her home-made soups, salads, and breads. The cookie jar was well stocked with his favorite peanut butter or chocolate chip cookies.

The newlyweds heard each other singing around the house or in the shower. At other times, John heard her playing the keyboard and singing hymns. He never tired of her lilting voice. Beth enjoyed hearing John play the keyboard or his guitar. One evening while she sat reading, John played a hauntingly beautiful melody. "What's the name of that song?" she asked. "I don't recognize it."

John smiled at her. "*I Love You, Beth.*"

"I love you too, honey, but what's the name of the song?"

He looked up. "The name of the song is 'I Love You, Beth.' It expresses how I feel about you."

Beth stared at him. "You composed a song?"

He continued playing. "Yes, I did."

Beth walked up behind John and wrapped her arms around him. "That's the most beautiful melody I've ever heard."

"I don't have words yet, I'm not sure I can put my feelings into words."

Beth kissed his cheek. "That's worth more than a million roses."

The couple found a few irritating habits to overcome. Beth cluttered the bathroom counters with her cosmetics, combs, and brushes. John occasionally left whiskers in the sink and sometimes forgot to put the toilet seat down. If the dishwasher was full, Beth left dirty dishes in the sink while John preferred to wash and dry them right away.

One morning Beth caught John drinking orange juice directly from the carton.

"John! What do you think you're doing?"

He flashed a sheepish grin. "I suppose you don't go for that, huh?"

"Don't tell me your mother let you get away with that."

He laughed. "Not on your life! But I've been on my own for quite a while now." Her disapproving glance told him those days were over.

They both had far too many clothes and agreed that they needed to set aside time to sort and give away outfits they no longer wanted. But when she donated his old high school letterman's sweater to charity, along with a few of her things, John came unglued. He barely spoke to her for the rest of the day. She didn't mean to upset him.

Beth was forever leaving CD's out of their cases, while John put them away each time. John sometimes left his shoes next to the sofa. Beth put them away, remembering her mother's wise saying, "An empty stable stays clean."

One Saturday morning, Beth sat carefully painting her fingernails.

John entered the room. "What's that awful smell?"

Beth sighed, "It's nail polish."

He wrinkled his nose. "It smells worse than airplane glue."

"Well, it's all part of my beauty regimen for you." John rolled his eyes and opened the window. Len was coming later to watch an afternoon of college football, something Beth could do without. She'd prepared sandwiches for them and set out a tray of vegetables. She was meeting friends at the mall for lunch and shopping.

Beth waved her hands back and forth through the air. "Honey, would you start my car for me?"

John looked puzzled. "I guess so—but why?"

"My nails aren't quite dry, and I don't want to ruin them." She blinked her eyelashes at him.

John chuckled. "Whatever."

She stood by while he started her car. "I have to hurry; my car is on fumes, and I need gas."

"No, you don't." John said as he exited the car. "I filled your tank this morning while you were still sleeping."

Her eyes lit up. "You did?"

"Yes, I checked your oil and tires too. You're good to go!"

"Oh, thank you, honey!" She kissed his cheek before entering the idling car.

He waved, "Have fun with the girls!"

Beth winked at him. "You, too!" John looked perplexed. She corrected herself. "What I mean is, have fun. But not with any girls!"

John shook his head. "Okay, no girls!"

Beth returned home from shopping just as Len was leaving. John was telling him goodbye. Beth got out of her car and greeted them. "Hi guys, did the Huskies win today?"

Len sadly shook his head. "I'm afraid not! I hope John doesn't beat you tonight."

"Huh!?"

Len laughed, "John will explain it to you." Beth watched as he got into his car and drove off. John greeted her with a bear hug. She kissed his cheek. "What was that all about?"

"Oh, that crazy Len; we watched a documentary on how some men beat their wives if their team loses."

Beth frowned: "I've heard about that sort of thing before; I hope I don't have to hide out tonight."

John laughed. "My plans for this evening don't include a beating; in fact, they're quite the opposite."

"Whew!" She sighed. "That's a relief. Help me with my bags, will you, dear? I bought you a new shirt today."

John peeked into a bag, "What are all these other things?"

"Oh, you'll see—just a few things we need."

"Did you keep the receipts?"

She frowned, "They should be in the bags." She really didn't think his questioning was necessary. He insisted he needed receipts for the taxes, but she wasn't used to anyone telling her what to do. She loaded John's arms with packages. He was happy to see her. He couldn't imagine ever laying a hand on her in anger. He helped her unload her packages and leaned against the counter. "You'll never guess what Len told me today."

"What? To beat me?"

John chuckled. "No, he said Rod and Marla are dating and it looks serious."

Beth put a carton of milk in the refrigerator. "No kidding!"

Emails and texts from Mr. Bickel filled John and Beth's inboxes. He'd shown the video of their performances everywhere he went. The scout couldn't understand why the couple turned down his offers. It made no sense at all. He made a nuisance of himself, calling daily. Finally, they gave in to one of his requests and agreed to perform in Branson, Missouri on Thanksgiving weekend.

The experience, though fun, proved to be very hectic. They were well received in Branson, but the thought of catching flights, staying in hotels, and flying back and forth didn't appeal to them. They knew that wasn't their calling. John was making applications to the seminary with the blessings of Pastor Sorensen and Pastor Phil. Beth and John felt that, for now anyway, their future didn't include traveling around the country performing. At least they earned a tidy sum to help with Christmas expenses.

Tiffany moved in with her parents until she could find a place to live. She shared Bill's office as he and John began her training at the main store. Tiffany caught on fast. The staff welcomed her and encouraged her to make suggestions. She shared some innovative ideas. She agreed that closing the nonproductive stores was the best plan of action. If they were to save any of the stores, the deadweight had to go.

Beth struggled with mixed emotions as her father and Gladys began to date. She tried not to resent Gladys taking her mother's place in her father's life. But as Grant explained, he'd kept his vows to love her mother until death parted them. Before she died, Christina had encouraged Grant not to mourn forever, but to get on with his life. He hadn't looked at a woman in almost three years.

Beth learned that Gladys and her late husband made their fortune in real estate. She took his death hard and, until she met Grant, she'd almost given up on happiness. As Beth prayed for her father, it became clear that Gladys just might be the answer to her prayers. It blessed Beth to see her father enjoying himself again. Gladys would often join them on the weekends to hear them play and sing. Beth hadn't seen her father so content in a long, long time. A twinkle had replaced the sorrow in his brown eyes.

Eighteen

On a crisp December morning, John entered the kitchen buttoning the cuff of his white dress shirt. Beth was setting the table for breakfast. He helped himself to a mug of coffee. "Beth, have you seen my navy blue suit?"

Beth thought for a moment. "It's at the cleaners."

John clenched his jaw. "It didn't need cleaning!"

"Yes, it did. Remember? You asked me to take it to the cleaners last Friday." She leaned against the counter while holding a fork in her hand.

He took a swig of coffee and put his mug down. "No, Beth, I distinctly remember asking you to drop off the *gray* suit."

"I could have sworn . . . "

"You weren't listening!" He snapped. "I said the *gray* suit!"

She fought the urge to snap back at him. "Can't you wear something else? I mean, what about the gray one?"

He rolled his eyes. "It needs cleaning, remember!"

She fired back, "Well then, what about the brown or black one?"

John gave a disgusted sigh. "I need to wear the navy blue one today. I have an important business meeting." He poured more coffee into his mug.

Beth stiffened as she looked him in the eye. "Surely you have something else suitable for your meeting."

John slammed his mug down on the counter, spilling its contents. "You just don't get it, do you? What cleaners did you use?!"

His anger startled her. She stepped back. "M . . . McGavin's cleaners."

John grimaced as though she'd thrown his suit in a mud puddle. "That place does a terrible job." His face flushed red. "From now on, leave my suits alone, I'll take care of them myself!" He noticed a flicker of pain in her eyes. She looked like she might cry. He didn't care. "Look, last month you ruined two of my favorite shirts and shrank a sweater. Not to mention turning my underwear pink! In fact, leave all my clothes alone." He abruptly left the kitchen. A few minutes later, she heard him slam the door on his way out.

Beth had never seen this side of John before. She grabbed a paper towel and soaked up coffee as she fought tears. Had she made a huge mistake marrying a man so vain and self-centered? She thought of how he reacted the time she left the iron on his shirt too long. "Beth, how could you do such a dumb thing?" The other shirt, his favorite red one, bled in the wash, turning his underwear pink. She thought he'd appreciate not having to take his clothes to be professionally laundered any longer. And the sweater was fine when it came out of the washer. She meant to let it air dry, but somehow it ended up in the dryer. His favorite sweater shrank to the size of a small child's.

She felt foolish and irresponsible as she tidied up the kitchen. She decided to head for the mall to buy him new shirts and a sweater. *But do his laundry again? Never!*

John fumed on his way to the cleaners. He tried not to think of the pain he'd caused her. Was she in tears? He shook the image from his mind. Couldn't she understand the pressure he was under these days? The future of the stores depended on the outcome of today's meeting.

He picked up his navy blue suit and inspected it carefully before leaving the cleaners. It looked fine, but then it wasn't dirty in the first place, he reasoned.

On his way back home, he pulled into a coffee shop drive-up window for a latte. He pleasantly addressed the clerk as she took his order. While sipping the frothy beverage, his anger subsided. He thought about his actions. He'd treated his wife like a numbskull, ordering her not to touch his clothes. But it probably would be best for him to take care of his suits as he had always done in the past. Beth's pain-filled eyes surfaced in his memory, and guilt prodded him to swing by the florist. He'd apologize and seek her forgiveness.

Beth was gone when he returned home. He focused on the cheery curtains she'd hung in the kitchen window and the matching placemats at the table. A prayer plant flourished on the windowsill. Honeymoon pictures graced the refrigerator.

She usually leaves for work at two in the afternoon; why isn't she home this morning? He looked for a note but found none. He placed the impressive bouquet on the kitchen table before heading for the bedroom. He dressed in his blue suit and stared in the mirror as he adjusted his striped tie. He put on his jacket and left for the meeting with his banker. He was hoping to get an extension to cover the Tukwila store. He had to make a good impression or risk losing the store to demanding creditors. It was getting harder and harder each month to meet the payroll.

His temper had gotten the worst of him this morning. He reminded himself that he shouldn't take out his frustrations on Beth, ever.

As Beth shopped, she mulled over their argument. The more she chewed on it, the bigger it grew. The initial hurt turned to anger, and the anger morphed into bitterness. Its tentacles choked her feelings for him as she drove home. Beth entered the house and dropped her packages on the sofa. She put the new shirts and sweater on the coffee table where John would find them when he came home from work.

She scribbled a note: *"John, this is to replace your damaged shirts and sweater. Sorry, your inept wife!"*

Beth walked to the kitchen with a small bag of groceries. She gasped as she caught sight of a huge bouquet on the table. At first, the delicate white roses with red tips took her breath away; they were gorgeous. Then anger pushed joy aside as she thought. *What is it with men? They think they can walk all over you and then fix everything with flowers!* Hadn't Reid done that very same thing after an argument? John was no different than any other man.

She snatched up the flowers and walked to the sink. She opened the cabinet door and tossed the flowers in the garbage can beneath the counter. She didn't need his peace offering of flowers or anything else he had to offer!

She finished her housework in record time as resentment simmered on the back burner of her soul. She tossed a load of laundry into the washer, being extra careful not to include any of John's things. His clothes could stay in the hamper until they rotted, or he got around to doing them himself. She dressed in her uniform and went to work.

John was exhausted when he came home that evening. The meeting with his loan officer had not gone well. The bank cut back on lending, and John had to justify every dollar. He received only a fraction of the money he was hoping for. He entered the house and removed his suit jacket. The hallway mirror reflected his tired eyes. He soon discovered the new clothes, along with Beth's terse note. She didn't need to buy him anything. She hadn't held it against him when he accidentally broke her grandmother's antique music box. He hoped the roses had smoothed things over a bit. He walked to the kitchen only to discover that the flowers were missing. Where were they? Did she take them to work? Was she still mad at him? He didn't blame her if she was. He acted like a jerk that morning.

He thought of calling her, but knew she wouldn't answer while working. He sent a text. *I'm sorry, honey.* He decided to see what she had left him for dinner. The only things on the stove were his cold breakfast eggs. There was nothing in the fridge either. He'd taken her wonderful meals for granted lately. He decided to make a sandwich. He decided to toss the cold eggs into the garbage when he discovered the roses. Pain pierced his heart like a razor blade. She wanted no part of him or his flowers. A lonely tear left his eye.

John's sandwich tasted like cardboard, but it satisfied his hunger. He hadn't eaten all day. He slumped into his leather recliner and clicked on the TV to the sports channel. Before long he fell asleep.

Beth spent the evening fretting about the beautiful roses in the trash can. She hoped and prayed that John wouldn't discover them. That was a terrible thing to do with a gift, especially a gift from the man she loved. So, he was picky about his clothes. Wasn't his sense of style one of the things that attracted her in the first place? She pondered his unusual actions. Surely something else must be bothering him besides his suit. As she mulled it over, she knew she would have to forgive him eventually. She wasn't looking forward to facing him when she returned home.

Beth let herself into the house late that evening. John was sleeping in the recliner. She tiptoed past him and headed for the bathroom. She quickly showered and put on her nightgown and robe. She thought she could avoid him until morning if she hurried to bed. But first, she needed to remove the flowers from the garbage. She went to the kitchen and looked under the sink. Her heart sank. The trash can was empty. The beautiful roses were gone. Shame and anger clashed within her. Her mind raced. John must have taken out the garbage. She heard steps behind her. "Are you looking for something?"

She spun around to face him as her cheeks flushed. "You scared the daylights out of me!"

His eyes held remorse as he reached for her. She froze in his arms. He sighed. "I'm sorry, Beth. I acted like a jerk this morning."

"You can say that again!" Tears stung her eyes, yet she remained rigid and unyielding. John felt like he was hugging an ironing board. He released her and sat down at the kitchen table.

"So, it's come to this."

She stared at him. Indignation flared, "Come to what?"

He sighed and leaned back in his chair. "To us hurting one another."

Thinly veiled anger spurred her onward. "I'm not the one who threw a fit this morning!" He didn't answer her, but his eyes held pain. Beth drew a deep breath. "I don't want to hurt you, John, but I am angry."

"I figured that much! What do I have to do to get out of the doghouse?"

She placed her hands on her hips. "Your own laundry! For the rest of your life."

He tilted his head. "Is that all?"

She paced back and forth. "John, I'll never touch any of your clothes again. Especially your suits! Not even if you're wearing them."

John crossed his arms. "Now that doesn't sound like much fun."

She glared at him. "Well, that's just the way it is!"

John tried another tactic. "Does that mean you'll touch me if I'm not wearing clothes?"

She snickered. "Why do you always do that?"

"Do what?"

"Make me laugh!" She sat down facing him.

John leaned towards her. "Because it's a whole lot better than making you mad."

She tried to keep her resolve. "Look, John, I'm sorry about ruining your shirts and sweater."

He threw up his hands. "It's water under the bridge. You didn't have to buy me new clothes, but thanks. They're nice."

She stayed rigid. "I'm glad you like them." She put up her hand. "But I still think you're wrong about the suit. You did say the *blue* one!"

He pursed his lips. "Maybe I did. I'm sorry."

Tears pooled in Beth's eyes. "When you chewed me out, it made me feel so stupid and . . . and incompetent."

John looked shocked as he studied her tearful eyes. His voice cracked. "I'm really sorry. You're anything but stupid and incompetent." He raked his fingers through his hair. "You are, without a doubt, the *smartest* woman I've ever known."

"You're just saying that."

"No, I am not! I mean it. I didn't realize how condescending my actions were." He reached across the table and tipped her chin upward. "Can you forgive me?"

She looked down. "Maybe, if you forgive me too."

He withdrew his hand. "For?"

She glanced towards the sink. "You know."

He arched his brows, "Trashing the roses?"

"Yes, they were beautiful, but I was so mad at you!" She rested her head in her hands. "Later I regretted what I'd done, but it was too late . . . and now they're gone." Tears streamed down her cheeks. She sniffed, "They'd probably be dead by now anyway." She took a napkin from its holder and dried her cheeks and wiped her nose.

John stood up and abruptly left the kitchen. Beth felt terrible. Had she hurt him too much this time? Why did relationships have to be so complicated anyway?

A minute later John returned bearing the vase of white roses. "I figured you might have second thoughts . . . so I saved them."

She gasped, "You saved them?!"

He shrugged. "Well, they were too expensive to line the garbage. I figured if you didn't want them, I'd take them to work tomorrow." Her jaw dropped as he set the bouquet before her. "Am I forgiven?"

She reached for the vase and slid it towards her. She buried her nose in the blossoms and drank in their fragrance. His waiting eyes begged for an answer. A weak smile played on her lips. "You're forgiven."

Relief flooded his face. She stood up and crossed the distance to his waiting arms. He drew her close. His gentle kiss erased all traces of her anger. Unshed tears glistened in his eyes. "So, we're good, Beth?"

Warmth and familiar love flooded her eyes. "We're better than good. We're married."

He smiled. "Shall we retire?"

She slipped her arm around his waist.

Nineteen

Beth and John looked forward to celebrating their first Christmas together. They had plans to gather at Ray and Pamela's on Christmas Day. Grant and Gladys were coming too. John's sister, Rochelle, and her husband were flying in for the holidays, as was John's grandmother, Marie.

As an only child, Beth was excited at the prospect of being part of a large family celebration. They had much to do to get ready for the big day.

On Saturday morning, the couple dressed in jeans, sweat-shirts, and warm jackets. John drove them to a Christmas tree farm in his dad's pickup. He parked and helped Beth step down from the truck. He grabbed his gloves and a small chainsaw before they set out. The two wandered back and forth through countless rows of fragrant green trees until she spotted the perfect one. "Over here, John!" Beth led him to a magnificent Noble fir. Her eyes sparkled. "What do you think about this one?"

John laughed. "It would never fit in the condo; it's too tall."

Beth frowned. "Couldn't we trim some off?"

John took her hand. "Let's keep looking." He led her further into the maze of trees. Before long, he found another fir just as nice as the first one, but shorter. "How 'bout this one?" he asked.

Beth stood back giving it a critical eye, then flashed him a bright smile. "I love it!"

"So, this is the one?"

"Yes, that's the one!"

He pulled on his leather gloves, knelt, and began sawing. Beth jumped up and down like a kid. When the tree fell, the couple dragged and hoisted it into the back of the pickup. They stopped at a farmhouse to pay for the tree. Beth helped herself to a pile of fragrant greens from a bin marked *Free*.

On their way home, they stopped at a hardware store to buy a tree stand, lights, and ornaments. Beth shopped for candles and poinsettias, while John set off in search of tools. Beth wandered up and down the warehouse aisles, pushing her cart. She had rarely shopped in such a place before. *Where are you, John?*

When they returned home, their neighbor Sam helped John carry the tree to the elevator. It barely fit inside, even tipped diagonally. Between the two of them, they got the tree to John's door. He worked on the tree outside until he had it firmly into the stand. The couple lugged it inside and set it by the bay window where it barely cleared the ceiling. "It's a good thing we didn't get the first tree," Beth remarked.

John winked. "It's a good thing you listened to your husband for a change."

Beth placed her hands on her hips. "Don't I always?"

John chuckled. "Sometimes."

Christmas carols played in the background while they decorated their tree with colored lights and pretty ornaments.

"These are cute; they look just like gingerbread cookies," John said as he placed one on the tree.

"I like this snowman," Beth said. "And the angels we got at the craft fair. They're so pretty."

John was enjoying himself too. "Christmas brings out the kid in us, doesn't it?"

Beth had a wistful look in her eyes. "Maybe by this time next year we'll have a baby to celebrate with."

John smiled. "Could be." John reached up and topped the tree with a large gold star.

Beth stood back to admire their handiwork. "It's just beautiful!"

"It really does look great," he said as he high-fived her. She began adorning the fireplace mantle with fragrant boughs and tall candles. After placing poinsettias and angels around the rest of the room, their home was transformed into a winter wonderland.

John asked Beth to sit down. "I have an early Christmas present for you." He disappeared into the office. Before long, he emerged bearing a large box. He placed it in front of her.

"Are you sure you don't want me to wait until Christmas?" she asked, hoping he wouldn't make her wait.

He shook his head. "Nope, you can open it now."

Beth sat down and lifted the lid. From a bed of shredded paper, she found an alabaster figurine of Mary holding the baby Jesus. She caressed the smooth stone with her fingers. "How lovely." She asked him to hold it while she removed the rest of the paper. She found a complete manger scene with Joseph, shepherds, angels, wisemen, and animals all intricately designed. Beth reached out and touched John's cheek. "Thank you darling—this is a precious gift. I absolutely love it!" She walked to the fireplace and carefully placed each figurine amongst the greens on the mantle. She stood back to admire the scene. "You have excellent taste."

He hugged her. "I know. I married you, didn't I?"

John and Beth kept busy shopping for gifts and practicing special numbers for their Christmas Eve service. John addressed cards while Beth baked cookies and nut breads for their friends and family. He gratefully sampled the goods to see if they were fit to give away.

Beth laughed. "How many do you need to try anyway?"

Beth mysteriously disappeared every other morning. She didn't even tell John.

On Christmas Eve, she prepared a spinach soufflé for their dinner, along with a chef's salad. The table was set with white dishes on red placemats. She'd made a festive centerpiece of holly and candles. The couple joined hands and asked a blessing over their meal.

"This looks wonderful, honey," John said as he began eating. He closed his eyes to savor the taste. "I'm so glad I married a good cook. This soufflé is delicious."

Beth jumped up. "I forgot the rolls!" She grabbed two potholders and removed a pan from the oven. She yelped as she slid the rolls on the counter. She sucked her painful finger on her way to the sink. She ran a stream of chilly water over her burn.

John came to her side. "What happened?"

She shook her finger back and forth and asked him to get an ice cube from the freezer. He did as she asked, and she held it on her burn for a few minutes. "It's okay, I'll live. Hold this plate, okay?"

John watched as she dished up four rolls and brought them to the table. "There's nothing as good as your homemade rolls."

"Be careful, they're still pretty hot."

"You do spoil me."

After supper, he helped her with the dishes before they finished wrapping the presents. At nine o'clock, they dressed for church. The service was scheduled for eleven p.m., but they planned to arrive early to get a good seat.

Beth appeared in a dark green velvet dress. "Zip me up, will you, darling?"

He smiled as he did so. "I love it when you wear a dress." He looked into her eyes. "Your eyes are green again!"

"That's what happens . . . ."

"I know, I know, when you wear green. I swear, you get more beautiful every day."

"Thank you, darling. So do you. Help me fasten my pearls."

John worked the clasp of her grandmother's pearls before he planted a kiss on the back of her neck. Her hair was done up in a French twist, and she was wearing the pearl earrings he'd given her as a wedding gift.

John stood before the hallway mirror, knotting his dark green tie. She folded the back of his collar over the tie and brushed a stray hair from his shoulder. As she helped him with his suit jacket, she laughed. John wrinkled his brow. "What's so funny?"

"Oh, nothing."

"Come on Beth, tell me why you're laughing."

She composed herself. "Well . . . I was just thinking of my vow never to touch your suits—even if you were wearing them."

A pained expression crossed his face. "I suppose I'll never live that down."

She checked her image in the mirror, turning from side-to-side. "You know I couldn't keep a promise like that. It was a silly vow." He stood behind her, watching her expression in the mirror. "A very silly vow, totally contradictory to the one you made on our wedding day."

She turned towards him. "And which vow might you be referring to?"

"The one to love me for better or worse."

She smiled as she leaned into his embrace. "Oh yes—that one."

John drove carefully through snow flurries on the way to church. Beth smiled. "Don't you just love Christmas with all the stores decorated so beautifully?" He nodded, and she continued. "And the pretty lights on everyone's houses? Even the streetlights seem happy."

John shook his head. "Sometimes you remind me of a little kid." He parked the car, and they joined hands. He began, "Lord, we ask your blessing on the service tonight and thank you that we can be a part of the celebration. We pray that our performance will bring glory and honor to you and bless the hearts of the listeners. Help with our nervousness and let us stay on key."

"Amen," Beth said.

When they entered the foyer, they were surprised to find their whole family waiting for them. John's parents, his two sisters and grandmother, as well as Grant and Gladys, welcomed them with warm hugs. Each person received a short, unlit candle as they entered the sanctuary. The family settled near the front of the church. Beth noticed Gladys and her father arm-in-arm.

The church was decorated with wreaths and garlands. A huge, flocked tree with tiny blue lights graced the altar platform. A gold banner hanging from the rafters proclaimed, "Joy to the World!"

The fragrance of cedar and pine filled the air. Overhead lights dimmed as candles flickered from the altar. Pastor Sorensen welcomed the congregation warmly before they stood to sing, "Oh Come all ye Faithful." Beth wanted to remember this Christmas Eve forever. Their voices proclaimed adoration to their Lord. When they sat down, John put his arm around her shoulder. They smiled at each other.

Beth never tired of hearing about the birth of her Savior. Pastor Sorensen read the Christmas story from the Bible, interspersed with various carols. She thought of Mary, traveling by donkey, large with child. How difficult that must have been, especially in those days.

Pastor Sorenson announced that it was time for Beth and John to sing, "Mary Did You Know?" The pianist vacated the piano bench as the couple walked to the front of the church. They sat at the grand piano and began playing. Their voices blended as the song's tender message moved the congregation to tears.

John's grandmother beamed. Her prayers had carried John throughout the years. Along with the rest of the congregation, Grant and Gladys seemed enthralled by their singing. Rochelle sniffed and wiped her eyes with a tissue, as did Tiffany.

The service continued with the pastor's sermon as he challenged his congregation to reflect on the best Christmas ever; the first one!

After the sermon, John and Beth went forward again. Beth sat at the piano while John stood before the congregation to sing a solo, "O Holy Night." His voice rang out with reverence and majesty. "Fall on your knees, O hear the angel voices, O night divine, O night when Christ was born." Together, they were truly magic. Only God could have brought about the combination of their talents for His glory.

The service continued with more carols and scripture readings. Now it was time for Beth's favorite part. Two ushers stood at the ends of each row with burning candles. The flame passed along as each person tipped their unlit candle towards the fire. Soon, all the candles flickered, and the overhead lights vanished, leaving only candlelight. The congregation began singing "Silent Night." Beth squeezed John's free hand. By now it was midnight. After singing the last stanza, they blew out their candles. The lights came on as the organist played "Joy to the World."

The Beaumont and Delaney families hugged goodbye in the parking lot.

It was one a.m. when Beth and John arrived home. "Wasn't it wonderful to see the whole family in church?"

John agreed. He hung up their coats and removed his suit jacket. He took his wife in his arms. "Merry Christmas, baby."

She snuggled close to him. "Merry Christmas."

The next morning, Beth served a breakfast of cinnamon rolls, quiche, freshly cut fruit, Greek yogurt, and coffee. Afterward, they sat by their Christmas tree and presented their gifts to one another. John handed her a small box. Beth looked towards the mantle. "You already gave me a present, remember?"

John looked her in the eyes. "Well, here's another one."

Beth slowly opened the box and lifted the lid. "Oh, my goodness!" She stared at a pearl bracelet that perfectly matched her pearl drop earrings. She slid it on her wrist. "Thank you, honey, it's beautiful! I'll wear it all day." She gave him a gentle kiss.

He held her close to his heart. "I love you."

"And I love you—so much!" She stood and walked to the tree and picked up a small flat package. As she approached the sofa, she held out her gift. "This is for you."

He felt it and held it up. "It feels like a CD."

Beth wanted him to hurry. "Open it!"

John began tearing the foil away. Sure enough, it was a CD. He stared at the label showing Beth's smiling picture. *"Songs for My Beloved, by Beth Beaumont."*

John asked, "What is this, anyway?"

"You'll see," she said as she put it into the CD player. Before long, he heard her playing the piano and singing his favorite songs.

He looked stunned. "When did you do this?"

She took his hands in hers. "It took a few mornings. I went to a recording studio, and had it made so you can listen to it in your car or wherever!" He listened to her lovely voice singing to him. "This is the coolest gift I've ever received."

They arrived at John's parents' home a little after 3 p.m. An aroma of roasting turkey, beef, and ham greeted them. John's father welcomed them warmly and took their packages. "Come in, you two—we've been waiting for you."

Beth presented a pecan pie to John's mother, along with some homemade rolls. "The pie is still warm."

Pamela smiled. "These look delicious!" She disappeared to the kitchen while the couple hung their coats in the entry closet. Tiffany's dog ran to John and jumped up on his black slacks. His tail swished back and forth. John knelt and gave the dog some attention. "Hey buddy, take it easy." He ruffled his fur while the dog licked his face.

Beth knelt and petted his neck. "What a beautiful golden retriever."

John smiled, "Beth, may I introduce you to Tiff's dog, Buffy?"

She reached for his paw; "How do you do Mister Buffy?" He licked the back of her hand.

Tiffany greeted them and called Buffy for a treat, and he dashed away.

John and Beth went to the family room to join the others. John stood by the crackling fireplace, rubbing his hands. "It's cold outside!"

Beth settled on a nearby sofa as Ray added their presents to others stacked beneath the tree. "What can I get you to drink?" he asked. They both decided on Pamela's signature eggnog. John joined Beth on the sofa while they sipped the frothy beverage from glass mugs.

"How was your trip out?" John asked Rochelle's husband, Jerrod.

"A nightmare. The flight was overbooked and three hours late!" Rochelle interrupted. "Traveling is no fun anymore."

A few minutes later, Grant and Gladys arrived. They'd spent the day next door with her grown children and grandchildren who were now on their way to visit other relatives. More presents were added to the pile. They sighed as they sank into a loveseat next to one another. Gladys let out a sigh. "I'm beat!" Tiffany told her to relax and enjoy a beverage. Beth wandered over to a table and began adding pieces to a nearby jigsaw puzzle. Tiffany joined her, gathering pieces into a pile. Her cell phone chimed, and she fished it from her pocket. She frowned when she saw who was calling. "Excuse me." She abruptly left the room. Buffy followed her down the hall.

Pamela joined the family and settled near her husband. Ray put his arm around her. "She's been slaving away in the kitchen all day."

She fanned her face with a napkin. "I couldn't do it without Martha's help. She's such a gem."

John asked if she needed any more help. His mother assured him that all was well. "The table's set, and Martha kicked me out of the kitchen to be with my guests."

John's grandmother began raving about last night's wonderful church service. She turned to Jerrod. "You should have heard John and Beth's performance."

"Is that right?"

"Oh my, it was so inspirational," Marie said. "They have the most beautiful voices."

Jerrod rolled his eyes. "From what I hear, they walk on water."

Rochelle closed her eyes. "See what I have to put up with?"

"Cool it, Rochelle," Jerrod warned.

Anger flashed in her eyes. "Don't tell me what to do!"

Beth looked bewildered. The rest of the crowd squirmed uncomfortably.

"That's enough, you two!" Ray snapped. "It's Christmas, for heaven's sake." Rochelle stormed out of the room. Jerrod sat scrolling through his phone.

Pamela made a feeble attempt to apologize to her guests. "Things have been a little tense around here today."

Gladys came to the rescue, "Tell me about it! We've had a trying day too, haven't we, Grant?" Though he glanced at her, he wisely remained silent. Gladys continued. "I think the stress of the holidays gets to everybody!"

John slid his arm around Beth's waist. His sister could be a real drama queen, and he didn't care much for her smart-aleck husband either. It wasn't unusual for them to ruin a holiday celebration.

Beth excused herself to the bathroom. She ran into Tiffany in the hallway. She looked as though she'd been crying. "What's the matter?" Beth asked.

"Derik called."

"Your ex?"

"Yes, he would call today! After all these months he's finally getting nostalgic." Tiffany sniffed. "I thought I was over him, and now he calls and I'm a basket case again."

Beth put her arm around her. "I'm sorry; do you want to talk about it? If so, I've got wide shoulders."

Tiffany shook her head. "Some other time maybe, but not right now." Beth fished a tissue from her pocket and gave it to Tiffany. "When you feel like talking, let me know."

Tiffany blotted her tears. "We'll talk after the holidays, when I've had a chance to sort out my feelings." Buffy followed behind them as they returned to the family room. John searched Beth's eyes as she sat next to him. She gave him a reassuring smile. Buffy sat at Tiffany's feet.

Martha appeared and announced that dinner was ready. The family gathered around the huge oak table in the dining room. Tiffany convinced Rochelle to come out of her room to join the family for dinner. Rochelle's blotchy eyes looked like she'd been crying too. She sat as far away from her husband as possible.

Beth detected pain in Jerrod's eyes. His cell phone rested on the table next to his plate. She prayed a silent prayer for him and Rochelle. Beth admired the floral centerpiece and the bountiful feast spread before them. She eyed heaping platters of ham, turkey, and prime rib with all the trimmings. Martha added Beth's rolls to the table before joining them.

John's father asked everyone to join hands while he prayed the blessing. Jerrod stared straight ahead, which Rochelle called to everyone's attention. Beth squeezed John's hand, sensing his embarrassment.

Bowls of mashed potatoes, gravy, and vegetables made the rounds along with salads and Beth's rolls. Everyone agreed that they were delicious. Gladys even asked for the recipe.

Buffy settled near Jarrod's feet as he fed meat scraps to him. Tiffany frowned but didn't make an issue of it.

The family laughed as John recalled some of his and his sisters' escapades. John's grandmother sighed. "I remember you kids as babies. It seems like only yesterday! I hope to get a great-grandchild one of these days." She glanced from Rochelle to Beth. Pamela and Ray exchanged looks.

Rochelle sneered. "Don't look at me. I don't need two babies!" Grandma Marie shifted her gaze to Beth.

Grant cleared his throat. "Give them time; they've only been married two months."

Beth assured Grandma that they hoped to have a baby before long. Marie smiled, placated for the moment. Beth began sharing a memory from her childhood when her father had searched all over town for a special Christmas doll. She tried to describe the doll's size with her hands. Gladys commented on Beth's lovely bracelet. Beth turned her wrist back and forth. "It's a gift from John."

"It's beautiful!" Tiffany said, "It matches your earrings perfectly! What did you get for Christmas, John?" He told the family about the CD of love songs Beth recorded.

Jerrod laughed and banged his fist on the table. "How corny is that?"

Tears stung Beth's eyelids. Rochelle snapped, "It's better than what you gave me!"

"Nothing ever pleases you," Jerrod said.

Rochelle turned to Beth. "Do you want to know what he gave me? A book on how to manage money. How special is that?"

Jerrod narrowed his eyes. "I suppose the trip out here was nothing at all."

"I'm sure you didn't mind spending money on your secretary!"

John raised his hand. "Stop! Just chill! Mom and Dad did a lot of work to make a nice Christmas for us. Let's not spoil it by slinging insults."

Rochelle's cheeks grew red as she pointed at Jerrod. "He's the one who insulted your precious wife!"

Tiffany was furious. "Beth *is* a precious wife to John. If everyone were like her, this world would be a much better place."

Rochelle threw her napkin down. "How touching!"

John's grandmother was aghast. Pamela was near tears. Grant had finally had enough of family dynamics for one day. "How 'bout we call a truce and enjoy our meal? Everything is delicious, Pamela."

Ray put his fork down. "Grant is right. No more negative talk! If you can't say anything nice, don't say anything at all!"

The rest of the meal was eaten in near silence, except for an occasional ping from Jerrod's phone. John was furious, but for his mother's sake, he pushed his anger down. Beth sensed his discomfort as she watched him from the corner of her eye.

Martha offered dessert, but the family decided they were too full and would have it later. Martha and Tiffany began clearing the table. John drew Beth aside. "Are you okay, honey?"

She stood tall and straight. "I'm fine."

"I'm sorry about Rochelle and Jerrod. Do you want to leave?"

She shook her head. "No, that's just what the enemy wants: to ruin Christmas and all your parents' hard work and plans. We'll stay because we're a family. All of us!"

He wrapped his arms around her. "You *are* my precious wife."

"And you're my precious husband. Now let's go spread some Christmas cheer."

They joined the group gathered in the living room, sipping coffee and tea. A crackling fire and the glow from the Christmas tree set a magical scene. John and Beth went to the piano and began to play. Before long, the family was caught up in the couple's enthusiasm and joined in. In addition to traditional carols, they sang jovial songs like "Jingle Bells" and "The Twelve Days of Christmas." Even Buffy joined in with an occasional howl. By the time they finished, laughter had replaced tension in the room. Pamela asked John and Beth to sing, "Mary Did You Know?"

"We don't have the music, but I think we can remember it," John said as he looked at Beth. She nodded in agreement. As they played and sang with their magical harmony, the message of the song touched hearts again. Even Jerrod seemed to enjoy listening. He didn't say anything but briefly made eye contact with John and tilted his head ever so slightly.

After the gift exchange, Ray gathered up the discarded wrappings and fed them to the fireplace. Flames danced and crackled as heat filled the room. He tossed on another log. There was nothing like a real wood fire as far as he was concerned.

The family gathered in the dining room again to enjoy slices of pie with whipped cream. Martha joined them as Pamela poured coffee and tea. Beth received raves about her delicious pecan pie. John beamed at his bride. "She spoils me rotten." Jerrod had heard enough. He and his trusty phone disappeared.

The family played Mexican Train for the next hour. John and Beth bundled up and bid everyone goodnight, except Jerrod, who hadn't returned. Rochelle cornered them before they left. She apologized for her and Jerrod's behavior. Beth gave her a gracious hug.

On the way to their car, a full moon illuminated their frozen path. They gazed up at backlit fluffy white clouds swirling beneath the golden moon's halo. The view of Seattle's distant harbor was breathtaking as thousands of lights sparkled like diamonds. John reached for her hand. "I'm amazed at how you handled everything, Beth, even giving Rochelle a hug."

"She's hurting, honey; her dreams have been shattered."

"You're right. Tiffany seemed a little distant, too."

Beth faced him. "Derik called."

"That explains a lot."

Beth sighed. "I guess our prayer list is growing longer." They listened to Christmas carols as John drove along, each lost in their own thoughts. They were almost home when John broke the silence. "I hope we never treat each other the way Rochelle and Jerrod do."

Beth faced him. "I can't imagine talking to you that way." She touched his arm. "Honey, what we have between us is so special. Let's do everything we can to preserve it."

"Deal." He said as he pulled into their driveway. "Tiff said something earlier about us all getting together for New Year's Eve. She wants to go to Seattle Center with the Space Needle crowd. I don't know about that. What would you like to do for our first New Year's Eve?"

Beth thought for a minute. "Let's spend it alone, together."

"Just the two of us?"

She gave him an ardent look. "I'll make us a romantic candle-light dinner."

John smiled. "It's a date!"

Three weeks later, John woke Beth with a kiss. He set a tray on the bed bearing two cups of coffee and a long-stemmed red rose. Beth stretched and rubbed her eyes. He fluffed her pillow. "Happy anniversary, sleepyhead." She stared at him. "It's not our anniversary; we've only been married three months!"

"How quickly you forget, my dear. It was exactly one year ago when you walked into the Bible class. I'll never forget that day."

Beth sat up. "Really? I didn't think you noticed me at all."

John sat beside her. "I noticed you all right. So did every other guy."

"Seriously?"

"Yeah, every week I fell more in love with you. I had to play it cool, though, because you wouldn't give me the time of day. I figured you had someone else."

Beth's brow was partially hidden by a dark curl. "The last thing you needed was another woman giving you encouragement."

John took a sip of his coffee. "That's what drove me crazy. The only woman I wanted to notice me didn't."

Beth tickled his chin. "A woman would have to be blind not to notice you. But I wasn't ready to date yet. I assumed you had someone else in the wings anyway." Beth held the rose to her nose. "Thank you, darling. It's beautiful."

John took her hand. "When did you first know you wanted to marry me?"

She smiled. "The first time you kissed me. In the church parking lot, remember?"

His dimpled smile appeared. "How could I ever forget?"

She continued. "From that moment on, I never wanted to kiss anyone but you."

John said, "I felt the same way. That was quite a kiss!"

"Yes, it certainly was." She gave him a knowing smile. "But then your kisses always affect me that way. When did you know that you wanted to marry me?"

"That's easy. When I woke up with you sleeping beside me."

Beth was incredulous. "On our honeymoon? That's when you knew?!"

John frowned. "No silly, on the van ride back from the hike. Remember? You fell asleep against my shoulder."

Beth laughed. "I was so embarrassed."

"I know, but I got a kick out of it."

She gave him a sideways glance. "You usually get a kick out of my embarrassing moments."

John kissed her cheek. "It's just that I find your naiveté refreshing—that's all."

She batted her eyelashes and kissed him back. "Happy anniversary."

Twenty

Beth insisted on celebrating Valentine's Day with a picnic lunch at John's office. John thought it a bit strange but indulged his wife's pleading. Her basket held sandwiches, two heart-shaped lemon meringue tarts, a bottle of Italian soda, and two fluted glasses.

John noticed how the staff exchanged looks as they entered the showroom. "Well, what brings you here on a Monday? I thought you had the day off," Bill said.

John mumbled in his cousin's ear, "We're having lunch in my office; don't ask me why."

Bill chuckled. "Okay."

Beth greeted the staff cheerfully, "Happy Valentine's Day, everybody!" She placed a box of heart-shaped cookies on the counter. The group crowded around, knowing how good her cookies were. "Thanks, Mrs. Beaumont," one of the younger staff members said.

John carried the lunch into his office and put the basket on his desk. He turned to his wife. Her beautiful eyes radiated love, causing his heart to flip-flop as usual. "Happy birthday, baby, and happy Valentine's Day."

"The same to you, darling. Well, *not* happy birthday." She handed him a large white envelope. "Don't open it yet." She began clearing John's desk. He helped her by putting a few items on a nearby shelf. Beth removed a white linen cloth from her basket. She shook it out and placed it over the top of his desk. "Close the shades."

"Just what do you have in mind anyway?"

She folded her arms across her chest. "Not what you think! I just want a candlelight lunch, that's all." John chuckled. He shut the blinds while she lit two candles and turned off the lights. Beth smiled. "There now, isn't this romantic?"

John drew up two chairs. "This looks wonderful." He held her chair as she sat down.

John reached for her hand and thanked the Lord for their food and her birthday. Beth added, "And thank you for Valentine's Day, too." Beth squeezed his hand before letting go.

They enjoyed light conversation while enjoying their lunch. John scooped the last of the meringue from his tart when she began.

"John! Guess what?" Her eyes danced in the candlelight.

She looked so lovely, he decided to play along. "What?"

"You can open your Valentine now!"

He shook his head. "Not so fast. I have one for you first." He scooted his chair back and reached for his briefcase. He set it on his lap and withdrew a heart-shaped box of candy, along with a card and a small box.

Her eyes lit up. "Chocolates!" She clasped her hands together before lifting the lid. She picked out a piece of candy and offered John one. After devouring the confection, she read the card.

"To My Wife." She read the verse that spoke of his undying love. He then gave her a small box. She sat very still as she opened the lid. She stared at a gold, heart-shaped locket, edged with tiny diamonds. Inside the locket, she found two miniature pictures of them on their wedding day. Tears filled her eyes. "I'll treasure this always."

He put his arms around her. "Read the back."

She turned it over and read the inscription. "Forever yours, John."

She held the locket by its gold chain. "Help me fasten this around my neck." He lifted her hair aside and fumbled with the clasp until it clicked. He began kissing the back of her neck. She turned to him, her face flushed. "John, stop it! Or we'll never make it out of here."

He sighed. "Okay honey, I'll behave."

"Now it's your turn." He picked up the card she'd given him earlier and removed it from the envelope. The front of the Valentine showed a beautiful sunset. It read "To My Husband on Valentine's Day."

He opened the card and began reading. "I thank God for the day I found you and for our love. You mean more to me every day. Happy Valentine's Day to my dearest friend and husband!" And in her handwriting were the added words: "And to the father of our baby."

John dropped the card and tilted his head to one side. "Does this mean what I think it means?"

Beth moved to his lap and wrapped her arms around him. She could barely contain her joy. "Yes, darling, we're going to have a baby!"

"No kidding?" John drew her closer and looked into her impish eyes. "How long have you known anyway?"

She felt heat in her cheeks. "I found out for sure yesterday. I almost told you last night, but I made myself wait. I wanted to tell you about it here, in your office, since this is such a special place for us. I mean . . . well, after all, you proposed to me here."

John's dimples appeared. "True! So, how far along are we?"

"About six weeks." She hugged his neck again. "Are you happy, darling?"

He leaned back so she could see his eyes. "I'm ecstatic! Way to go, Beth."

"Well, I had a little help."

"It was my pleasure to assist you, Mrs. Beaumont." He brushed a stray curl from her forehead. "Shall we tell the others?"

"Let's wait until after tonight's birthday party. Our family should hear it first."

They met John's parents and Tiffany that evening in a small private room at the Lighthouse restaurant. A round table was set for seven people. A balloon bouquet rose from the back of Beth's chair. Red and yellow roses graced the table.

"With this being your birthday and Valentine's Day, John better never forget this day!" Ray teased. Beth gave a sly smile. "Oh, he won't, I'm sure of that."

Tiffany hugged her sister-in-law before giving her a present. "Happy birthday, Beth!" She stopped to stare at her neck. "What a beautiful locket."

Beth smiled. "It's from John."

"Of course, who else? May I look inside?"

"Certainly."

Tiffany carefully opened the delicate gold heart and called Pamela over. "Look, Mom, isn't this cool?"

Pamela agreed. "What a thoughtful gift."

Before long, Grant arrived with Gladys on his arm. He hugged his daughter. "Happy birthday, my little valentine."

Beth laughed. "You say that every year."

John slid his arm around Beth's waist. "She's my valentine now."

Grant chuckled. "I suppose she is."

The group enjoyed a festive meal before the waiter brought in a German chocolate cake. Twenty-seven candles flickered while John led the group in singing "Happy Birthday." After Beth blew out her candles, Tiffany asked, "Did you make a wish?"

John stood and cleared his throat. "Beth and I have an announcement to make."

All eyes were on him as he tenderly touched his wife's shoulder. "We're expecting a baby!"

A chorus of cheers went up along with applause.

"When is the baby due?" Pamela asked.

"In September," John said.

The couple received heartfelt hugs accompanied by tears of joy. Pamela could hardly wait to hold her first grandchild. Ray and Grant agreed that what the baby really needed was a college trust fund.

Tiffany put her arm around Beth and asked, "Is it a boy or a girl?"

Beth shook her head. "We don't know yet. We might wait to be surprised."

The Beaumont baby would be a very welcome addition to the world. Beth stifled a smile as John strutted across the room. Grant proposed a toast to the happy couple and the growing family. Cheers went up.

It was soon time for Beth to open presents, but none of the gifts matched the joy of the gift she had been given from God.

Over the next few weeks, news spread throughout the community. Beth's life was full and content. Though she struggled with morning sickness, she radiated joy. She cuddled in John's arms nightly as they talked endlessly of baby names, their future, and their perfect lives.

John submitted his application to the seminary. If accepted, he might be able to attend the Seattle campus next fall. Otherwise, they would have to sell the condominium and move to California. They knew that might be a problem as the real estate market was at a standstill, especially for condos. Besides, they wanted to be near their family.

Beth wondered how long they could continue living at the condo anyway. A baby meant a crib, changing tables, strollers, toys, and a host of other paraphernalia.

John knew he was a blessed man, but was he ready to be a father? How much time would he have to study, and would they suffer financially? Would Beth stay home with their child or keep working? Did he have the patience to endure a crying baby? What if the baby were sick or deformed? He'd valiantly tried to adjust to Beth's work schedule without complaining. In the evenings, he kept busy on his computer with work matters or playing the piano. He watched TV and studied his Bible, but he really missed his wife. He worried about her driving home so late, especially on a stormy night like this. John looked at the clock. It was 11 p.m. Beth was due home in half an hour. He had a fire going, music playing, and candles lit. He'd purchased flowers earlier, along with her favorite chocolate cherry ice cream. When she wasn't home by 11:45 he dialed her phone. It went to voicemail. He turned off the music and turned on the television. After channel surfing for fifteen minutes, he began pacing the floor. Where could she be? He looked out the window for the tenth time. He prayed she wasn't stuck in the rain some-where. Maybe she stopped at the store—but she'd have called to let him know by now. He began imagining all kinds of things.

Perhaps she had an accident or a flat tire. Maybe she was sick or had engine trouble. Had her car plunged down a ravine? He prayed fervently, asking God to watch over her as rain beat steadily on the metal roof. She'd been late before, but never *this* late. He tried calling and texting her cell again. She still didn't answer. At 12:30 a.m., he called the hospital. An automated voicemail played. "All clerks are assisting other callers. If this is an emergency, hang up and dial 911."

John continued pacing the floor and looking out the window at the pouring rain. He decided to go out and look for her. He blew out the candles and donned his raincoat, before taking off into the night. He carefully navigated the stormy route, looking for any disabled cars. His windshield wipers swished full blast as the glare from oncoming headlights blinded him. He was a mile from the hospital when his phone rang. He exhaled a sigh of relief. "Hello, Beth?"

Her voice sounded curt. "Sorry, John, I can't talk long, my battery is almost dead—be home soon." Her phone broke up and died before he could say anything.

John fumed as he made a U-turn. There was absolutely no excuse for this. She could have called earlier instead of letting him worry his head off. His anger mounted as he sped home. He parked his car and got out just as his neighbor, Sam, drove up. He greeted John in the parking lot. "Nasty weather out there, huh?"

"It sure is," John said as he shivered. "Better make a run for it."

John unlocked his door, went inside, draped his raincoat in the bathroom shower, and turned up the heat. His thoughts alternated between relief and anger. He switched on the television. An infomercial guru was expounding on how to make a large profit in the foreclosed real estate market. The later it got, the madder John became.

Beth arrived at one-thirty wanting only the comfort of her husband's arms. John met her at the door. "Where on earth have you been?" His harsh voice frightened her.

"At the hospital—where do you think I've been?"

John glared, "I called the hospital. If you were there, why didn't you call me?"

Her jaw dropped. "I did call you!" His face flushed as he

nailed her to the wall with angry eyes. "Yeah, finally at one o'clock in the morning, with no explanation whatsoever! One thirty is a ridiculous time to come home!"

"I didn't know I had a curfew! In case you haven't noticed. I'm a grown woman, John!" She felt foolish as soon as the words left her mouth.

He fired back. "Yes, you are. But you're also my wife. And I deserve an explanation!"

"Well, you're not going to get one by yelling at me!"

"I'm not yelling," John said evenly.

Beth struggled to keep it all together as she went to the kitchen for a glass of water.

John followed her. "Where have you really been?!" She silently counted to ten as she removed a glass from the cupboard. She pressed it against the ice dispenser on the refrigerator door. John glared, his hands resting on the counter. She fought tears as she filled the glass with water and began to drink. John continued waiting for an answer. When she finished, she put the glass down and headed straight for the bedroom.

She closed the door behind her and locked it. He heard muffled sobs.

John tried the knob. "Beth, open this door!" He raked fingers through his hair. This wasn't how the evening was supposed to end. He banged on the door and raised his voice. "Let me in, I want to talk to you."

She sobbed, "Just go away!"

John muttered something under his breath as he walked to the sofa and dropped onto the cushions. He grabbed a throw pillow and pounded it with his fist before placing it beneath his head. It was useless. It felt like a block of cement. He threw the pillow across the room, knocking over the vase of flowers.

He tossed and turned on the sofa. It was impossible to straighten out his long legs. After feeling sorry for himself for a while, he decided to pray. *Lord, I think I blew it big time. I'm sorry I made her cry. But how could she be so selfish as not to even call me? And now she's locked me out of our bedroom! Yes, I'm mad, and I have a right to be. But it feels terrible having her mad at me. Please bridge the gap between us until we reconcile. You know how much I love her. Help us work things out.*

John thought how things might have gone differently had he welcomed her home the way he usually did, with a bear hug. He sighed and went to the closet for a quilt. It looked like he was going to spend the night on the sofa. He spread the quilt over the sofa, folded it in half, and got between the covers. He turned off the lamp and curled up in a fetal position. He closed his eyes, but sleep wouldn't come.

He stared into the fireplace as he longed for her arms. He felt a sinking in his gut. The wall clock beats were out of sync with the rain on the roof. The fireplace flames mocked his thoughts. *She's fed up with you! She doesn't have a curfew! Who do you think you are? Your feelings aren't important to her. She wasn't thinking of you at all. She'd rather be with someone else after work.*

Other thoughts battled for attention. *"Love is patient and kind; love does not envy or boast; it is not arrogant or rude. It does not insist on its own way; it is not irritable or resentful; it does not rejoice at wrongdoing, but rejoices with the truth. Love bears all things, believes all things, hopes all things, endures all things."*[i] John squirmed uncomfortably, trying to find peace for his soul. After a while, the bedroom door clicked open. John heard her go into the bathroom and shut the door. A few minutes later, she was kneeling at his side.

In a nasally voice, she asked, "John, do you still want to talk?" Firelight illuminated her sad face.

"Come here, baby." John said as he reached out and drew her up beside him. He kissed her tear-stained cheeks. "I'm sorry I jumped all over you the minute you walked in the door."

She didn't comment.

John heaved a heavy sigh. "I was worried sick! I thought

something terrible happened to you. What if I came home two hours late?"

Beth drew a deep breath. "I'd be worried."

He continued. "I hate being alone every night. I'd really like you to be here when I get home from work." He knew his demands might lead to a full-blown argument, but he'd been holding his feelings in check far too long.

Tears pooled in her eyes as she touched his cheek. "I don't like being away from you either." Her gentle caress totally disarmed him.

John took her hand and kissed it. "Honey why can't you work the dayshift?"

Beth swallowed tears. "I saw an opening earlier today. I'll apply tomorrow."

John arched his brows. "No argument?"

She shook her head from side-to-side as huge tears streamed down her cheeks. She buried her face against his chest and sobbed.

John tightened his arm around her trembling shoulders. "I'm sorry I was so cross with you, babe. Please forgive me."

Her tears continued, forming a wet circle on his shirt. "Oh John, it was just terrible! Two ambulances came in at ten thirty. There was a head-on collision. A young father was dead on arrival." She shuddered. "He was about your age. We tried to revive him . . . but . . . and we almost lost a darling little boy. The other family was covered in blood. I just couldn't leave! And there was no time to call you. We needed every one of us." Her beautiful eyes mirrored pain. "The baby has serious internal injuries, and his mother has a broken pelvis." Beth's copious tears continued, and her nose was running. John paled as he reached for a Kleenex box on the end table. She took a tissue and blew her nose.

John felt like a heel. He closed his eyes and sighed. He scolded her when she was only doing her job. Watching her sob was heartbreaking. He held her in his arms until her tears subsided. "I should have realized you had a good reason for being late."

Beth drew several short breaths in succession. "You had no way of knowing." She looked him in the eyes. "I'm truly sorry." John sighed. She took his hands in hers. "Honey, I can't promise that it won't happen again; but I'll do everything in my power to reach you in the future."

He kissed her forehead. "It sounds terrible. And you must be exhausted. Can I get you anything?"

She blew her nose again. "No. I just need some sleep." She lowered her eyes, "but I couldn't sleep without you."

John stroked her hair, "I couldn't sleep without you either. Does this mean I can come to bed now?" She gave him a feeble nod.

"Let's pray for those families before we go to bed," John said. She squeezed his hand.

John still couldn't sleep in the comfort of his bed. He cradled his melancholy wife until she fell asleep. He silently prayed for her and the families lying in the hospital in crisis. He realized that, more than likely, he'd minister at just such a scene in the future. He prayed for patience with Beth and wisdom to be a better husband.

Early the next morning, the couple awoke to a ringing phone. John winced as he fumbled for his cell. "John, it's Dad. The Tukwila store went up in flames last night. Meet me at your office as soon as possible."

John gasped. "I'm on my way."

Beth reached for his arm. "Honey, what's the matter?"

"There's been a fire, Beth. The Tukwila store. I have to go."

She threw off the covers. "I'm going with you."

The rain had let up considerably. The couple ran as they headed for John's car. "What I wouldn't give for a cup of coffee!"

Halfway there, Beth warned, "John, slow down! The roads are slippery; we want to get there in one piece." When they arrived at the store, Ray met them at the entrance. John didn't give any polite greetings. "When did it happen?" he asked as he approached the coffee pot and helped himself to a travel cup.

"Sometime late last night."

"Was anyone hurt?"

"I heard something about a firefighter."

John rubbed his temples. "Let's go!"

Beth capped an extra cup of coffee for John before leaving the showroom. They piled into Ray's SUV and headed for the freeway. The morning traffic was horrendous as Ray navigated the gridlock. Thirty minutes later, they reached their exit and headed towards the Tukwila store. The street in front of the store was taped off to traffic, so they parked two blocks away. Thick gray smoke and particles of debris clogged the air. Six fire trucks were still on the scene of the smoldering rubble. John and his father joined a host of people gawking at the remains of what had been an elegant old store. The building had recently been stocked with overflow inventory for a liquidation sale.

Television crews filmed the firemen's attempts to douse hot spots of the fire.

Light rain from a sodden sky helped drench the remaining embers. A host of firefighters canvassed the scene. Ray approached one of the men. "I'm Ray Beaumont, and this is my son, John. We own this store."

The firefighter raised his arm. "Stand back."

John persisted, "Does anyone know how it happened?"

Ray coughed. "I heard a firefighter was injured, is that true?"

The fireman said, "Yes, one of our rookies is in the hospital, burning timbers fell on him."

"This is devastating!" Ray paced back and forth. Beth watched John put his hand on his dad's shoulder.

One of the firefighters said, "You'd better talk to the detectives. I'll let them know you're here." John was talking with a reporter when two men drove up in a black sedan. They stopped the car and exchanged words with Ray Beaumont. He called his son over. "The detectives want to talk to you, John." Beth followed as John approached the men.

"Hello, I'm John Beaumont and this is my wife, Beth."

The first man offered his hand. "I'm Detective Brown. Let's get out of this rain so we can talk." They agreed to meet at the Evergreen store.

Tiffany greeted the detectives and helped Beth out of her damp coat. "There are towels in the back; I'll get one for your hair."

The detectives canvassed the store. They wandered through various furniture suites and stared up at the ceiling. Detective Brown asked, "Are all of your stores alike?"

John shook his head. "No, but they all have sprinkler systems if that's what you're referring to."

John's father added, "This is our newest store. We spent a bundle updating the older stores with sprinkler systems. I don't understand why they didn't prevent the fire."

The second man, a wizened old detective, stared at Beth. "What did you say your name is?" His eyes traveled over her body.

She'd seen his type before. "Beth Beaumont."

"Detective Jake Adams," he bowed slightly. He stared at her a little too long for John's liking. Tiffany returned with a towel for Beth and introduced herself to the detectives. Now Jake had another beautiful woman to stare at. Beth began blotting her hair. Detective Brown addressed John. "What can you tell us about the fire?"

John blanched, "Me? Nothing."

"Is that your black BMW outside?" Detective Adams asked.

"Yes."

"Mind if we have a closer look?"

"Not at all, but why are you asking about my car?"

"Just covering our bases," Adams said.

Ray's face flushed. "Are you accusing John of something?"

The detective ignored him and addressed John, "So where were you last night around midnight?" John was losing patience. "I was home, where I live by Salmon Bay."

Detective Adams turned to Beth. "Can you verify that?"

Beth put the towel aside. "Yes, of course I can."

The detective remained calm. "So, you were together last night?"

Beth glared. "I just told you I was with him."

"The whole evening?"

"Yes, but . . . ." Beth stopped talking mid-sentence.

"That's enough questions for now," Ray Beaumont said. Jake Adams' eyes narrowed.

"We'll see you later, Mr. Beaumont." Ray showed them to the door. "Of all the nerve!"

John was flabbergasted. "Surely, they don't think I had anything to do with the fire. Do they?"

"That's absurd," Ray said. "Why on earth would anyone think that?"

Beth was on the phone to her father. He advised them to play it cool until John was charged with something. He said the detectives were probably grasping at straws. He promised to see what he could find out.

Later that evening, Beth, and John read newspaper accounts of the fire.

Tukwila — A long-standing Tukwila business, Beaumont Home Furnishings, went up in flames last night. The fire attracted more than 125 firefighters from King and neighboring counties to fight the stubborn five-alarm blaze. Starting just after midnight and extending throughout the night, firefighters battled the fire that claimed a local business that has operated since 1935. By Wednesday afternoon, all that remained of the sprawling building were mostly charred remains. The fire investigators do not yet know what started the blaze.

"We have to sift through the rubble piece by piece," Tukwila Fire Marshal Charles Tucker said.

The investigation could take weeks.

By the time the first firefighters arrived, the blaze had already burned through the ceiling. One firefighter, injured as he tried to enter the building, is recovering at a local hospital.

"The rest of the crew retreated because of the danger of the collapsing roof," Fire Chief Moore said. Some of the company's employees arrived on the scene and expressed shock.

Owner Ray Beaumont said, "It's devastating; we're all just stunned."

Clem Morgan, who manages the Tukwila store, expressed shock as well.

"I'm just thankful nobody was inside the building," Morgan said. He added that the store was scheduled to close forever within the next month. Investigators are encouraging anyone with any information about the fire to call Tukwila police detective Richard Brown.

Twenty-One

B eth and John checked on the injured firefighter at Harborview Hospital the following day. They introduced themselves and told him they were praying for his recovery. His collarbone had broken from falling debris, but his injuries weren't life-threatening. Miraculously, he'd escaped major burns. John and Beth checked on his progress daily until he was released.

Beth was able to transfer to day shift the following week. At least now she could be home with John in the evenings.

One Sunday afternoon, their neighbor, Sam, came to the door. "I need to talk to you guys."

"Sure, come on in," John said. Beth offered him a cup of coffee, but he declined.

"I don't quite know where to begin except to say that some detectives have been asking the neighbors if they saw anything suspicious the night of the furniture store fire. I mentioned that I saw John arrive home around one fifteen in the morning . . . but I surely don't think you had anything to do with the fire. They told me I might be subpoenaed as a witness."

John exhaled a deep sigh. "It doesn't look good, does it?"

"Where were you that night anyway?"

"Out searching for my wife. She was tied up with an emergency, and I was worried enough to go looking for her."

Sam shook his head. "That might be a tough one to swallow."

John's face turned red. "Well, it's the truth."

"Oh, I believe you, but those detectives are on a rampage. Look, if I can be of any help, just holler."

"I'll do that. Thanks for coming over." They shook hands before he left.

Over the next few weeks, John answered multiple questions to the press and to concerned customers regarding the fire. Firefighters were still sifting through the rubble to determine the cause of the fire. Several calls were received by the police with anonymous tips. Some of them pointed straight to John.

Bill and Tiffany were arguing. "There's no way in the world that John is involved with the fire; I don't care what anybody says."

Bill's intense brown eyes sought hers. "I didn't say he was, but that's what the detectives suspect."

Tiffany stared at her cousin. "Why, because of anonymous tips by crackpots? Look, if John says he was home, then it's true. Besides, John is one of the gentlest people in the world. He's just not capable of such an awful crime."

Bill sat beside her. "I know that, and you know that, but what I'm trying to say is that John is a suspect. And if he's a suspect the insurance company won't settle any claims."

"It's not fair. Beth worked late that night and John has no alibi."

Though they usually took weekends off, Beth and John both had to work the following Saturday. The stores were having blowout sales; and the hospital needed an extra nurse. She was at work when a co-worker showed her the latest article in the Seattle Times. Dr. Martin said, "You'd better sit down."

Beth shot him a worried glance as she took the paper from him. She sank into a chair in the nurses' lounge.

The Tukwila, Beaumont's Home Furnishings, store went up in flames shortly before it was due to close forever. The fire marshal determined the cause of the fire to be arson. Detectives reported that the current manager, Clem Morgan, said the sprinkler system had been inspected and disabled earlier the day of the fire. The unnamed inspector disappeared before anyone realized that the system had not been reactivated. An anonymous tipster called the police the night of the fire describing a black BMW fleeing the scene at 12:30 a.m. A suspicious item was found nearby with a clear set of fingerprints. The suspect's fingerprints are still in the county database from an earlier arrest.

Color drained from Beth's cheeks as she dropped the paper. "How could they print such a terrible lie? It is not true. It's just not true!" Dr. Martin advised her to take the rest of the day off. The first thing Beth did was call her father.

John was assisting a customer when Detective Brown and his partner, Jake, entered the store. Jake approached John. "I have a warrant for your arrest."

John's eyes grew wide. "What for?"

Jake applied handcuffs. "For the crime of arson in the first degree. You have the right to remain silent. Anything you say can and will be used against you in a court of law. You have the right to an attorney. If you cannot afford one, one will be appointed for you."

A startled customer stared as John was escorted out of the store.

Bill immediately called John's father. Tiffany shed tears as she watched her brother. He helplessly looked at her as the detective slammed the back door of the police car.

John was taken to jail, fingerprinted, and held for questioning. He was no longer in cuffs while the detectives grilled him mercilessly. "Admit it, John. Times are tough. You need the insurance money! Your prints are all over the place."

John clenched his jaw as his face flushed beet red. "You're crazy! How could my prints be all over a burned-down store?"

"You left a few clues behind," Jake said as he shoved him aside.

"Keep your slimy hands off of me!" John warned, resisting the urge to fight back.

"Face it, John! This isn't your first brush with the law, is it?"

John threw up his hands. "No! I smoked a couple of joints when I was a teenager! I paid my debt to society, and I haven't touched marijuana since!"

"It says here you were a drug dealer."

"What?!" John asked.

"Yep, a dealer."

"That's a bald-faced lie and you know it!"

"Computers don't lie, John."

John shook his head from side to side. "Why are you so hell-bent on pinning this crime on me anyway?"

"More than one person saw your car leave the scene of the fire."

John's eyes narrowed. "I told you I was home alone."

"I thought your wife was with you!"

Just then, Grant Delaney walked into the room. "The show's over, folks. He's done talking for now."

"He's not going anywhere but to jail. He's under arrest."

Grant promised John that he'd get an arraignment as soon as

possible. He accompanied two police officers as they escorted John to a jail cell. John flinched as the iron bars slammed shut behind him. He looked around the stark cell and back at his father-in-law. "What a nightmare!"

"Sit down, son," Grant said.

John slumped on the edge of an iron bed. Grant sat next to him. "Hang in there, John. We're all pulling for you. I'm getting you a great defense attorney."

John stood and paced his cell. "I don't get it! How could they have my fingerprints?"

Grant shook his head. "They haven't got proof of anything. I'll get to the bottom of this."

As he was about ready to leave, John grabbed Grant's arm. "Take care of Beth for me. She'll be out of her mind with worry." Grant promised he would.

John tried to ignore the sounds of men yelling at each other. He scrutinized the small cell holding a stainless-steel toilet and a sink. He stared at the ceiling, counting the tiles one by one as he tried to make sense of his last few hours.

Anger swelled like a tidal wave in his soul. He thought of Beth. He knew she'd be terribly upset. How he longed for her. He tried to pray, but his anger intensified as men in neighboring cells whistled and gave cat calls. "Hey pretty boy! You like playing with matches?"

Besides anger, John felt fear like never before. His body ached on the rock-hard bunk. *Why, Lord, why?*

John's parents and Beth's father insisted that she come home with one of them, but Beth stubbornly refused. She wanted to be alone. She took a hot shower and drank a glass of warm milk. Janet called and offered to come over. Beth refused her offer.

Beth felt lost in their big bed, pining for John. She prayed fervently as she hugged his pillow, savoring his woodsy scent.

The tear-soaked pillow cradled her distraught head as she cried out to the Lord. *Please deliver John from evil!* She thought of the night she'd locked him out of their bedroom with remorse. She got up and walked the floor most of the night. She rubbed her abdomen. *Don't fret, little one.*

Was God saying that very thing to her? The thought of her beloved husband in jail, of all places, broke her tender heart. *What can I do, Lord?* She opened her Bible. As she read from Psalms, she drew comfort from God's Word. "Be still, and know that I am God."[i]

She decided to write John a letter. She'd have her father deliver it the next day.

After she'd emptied her heart onto the page, she felt better. Peace settled over her like a down quilt. Mercifully, sleep came as she cradled John's pillow in her arms.

The following morning the jailer unlocked John's cell. "Your attorney is here." He led John to a private room for their meeting.

Grant shook John's hand and handed him his Bible. "Beth sent this, along with a letter."

John's anxious eyes sought his brown eyes. "How is she?"

Grant motioned for John to sit down. "She's a strong woman John; she's doing better than I thought she would."

"Did she stay with you?"

Grant shook his head. "No. She wanted to stay home. I tried to get her to come with me, and so did your parents. Her friend Janet is going to stay with her tonight."

John stood and paced back and forth. "When can I get out of here?"

Grant rubbed his chin. "Hopefully tomorrow. Getting booked on a Saturday is never a good thing. The court docket is packed, but I'm shooting for early Monday."

Grant spent the better part of an hour talking and reassuring his client. He hugged his son-in-law goodbye before walking him back to his cell. John gripped the bars of his cell as Grant slowly walked away. Had his father-in-law's shoulders always slumped that way?

He settled down on his bunk and opened Beth's letter. Her fragrance drifted from the page.

My Darling Husband,

I miss you more than life itself. My prayers for you never cease. Hang on to all that is good: God's love, my love, your family's love. You are the finest, gentlest, most godly man I've ever known. I am so privileged to be your wife. Honey, stand on God's promises while you lean on his everlasting arms. Remember, darling, that nothing can separate you from the love of God. As Paul's words from Romans reminds us: "For I am sure that neither death nor life, nor angels nor rulers, nor things present nor things to come, nor powers, nor height nor depth, nor anything else in all creation, will be able to separate us from the love of God in Christ Jesus our Lord."

Also, I might add, "nor false accusations, nor jail cells." I am convinced that God arms us with His word for just such a time as this. And nothing can separate you from my love either. If I know you, John, you're worrying about me. But I lean on the same wonderful Lord that you do, and believe me, I'm learning to lean like never before. He will sustain me as well as you. Soon the truth will come out, and you will be exonerated. In the meantime, stand on your faith. And John, I think God wants me to tell you something. "His call on your life does not cease in the hour of trial. That call gets louder, clearer, and stronger than ever before." Please feel my arms around you as I send kisses for your lips only. I will always love you.

Beth

John drew mammoth strength from her words. Tears spilled

down his cheeks onto his orange jumpsuit. *Be with her Lord. She's one in a million.* He then opened his Bible and began to read.

Monday morning Beth brought John's blue suit, a white shirt, and a tie for him to change into for his arraignment. Along with John's parents, she watched as Grant and John entered the courtroom. His eyes sought hers briefly before he looked away. As he stood before the balding judge, he held his head high, looking like the successful man that he is.

The deputy prosecutor accused John of everything short of murder. He embellished the charges, saying John had a long history of crime and was a flight risk. The judge asked, "Mr. Beaumont, how do you plead?"

John made eye contact. "Not guilty, Your Honor."

Grant Delaney pressed for John's immediate release. He pointed out that John was a respected member of the community, a business CEO, a lay minister at his church, owned his own home, and he was married and expecting a child. The risk of flight was minimal.

Much to the prosecutor's disgust, the judge released John on his own recognizance. He was ordered to surrender his passport and not to leave the county. He was to report weekly. The trial date was yet to be determined.

Beth waited while John was fingerprinted again and signed out of the courthouse. When he finally appeared before her, she wrapped her arms around him. "Come home, darling." John drew comfort from her arms. When she finally let go, John's parents and sister took him in their arms. They, too, had spent sleepless nights praying for him. Beth took his hand as they walked to her car. John was silent as she drove him home.

When they entered the condo, John collapsed onto the sofa. His once confident eyes appeared fearful as he related his jail experiences. "I just don't get it. How could my fingerprints be at the scene? And who said they saw my BMW? It doesn't make any sense at all!"

Beth knelt in front of him. "Honey, God knows you didn't do this, and so do I. The truth will come out eventually. We must trust the Lord. I'm confident that He will know what to do.

John sighed and drew her close to him. "I'm scared Beth, really scared."

"I know." She stroked his hair as she held him. "You're not alone in this. God promises he'll never forsake you, and I won't either."

"Thanks for the letter, honey. Your love flowed through like a transfusion to a dying man. What did I ever do to deserve you?"

She snuggled closer as he cuddled her. "I love you."

The couple spent the following days and nights praying for wisdom and guidance. John's parents and Grant were busy trying to track down facts. In the meantime, Grant located a pit-bull defense attorney, Mr. Seth Andrews. He interviewed John extensively and appeared at the next court hearing.

The prosecutor trumped up the charges, saying they had an eyewitness willing to testify to John's fleeing the scene. Another anonymous tip was received describing John's car and license plate number, leaving the area around 12:30 am. Besides that, they had an additional witness who saw John returning home about 1:15 a.m. on the morning of the fire.

Mr. Andrews argued convincingly that the tips could very well have come from the real arsonist to frame John. He further pointed out the reason John arrived home so late. The judge set a trial date for six months later.

John was beside himself as he left the courthouse. "How could this be happening? Who on earth would say they saw me leaving the scene? It's an outright lie!"

Grant paced back and forth. "Anybody with half a brain can

see that you've been framed! We'll find the underlying cause of this as soon as possible!"

A few days later, Grant came to them with more information. He sat across from John and Beth at their kitchen table. He clenched his fists as he explained what he'd been able to find out. "I've seen his kind before," he said of the newly elected district attorney. "He's out to make a name for himself and he sees John as a real catch. He's never met me before and, frankly, he was quite rude. He bragged that his motto is, 'You do the crime; you do the time!' The only problem is that in his zeal, everybody's guilty until proven innocent!"

Beth fought tears. "But what can we do?"

"He has an aggressive staff of hungry prosecutors who think nothing of embellishing their stories to get a conviction. It's all a game to them. To hear them tell it, John is a danger to society, and they want him locked up for good." Grant assured the couple that he'd do everything in his power to help John. "You've got a good defense attorney. We're working together to figure things out."

The story landed on the six o'clock news and splashed across the papers. John felt a churning in his gut that made him nauseous. The floor beneath him felt like sponge rubber. He was in danger of losing everything he'd ever worked for, including his family's good name. John doubted he'd ever get to seminary now.

Beth was furious. "Instead of blaming John, they should be out looking for the real arsonist!" She cradled her distraught husband in her arms. "God is a very present help in time of trouble, honey. We have to keep our eyes on Him."

John was completely bewildered. He couldn't eat or sleep. He paced the floor endlessly. "Who would do this, Beth? And why?"

"God knows, and He will bring out the truth."

"I sure hope you're right. At least you believe me."

"Oh John, nobody believes you're guilty."

"The prosecutors do!"

"That's because they don't know you."

John's parents were on their knees daily, pleading with God for justice. They too tried to console John. They attended court appearances as his attorney poked holes in the prosecutor's accusations.

Grant Delaney tried to reassure John. "Son, they have no supporting arguments. It's just circumstantial evidence and they can't link it to you. Hang in there. We'll beat this thing."

Pastor Sorensen was greatly distressed, too. He met John and Beth in his office. "John, I don't believe a word of these accusations, and neither does anyone who knows you."

He shared a scripture from Psalm 109.

> "Be not silent, O God of my praise!
> For wicked and deceitful mouths are opened
>   against me, speaking against me with lying
>   toungues.
> They encircle me with words of hate, and attack
>   me without cause . . . but I give myself to
>   prayer."[ii]

The pastor prayed with the couple and asked his congregation to pray.

Most people were sympathetic, but not everyone. One woman declared to an audience of listeners, "You never know about people; he could be guilty. I heard there was a big insurance policy." Another woman added, "It's always the good-looking ones you can't trust! The store was going to close, you know. I bet it's for the insurance money, too."

In fact, the store was fully insured. But if John were found guilty of arson, the policy wouldn't pay a thing. John would be in prison for a long time. That thought terrified him and Beth. She grew more distraught as John became withdrawn. He said little as he worked through his anguish. He no longer reached out for her at night. Instead, he stayed close to the edge of the bed, curled up in despair.

Beth could not break the cruel wall of pain between them. One evening she crossed the invisible line of their bed and snuggled up to his back. "John, please don't shut me out. Remember our wedding vows to love each other for better or worse?" He didn't answer. "We're one flesh, John, so if you're hurting, I hurt just as much as you do."

John mumbled, "I'm sorry, Beth . . . you don't deserve this."

She continued to hold him. "Neither do you darling. Neither do you."

John sank deeper into hopelessness with each passing day. The papers were filled with speculations about John's involvement in the fire. Letters to the editor, both pro and con, filled the editorial column. John dreaded answering the phone. He stopped going to the office.

He directed his anger towards God. *Is this what I get for deciding to serve you? It's not fair! How could you let this happen?*

One evening, Beth knelt beside her husband as he lay on the sofa suffering a bad headache. She massaged the muscles of his back and shoulders. "Pray with me, John." He sat up and gave a feeble attempt at prayer, but he felt like his prayers were going nowhere. *Did God care anymore?* For the first time in years, he doubted if God loved him. *Would a loving God desert me in my darkest hours?*

Beth cried out to the Lord: Where was her darling John? He was sinking into a black hole of self-pity and despair. His eyes held mostly sorrow. But there was something else in his eyes that worried her even more, an unfamiliar hardness.

She had worries of her own. Mild contractions added fear to her anxiety. It was much too early for contractions. She was only four and a half months along. She tried to put it out of her mind. It was springtime, May, the month they first began dating a year ago. She brought it up at the dinner table. "John—remember last year when we went on the hike?"

He smiled at the memory. "Yes."

"Let's go back there, just the two of us."

He stroked her hair. "I can't leave the county, remember?" She shook her head, she didn't remember. "It's no use, Beth. We're not going anywhere, anytime soon."

Many people were praying for the couple. Cards and letters arrived from the Bible study group. John's father and mother stopped by the next afternoon while Beth was at work. They rang the doorbell several times. They knew John was home because his car was parked outside.

When John finally answered the door, his parents were shocked at his disheveled appearance. Charcoal shadows beneath his eyes matched his mood and the gray sweats he wore.

He hadn't shaved in days. He brushed hair away from his eyes with his fingers.

Ray and Pamela wrapped their arms around their distraught son. He clung to them like a small child. Pamela found it hard to release him. They followed John to the kitchen, where he offered them a cup of stale coffee. The place was hot and stuffy. Pamela opened the window to let in fresh air and began loading the dishwasher. She made a fresh pot of coffee.

Ray Beaumont faced his son. "John moping around the house won't help anything. Go back to your office. You need to keep busy."

Pamela looked him in the eyes. "Honey, you can't continue this way. Beth came to see me today; she's terribly worried about you." A deep sigh escaped John's lips. Pamela dried her hands on a paper towel. "She loves you so much but feels like you're shutting her out."

John took a deep breath. "I can't go back to the office with this hanging over my head. Beth shouldn't have dragged you into this. She doesn't need more stress either."

Ray Beaumont firmly grasped John's shoulders. "Listen to me, son. What Beth needs is her husband! She's carrying your child. This can't be easy on her. She needs your love and support more than ever."

"Yeah, I know."

Ray continued. "It takes courage to face things head on. Everyone at the store cares about you. Don't you know that?"

John shrugged. "I don't know anything anymore."

"It's times like these that test our faith. You can either go through this trouble trusting Jesus or go it alone. A man has no more faith in life than he does in the hour of trial, John. The choice is yours."

John sat at the table resting his elbows.

Ray placed his hand on John's shoulder. "Let's pray."

A while later John walked his parents to their car. They hugged him goodbye. He watched them drive away before returning to the house. He stood in the kitchen pondering his father's words. He went to the bedroom and knelt beside his bed. Tears streamed down his unshaven cheeks. He prayed the same prayer he'd prayed for days. "Where are you, God?"

My Spirit dwells within you. John opened his eyes. He knew that voice. It always came a little louder than a thought.

"Oh Lord, I don't know what to do. I just can't go to prison . . . especially for something I didn't do."

I, too, was unjustly accused.

"Why is this happening? My reputation is shot. I may never get to seminary."

Fear not! One day, you will search for your enemies and not be able to find them.

"People say I'm an arsonist."

But who do I say you are? Fear not, for I have redeemed you; I've called you by name; you are mine.[iii]

"I'm so weary. Do I really have to go through this?"

There will be dark days ahead, but when you pass through the waters, I will be with you; and when you walk through the fire you shall not be burned, and the flame shall not consume you[iv]—*for I am your God, and you are my servant, I have chosen you and not cast you off.*[v] *Weeping may endure for the night, but joy cometh in the morning.*[vi] *Do not let this trial consume you; instead, let my love consume you.*

John wept. "Forgive me for blaming you. I do love you, Lord."

My love is with you always. I will never forsake you.

Beth felt distracted at work; she should be home with John. It hurt so much watching him sink deeper into despair every day. She stopped at a deli on her way home. John was sitting at his computer when Beth walked up behind him and put her arms around him. He didn't resist her kiss. She was relieved that he'd showered and shaved. He rose from his chair and embraced her. They kissed tenderly; rather than a kiss of passion, it was a kiss of compassion.

John was quiet during dinner, but his face was no longer anguished, and he seemed at peace. He reached for Beth's hand. "I'm very tired, honey, I hope you don't mind, but I'm going to turn in early."

She squeezed his hand. "Of course not. I'll join you in a little while." He was fast asleep when she slid into bed.

Beth wasn't feeling well. An awful backache shot arrows of pain down her legs. Sleep eluded her like a forgotten promise. She tried not to disturb John as she shifted from side to side with intermittent cramping. She finally got up and went to the kitchen to warm some milk. She opened her Bible as she sipped the beverage, hoping it would help her to relax. The words on the pages blurred; she couldn't concentrate. She put the book aside and turned on the television, but nothing interested her. She headed for her bedroom. As she lay next to John, she placed her hand on his back and silently prayed for him. Worries for their future plagued her thoughts before she finally drifted off to sleep.

She and John were going down the freeway in his sports car. But they were in the back seat, frantically trying to reach the controls. The car accelerated to a breakneck speed. It was pitch black, and they had no headlights. Beth panicked because she couldn't see where they were going. A semi-truck with blinding headlights came barreling towards them. An angry face glared from behind the steering wheel. Beth screamed. "John, look out! John, John!"

He sat up and gently rocked his trembling wife while she sobbed. John stroked her forehead. "Honey, it was just a bad dream." She clung to him as she cried. "Oh, dear God. Please help us get through this."

John's tears fell silently. Nothing mattered now except his wife's peace of mind. He shared some of the things he had heard from the Lord earlier. She relaxed as he cradled her in his arms, stroking her hair and kissing her cheeks until she fell back asleep. When he heard the rhythm of her breathing, he vowed to never let go of her again.

He cherished the time he'd had earlier with the Lord. God called him *his servant*. John knew without a doubt that God loved him.

John was dressed by the time Beth got up. She cried in his arms. She cried so much these days that John thought he'd go crazy. He vowed that somehow, someway, he would make it up to her.

After John left for the office, Beth pulled herself together and went to the kitchen. Though she felt nauseous, she managed to get down a cup of yogurt and a piece of toast. She felt twinges in her abdomen as she showered but dismissed the pain. *Please, God, let it be nothing serious.* She'd just been under too much stress lately. She grabbed her sweater and headed out into the morning sunshine. Everything would be fine once she got to work.

When John arrived at the store his coworkers crowded around him. "Welcome back, John. We miss you."

Tiffany rose from her place at the counter and embraced her brother. "Oh, it's so good to see you."

John looked around. "It feels good to be back."

Bill touched his shoulder. "Come and have a cup of coffee. We're all pulling for you. We know what a man of integrity you are." He led the way to the coffee pot and poured a cup for John. "There's a stack of mail on your desk."

"Thanks."

John spent the morning catching up with things. He leaned back in his chair, reading encouraging cards and letters from former customers and loyal friends. He was overwhelmed by the number of people holding him in prayer.

The defense attorney, Seth Andrews, called saying he wanted to meet with John to share some information he'd obtained from the prosecutors. They agreed to meet at the store around noon.

The burly man entered John's office and dropped a file on his desk. He removed a glossy photo and handed it to John. "Have you ever seen this before?"

John stared at an 8x10 picture of a red gas can. "Why yes, I have."

Seth stared at him. "When and where?"

John scratched his head. "Well, it was a long time ago. Before Beth and I were married. In fact, we spent that morning with our pastor for a counseling session."

Seth frowned and rubbed his chin. John continued. "Beth's car had a flat tire, so I changed it for her. We went to the dealership to get it repaired. We dropped off the tire, and I waited with Beth inside the shop." He narrowed his eyes as he tried to remember. "She asked me to get something from my car. I went outside and a gas can was on the hood of my car." John grimaced. "It left a scratch too."

"Did you touch the can?"

"Well . . . yes. I removed it and set it on the ground."

"Then what?"

"I went back inside the shop and asked about it."

"And?"

"When I came back to my car it was gone."

"It was gone?"

"Yes, it vanished into thin air."

Seth furrowed his brows. "So, it just disappeared?"

"Yes. The strange thing is that later we learned that Beth's tire had been punctured in three places."

"Beth's tire was punctured?"

"Yes, it was the oddest thing; the mechanic suggested I make a police report."

"Did you?" Seth asked.

John paced back and forth. "Yes, yes, I did."

Seth tilted his head to one side. "Did you keep a copy?"

"I'm sure I did." John went to his filing cabinet and rummaged through various folders. "Here it is." He placed the paper in front of his lawyer.

"Make a copy for me and let me do some digging."

John photocopied the report and handed it to the lawyer. Seth shook John's hand and promised to get back to him later.

John decided to do some digging of his own. He sat at his desk reading and rereading the charges against him and the so-called evidence. The fire marshal concluded that someone poured gas over the sofas, bedding, and wooden furniture. It appeared that the sprinkler system had been disabled. John decided it was up to him to figure out the rest of the story. First, he needed to talk to Clem.

Twenty-Two

Beth was dragging by mid-afternoon. While hooking up a patient's IV, the room began to swirl. She quickly finished the procedure and dismissed herself. She staggered through the door into the hallway. As she gripped the handrail, the walls seemed to cave in on her. She dropped to the floor. Another nurse ran up to her, shocked to see a puddle of blood. "Beth, what happened?"

She groaned. Her eyes held sorrow. "I'm hemorrhaging, Betty." Reality swirled into darkness as she lost consciousness.

Beth was rushed to the emergency room, but it was too late to save her baby. The tiny child was no longer alive. The doctors fought to stop the bleeding. Thankfully, a gynecologist was on duty at the time. Hospital staff tried to reach John, but there was no answer. They called his store, but he wasn't there. Bill found John's cell phone lying on his desk. He didn't know where John had gone. The head nurse telephoned Grant, who in turn contacted Ray and Pamela. When Beth finally opened her eyes, Dr. Martin broke the news as gently as possible. Pamela, Ray, and Grant were at her bedside. Beth's tearful eyes searched the room. "Where's John?"

Pamela embraced her daughter-in-law. "We can't find him, honey. He left his office earlier this afternoon, and his cell phone was still on his desk."

Beth turned towards her father.

He took her hand. "I'm so sorry."

Tears spilled down her cheeks. "Oh Daddy, how could this be happening? My baby!"

It was times like these when the old lawyer finally ran out of words. His salty tears mingled with hers as he kissed her cheek. "I don't know, darling. I just don't know." He was devastated to learn that she lost the baby they had all been looking forward to. Nothing hurt more than seeing his child suffer. *These kids have been through enough!*

Ray touched her shoulder. "I'll see if I can find him for you." He blinked back tears. After all, he'd lost his first grandchild, too. He dreaded having to tell his depressed son this latest bad news.

Clem and John were arguing in a secluded parking lot. "You threatened to do something if the store closed; I still have your letter!"

Clem looked defeated. "It was all bull, just empty talk. How was I supposed to know this would happen? I may be a jerk, but I'm no arsonist."

John glowered. "I suppose you think I did it too!"

Clem shrugged. "At first, I thought it might be you, especially when the detective said someone saw your car fleeing the scene. Given what I know about you, I doubted it."

"The prosecutor thinks I did it."

"Yeah, the cops have been nosing around here for weeks. They think we might be in cahoots."

John raked his hair with his fingers. "That's ridiculous!"

"Look, John, I've worked for the Beaumonts for years. Your family has been good to me. I kind of lost it when I first heard about the store closing and said stupid things I regret."

John sighed. "I've never known you to hide your feelings."

"Do you have an alibi?"

"Beth was working late; I was home alone."

"No phone calls or nothing?"

"It's complicated. Beth was late, so I went looking for her. She finally called, but it was after one in the morning."

"Did you tell the cops that?"

"Yes, but they don't believe me."

"That's a tough one."

John agreed. "It sure is." He glanced at his watch. "Hey, I better get going. Keep in touch." John felt better after talking to Clem. He'd known him since he was a kid and didn't think he was capable of arson.

On his way back to the office, John decided to grab a bite to eat at a nearby cafe. He parked his car and reached into his pocket for his phone. It wasn't there. After searching his car, he let out a long sigh. He must have left it at the office. *How could I be so forgetful?*

At the café, he ordered a club sandwich. While sipping coffee, he thought of the baby and Beth and how she'd cried the night before. He felt shame at the way he'd been shutting out the person who meant the most to him. He vowed that they would pray together tonight, and he'd tell her more about his encounter yesterday. John was finishing his meal when Len walked in. "Hey there, John, how's it going? We've been praying for you at Bible study."

John motioned to his friend. "Have a seat."

Len slid into the booth across from John and ordered a burger. They talked for the next half hour. John confided that things were going from bad to worse lately.

Len was serious. "I know it sounds trite, John, but try to keep your eyes on the Lord. I know He's there for you."

"I know it too. We had a good talk yesterday."

Len tilted his head. "Who did?"

John smiled. "God and I did."

"Is that right?"

"Yes, but I don't want to discuss it until I tell Beth everything first."

"Fair enough," Len said. John pushed his chair back and excused himself to the restroom.

Len's cell phone rang. He frowned as he saw who was calling. "Hello?"

"Is this Len? John's friend?"

"Yes."

"This is John's dad. I've got his phone and I'm calling his friends. By any chance do you know where John is? It's urgent."

Len sat up straighter. "He's with me now; he just went to the restroom. We're at the Shipside Diner."

"Can you keep him talking until I get there?"

"Aw, sure. I think so."

"Good, don't let him out of your sight, please."

"Okay, I'll keep him here even if I have to hog tie him."

John was lost in thought when he returned to the booth. "Hey Len, I'd better get going."

"Sit down, John, we need to talk."

"I should get back to work. I've been useless lately. It's a good thing Tiffany and Bill are so efficient. They work well together." Len kept John talking, even though he could see he was getting more and more restless. Their server offered them more coffee. Len said, "Give us each a little more."

John was surprised. Len didn't usually ask for refills on *his* coffee. He looked at his watch. "Hey buddy, I've really gotta run."

"Stay here a bit longer, John; I need to run something by you."

John knitted his brows. "What?"

"It's about Mindy. I'm thinking of asking her to marry me."

John looked up. "Are you serious?"

"I'm thinking about it. I don't know if I'm ready, though."

"Is she ready?"

"She gives me subtle hints. What do you think? Is marriage all it's cracked up to be?"

"Speaking for myself, yes. I'm glad I married Beth, but if you're having reservations . . ."

"Well, we love each other but have some issues we don't agree on." John listened to his friend ramble on about their political differences. Len kept looking towards the entrance.

John was surprised to see his father come through the door. He had a worried look on his face. "Hey, Dad. What are you doing here?"

Ray sighed. "Thank God, I've found you. Beth is in the hospital."

"She's at work, right?"

Ray sighed. "John, we've been trying to reach you. She had a miscarriage this afternoon."

The color drained from John's face as he closed his eyes. "Take me to her."

Ray let his son out at the entrance to the hospital. "She's on the second floor, room 202."

John raced through the double doors and towards the elevator. *Oh Lord, give me the right words to say.* He pushed the button that took forever to engage. He gave up and ran up the stairs. He skirted the nurses' station on the way to Beth's room.

"Sir! Where are you going?" a nurse yelled.

"My wife, Beth Beaumont, is a patient here. I've got to see her."

"I need you to sign in and see your identification."

John took a deep breath and pulled out his wallet. He signed in and waited. The nurse studied his license and was satisfied. She gave him a visitor badge and pointed down the hall.

John paused outside of her room long enough to draw another deep breath. He opened the door and hurried to her side.

Beth was sitting up in her hospital bed. An IV pierced her wrist while monitors recorded her vital signs. John bent down to kiss her tear-stained cheek. Their eyes met in a valley of pain as he reached for her. "I'm sorry; I didn't know."

Her sorrowful face turned away as dark hair spilled across the pillow. John sat on the side of her bed. She buried her head against his chest and began to weep. He held her close to his heart, cradling her as gently as possible. "There, there, darling." Tears spilled down his cheeks.

"Our baby, John, our baby." She let loose with gut-wrenching sobs as sorrow consumed her entire being. John could barely speak above a whisper. "I know, darling, I'm so very sorry."

She moaned softly. "Why, John, why?"

He stroked her arm. "I don't know, honey. But I hope you can find it in your heart to forgive me someday."

Her sad eyes met his, "Forgive you?"

"Yes, this is entirely my fault. You've been under so much stress lately."

Her glistening eyes grew serious: "John, please don't *ever* say that again. You didn't cause this. I've been a nurse for a long time, and believe me these things happen every day. It's nobody's fault."

John reached for a tissue on the bedside table and dabbed his eyes. With another tissue he blotted her tears. She took it and wiped her nose. John and Beth sat a long time, just holding one another until the door opened.

Dr. Martin stopped by to offer his condolences. Beth was the best nurse they had, and it pained him to see the young couple in such heartache. He took John's hand in his. "My wife and I are praying for you."

"Thank you, doctor. We appreciate that."

Pamela, Ray, and Grant entered the room. Each one embraced John as he struggled to keep from falling apart.

Later that evening, Tiffany appeared with a small bouquet of flowers. She wrapped her arms around her brother and cried with him. Next, she hugged Beth and shed more tears. "I'm here for you guys if you need anything at all."

"Can you take me to get my car later?" John said.

John spent the night on a recliner next to Beth's bed. His legs spilled over the end of the chair. Nurses were in and out all night long, checking her vital signs, fiddling with the IV, and taking blood samples. She'd lost a lot of blood and was getting weaker.

He never left her side for more than a few minutes. "Nothing means more to me than you, Beth. Absolutely nothing."

Beth caressed his cheek in her own intimate way, the way that spoke volumes to his heart. "Don't make an idol of me, honey. God must always come first."

He took her hand and kissed it. "You're right, darling."

She sighed. "He's taking care of us, honey. At least it happened here, in the hospital, where I got immediate help. Had it happened at home, I might have bled out." She sniffed. "I should have sought help sooner. I denied that anything was wrong. As a nurse, I should have known better."

"Denial is a strong coping mechanism. Don't blame yourself either."

Beth pointed outside the window; a beautiful rainbow arched

in the sky. "All I know is that we have a baby waiting for us in heaven."

John teared up, "Yes, we do."

"I read the lab reports; it was a boy."

John closed his eyes. *My son.* He whispered hoarsely, "Shall we give him a name?"

"I'd like to name him after you."

More tears escaped his eyes. "Okay."

"John?"

"Yes, darling?"

"If we have another boy someday, could we name him after our fathers?"

"They'd be honored." Though he tried to be strong for her, a few more tears escaped his eyes. He put his arm around her. "We might never know the reason we lost our baby. But little John is now in God's arms."

"Just hold me, honey."

John wrapped her in an embrace; "There's nothing I'd rather do."

Pastor Sorensen visited later that morning to discuss a private funeral service for baby John. He felt so sorry for the newlyweds. Their wedding vows for better or worse had been tested early on. He knew that trials either strengthened a marriage or destroyed it. Somehow, he felt this couple would grow stronger through their ordeals. Their devotion to one another touched him. With all they were going through, they treated each other with great tenderness. He'd seen them worshiping on Sunday mornings, upholding one another in prayer. Why God had allowed this additional trial was beyond him. He'd stopped second guessing the Lord a long time ago. He relied on the promise from Romans 8:28: *"And we know that all things work together for good to them that love God, to them who are the called according to his purpose."* Repeatedly, he'd seen that prove to be the case.

Pastor Phil brought a bouquet of flowers from the Bible study group. Each member had signed a card. Dr. Martin decided to keep Beth another day or so because she'd developed a fever. Pamela came to visit while Ray took his son out to lunch.

Pamela sat in the chair next to Beth's bed and reached for her hand. She told her about the baby she'd miscarried thirty-eight years ago as the result of an auto accident. She'd been ejected from the car. She looked deep into Beth's eyes. "I know the pain you're feeling."

A tear rolled down one side of Beth's cheek. She squeezed Pamela's hand. "You've been like a mother to me."

Pamela hugged her. "I love you like a daughter."

Beth's father walked into the room with a bouquet of roses. "How's my girl today?"

"Better Daddy, better."

Beth was released the following day with instructions not to return to work for a few weeks.

John drove her home and helped her navigate the elevator. He unlocked the condo and held it open. She stumbled on the threshold. John picked her up and carried her to their living room. He gently placed her on the sofa, sat down next to her, and held her. She sighed, "It's so good to be home."

Instead of getting better, Beth grew lethargic as she mourned the loss of their baby. She worried about John's arson charge and the upcoming trial. She pondered their uncertain future and had troubling dreams.

John forced himself to return to the store. He worked hard so he could come home early. Beth spent her days dragging around the house and watching mindless television programs.

She usually opened a can of soup for dinner or made peanut butter sandwiches. John tried to tempt her to eat, but she kept insisting she wasn't hungry.

John called his mother. "I don't know what to do with her. She won't eat, and she's so listless." Pamela arrived the next day with a chicken casserole and a cake. Beth smiled weakly and thanked her. She turned away and headed for the bedroom. "I need to lie down."

Pamela ran a load of laundry and tidied up the place. She thought Beth might be suffering from postpartum depression. *It's no wonder with all that's been going on.* She was fighting depression herself. Her only son was in so much trouble. Her prayers grew more desperate daily. She went to the bedroom to check on her daughter-in-law. Beth was staring at the ceiling. Pamala sat next to her. Beth's pale face accentuated the dark shadows beneath her eyes. Pamela took her hand. "Honey, you shouldn't still be this tired. I think you should go back to your doctor." Pamela prayed with her before she left.

That evening, John tried his best to tempt his wife to eat some casserole. She ate what she could, which wasn't much. John coaxed her to eat more. "Look honey, chocolate cake." Beth nibbled at a few bites before pushing the plate away.

After dinner, John made a pot of spiced tea and brought it to the sofa where Beth was sitting. He offered her a cup. Beth stared into space. John snapped his fingers in front of her. She turned to him with vacant eyes.

John began, "I made you a doctor's appointment for tomorrow afternoon."

"I'm fine, John, just a little tired."

John was firm. "No Beth, you're not fine. The stress of everything has gotten to both of us. I know how desperate you feel. Remember when you told me I was shutting you out?"

"Yes, I remember."

"Well, now you're doing the same thing to me." John put his arm around her. "I promised to love you in sickness and in health. Part of love demands action. You challenged me, and now I'm challenging you." She leaned into his embrace and started to cry. Nothing made John feel more helpless.

Beth's medical tests showed that she was anemic. Her poor diet only made things worse. She was advised to eat iron-rich foods and given shots and supplements. Her doctor prescribed a mild antidepressant and encouraged her to get therapy to work through her grief.

Beth was unable to get a counseling appointment for several weeks. John realized that they both needed help. He took her to see Pastor Sorensen. Not only did he show them ways to deal with their sorrow, but he also tackled their communication styles. Part of his advice encouraged face-to-face discussions, without judgment; just listening and acknowledging each other's feelings. As they dealt with emotions of anger, sadness, and resentment at the injustice of their lives, they were urged to take their burdens to the cross. Their pastor suggested that they pray for the prosecutors, and whoever committed the crime. They worked on forgiving their accusers rather than being consumed with bitterness.

Through it all they gained insight into another dimension of intimacy; the intimacy of their spirits as they truly became one —yet honoring their individuality.

In time, Beth began to recover. As she regained strength, her optimism slowly returned.

John and Beth took time to minister to one another, praying daily, going for walks, holding hands and just being friends. There were no demands placed on one another. Their physical intimacy had been on hold for a long time. After one of their counseling sessions, it was suggested that they take their burdens to the cross and leave them there.

On their way home, Beth confessed her doubts about God. "Why did He let my mother die of cancer? Why did He let our innocent baby die? And why did He let you be accused of a horrible crime? What did we do wrong? I feel like He's punishing us."

John stopped for a red light and faced her. "I've wondered the same thing. I feel like such a failure."

"Oh, John, no, you are *not* a failure!"

He smiled. "I'm glad you think so."

"So how do we take our burdens to the cross?"

John thought for a moment. "Honey, either God's teachings are true or they're a lie. He doesn't say we will always have smooth sailing, but He does promise to be with us in our trials. We see through a glass darkly. What have we got to lose?"

The next day, John and Beth entered the empty sanctuary and walked to the front. A large wooden cross dominated the wall behind the altar. They knelt next to each other. John reached for her hand as he whispered, "This is the church we were married in."

How many songs had they sung in this place? How many prayers had been answered?

John suggested they lift open hands as they released each burden to the cross. They took turns naming their concerns as tears trickled down their cheeks. It was as if they let go of buckets of cement they'd been carrying for a long time.

A subtle peace settled over them like a down comforter. Neither of them moved as they basked in God's love. A brilliant shaft of sunlight pierced a stained-glass window, spotlighting the couple. Beth gasped and started weeping. Next, she smiled and began to laugh. Her eyes were closed. John put his arm around her. "Beth, what are you seeing?"

"I'm not quite sure, but it looks like my mother, sitting on a beautiful beach. It looks like she's cuddling a baby. It's our baby. They both look so joyful."

Twenty-Three

A few weeks later, John returned home to a wonderful aroma. He went to the kitchen and lifted the lid of their shiny stockpot. Beth had made one of his favorite dishes, a tantalizing chicken stew with dumplings. She walked up behind him and wrapped her arms around his waist. He turned to face her. She was wearing a dress. Her shiny hair cascaded down her back. She gave him a lingering kiss. "John, I'm so excited! My song is back."

John tilted his head. "Your song?"

"Yes, darling, I haven't felt like singing for such a long time. But today, while playing the keyboard, a hymn just flowed out of me."

"What song was it?"

Beth took his hand. "Follow me. I'll play it for you." He sat nearby while she found her place. She played an introduction and began singing:

> When peace like a river, attendeth my way
> When sorrows like sea billows roll;
> Whatever my lot, Thou hast taught me to say,

It is well, it is well with My Soul.

He joined her singing the other verses that ministered to his weary soul.

Not only was her song back, but joy returned. Though she was thinner than usual, she looked ravishing. John gently kissed her again and whispered in her ear. "Welcome back, baby. I've missed you."

There was now an added dimension to their love that only comes with a marriage that's been tried and tested.

Beth returned to work with even more compassion for the sick and suffering. She knew the fear and uncertainty that illness brings firsthand and the vulnerability of her patients. Some were all alone with no one to comfort them. She prayed for them silently, and sometimes patients asked her to pray at their bedside, which she willingly did. One of her coworkers tried to make an issue of it, but her complaints were ignored. "Wait until you're sick; you'll be the first one wanting Beth at your bedside," her supervisor said.

Bill and Tiffany were hashing out claims with the insurance company. There would be no settlement while John was a suspect. They were at odds as to how to manage the stores. Nothing was going the way Bill thought it should go. After all, he was the most qualified to take John's place, not Tiffany.

John was trying his best to keep his eyes on the Lord—yet his feet on the ground. The possibility of losing his bid to the seminary was very real. He could be found guilty by a jury and sent to prison. *Would God let that happen?*

John thought of his father's words the last time they prayed together. *"Lord, lift John above the circumstances and seat him in heavenly places with you."* Countless thoughts swirled in John's mind. He pictured Beth's face, heard her prayers, and felt her arms around him. He saw his father's compassionate eyes. *"Grant him peace, Lord."*

At times, John felt strangely detached from his troubles. He couldn't explain the peace he felt, except for God's promise that He would never forsake him. Though things were a mess at the office, thankfully, they were much better at home. Beth was back to her loving self, which meant the world to him. He couldn't imagine going through something like this without her love and support. She was an amazing wife.

Twenty-Four

Beth heard groans coming from her new patient's room. Her heart went out to the poor woman who'd obviously been beaten. Her purplish face was swollen beyond recognition. Her eyes were puffy slits. Red streaks covered her throat, and she could barely speak above a whisper. She was hooked to an IV and monitors while another machine pumped painkillers.

Beth checked the chart and gasped in horror. The woman with two cracked ribs was her former coworker, Susan Foster. Beth felt nauseous. "Susan, what happened to you?"

Just then an older woman entered the room. Susan groaned as tears spilled down her swollen cheeks. "Mom," she whispered. Her mother bent to give her a gentle kiss on her forehead.

"Tell her what happened."

Susan shuddered, "It was my fault, I tripped and fell."

Her mother rolled her eyes and raised her hands up. They both knew Susan was lying.

Beth gently touched Susan's shoulder. "We'll do everything we can to make you comfortable. Can I get you anything?"

"Water." Susan whispered. Beth poured ice water into a glass and held a flexible straw to her swollen lips. Susan groaned. Her mouth throbbed where her upper lip had been stitched.

Beth was gently dressing Susan's wounds when Reid Harper walked through the door with a bouquet of flowers. He went to Susan's side. "How are you doing, doll?" Susan flinched as more tears flowed. Reid turned on the charm. "I brought you flowers." She turned her face towards the wall. Her mother abruptly left the room.

"Nothing's too good for my girl!" He said while looking directly at Beth.

She felt like decking him. Instead, she turned and walked out into the hall. Sensing her anger, Reid followed her. "How's that husband of yours? I heard he's in a heap of trouble!"

Beth tensed. "Trouble? Not that I know of." She continued down the hall.

Reid was close behind her. "Maybe you should read the papers, honey."

Beth spun around facing him. "You should be more concerned about Susan's welfare than my affairs. What happened to her, Reid?"

His eyes flashed anger. "What's it to you?"

"I feel sorry for her. Nobody should have to endure a beating like that."

Reid glowered. "What are you talking about? She fell down the stairs."

"Yeah, right!" Beth felt hatred for the man.

"She falls a lot! She's a klutz!"

"Is that so?" Beth was livid. "I don't believe a word you've said!"

Reid shrugged. "Are you still jealous of her?"

Beth shook her head from side-to-side. "You're pathetic, Reid, just pathetic. This isn't about me. And you won't get away with this."

Reid laughed as if she'd said something hilarious. He winked at her. "You'd be surprised what I get away with!" He turned and walked towards Susan's room.

Beth fumed while she considered her next moves. Susan's mother appeared in the hallway. "Can we talk?"

Beth ushered her into a private room and pointed to a chair. "Please have a seat."

The woman's eyes glistened with unshed tears. "As you know, I'm Susan's mother, Joyce Foster."

Beth sat across from her. "Mrs. Foster, do you know who did this to her?"

She grimaced like she had something bitter in her mouth. "That scumbag she lives with, Reid Harper!"

Beth sighed. "Reid is with her now. He brought flowers."

"He always does that after knocking the daylights out of her."

Beth scowled. "This has happened before?"

Mrs. Foster was close to tears. "The first time he hit her because she burned his pancakes. I swear there's something terribly wrong with that guy."

Beth agreed. "She needs to press charges and get a restraining order."

"I wish she would, but he always comes crawling back with flowers and crocodile tears. He begs forgiveness, and she goes right back to him."

Beth touched her hand. "This is serious; he could have killed her. Somehow, we've got to make her see the light." Susan's mother began to cry. Beth handed her a tissue, "Can I pray with you about this?"

She dabbed her eyes, "Okay."

Beth held Joyce's hands as she prayed for God's protection over Susan. Among other things, she prayed for Susan to be strong enough to do the right thing and press charges.

Susan's mother tearfully said, "She did break up with him once. I was so relieved when she moved back home."

Beth looked into her sad eyes. "Oh?"

"But Reid called her constantly and parked outside of our house. He harassed her at work, too. One day she had a flat tire and Reid offered her a ride home. Instead of bringing her home, he took her to his place, and they took up where they left off."

Beth sighed. "What a shame."

"That creep even admitted he punctured her tire on purpose!"

"He punctured her tire?"

Mrs. Foster stood up. "Yes. I was literally sick when she went back to him." She wrung her hands as she paced back and forth. "Their truce lasted a month before he whacked her again for talking to some guy at the hospital. She left him again and finally had to leave her job. Even that didn't stop him. He bugged her until she went back to him last month."

Beth urged her to contact the hospital social worker with Susan's story. "Perhaps she can convince Susan to tell the truth about Reid."

Joyce wanted to see her daughter first. Reid was just leaving as she entered Susan's room. He wore a silly smirk.

That evening, Beth thought about Susan and her encounter with Reid. She felt terrible. How could she have ever considered marrying him? She thanked God for closing that door in her life. She had the dearest husband in the world.

The next day, Beth headed to work, anxious to check on her patient. Susan's best friend, Kelly, was sitting at her bedside. The perky redhead spent the next hour talking with Susan.

Beth took her aside after their visit. "Kelly, have you had any success in getting Susan to admit what really happened?"

Kelly scowled. "Not quite, she's still protecting Reid. I think she's afraid of him."

"As well she should be! She just can't go back to him."

"He's a strange one. He can be charming until he doesn't get his way."

Tell me about it! Beth thought.

Kelly went on, "One time he burned a collection of her family pictures because she wanted to attend a family reunion. Can you imagine?"

Beth shook her head. "He sounds like one sick puppy."

"He is! It makes me furious that she won't break up with him. Every time she tries, he stalks her continuously." Beth recalled how he'd shadowed her after their breakup. Again, she shuddered to think that she'd almost married him. It might have been her in that hospital bed covered with bruises.

"Let's talk to her together," Beth said.

Susan was sitting up, taking nourishment when they entered her room. Purple bruises distorted her pretty features. Beth gently touched her arm, "Susan, Reid can't hurt you here. There's a security guard outside the door, and Dr. Martin has limited your visitors to Kelly and your mother."

Susan whimpered. "You don't believe me, do you?"

Beth shook her head. "About falling down the stairs? No."

Susan turned her head towards the wall. Tears flowed over her bruised cheeks. "It's all my fault."

"How is it your fault?"

"I just can't please him. I'm no good."

Kelly spoke up: "He's the one who is no good! Think about all the stuff he's done to you. Love shouldn't hurt, Susan."

Susan directed her gaze towards Beth. "You used to be his fiancée, didn't you?"

Beth sighed, "Yes, we were once engaged."

Kelly's jaw dropped as she stared at Beth.

Susan trembled. "I believed the awful things he said about you."

"Things about me?"

"He said you lied and cheated on him, and that's why he broke up with you."

Beth frowned. "It was the other way around."

"All he talks about is you and how much he hates your husband."

Beth squared her shoulders. "He has no reason to hate John. I didn't date him until long after Reid and I broke up."

Susan reached for a tissue and wiped her nose. "Reid has newspaper clippings of you. He saved your engagement and wedding announcements, and he has articles about you two singing as well as clippings about the furniture store fire."

Beth sat down on a plastic chair, her mind reeling. Susan continued. "He said if John goes to prison, then you will be free."

"Free?" Beth could barely comprehend what Susan was saying.

"He's still in love with you."

Beth felt the floor buckle beneath her. "Then why do you stay with him?"

Susan shook her head slowly. "I . . . I don't know." Fresh tears stung her eyes. Kelly just stared at them.

Before the morning was over the social worker, along with Kelly and Beth, convinced Susan to press charges. Two women detectives came to the hospital to take her statement and photograph her injuries. They counseled Susan for over an hour. Finally, she agreed that Reid was a deranged man. She added that he'd bragged about puncturing Beth's tire too, the way he had hers. He'd shown her a special device he used.

Reid was sipping coffee in the break room when the female detectives entered. Beth watched as he was handcuffed and escorted to a waiting police car. Reid looked furious to be so roughly handled by women. He scowled out the window as the car pulled away.

Beth phoned her father to tell him what happened. Grant advised her to contact John and meet him at his home as soon as possible.

John was talking with Bill and Tiffany about a problem with one of their flooring suppliers when his phone rang.

"John, meet me at Daddy's as soon as possible. It's urgent!"

"I'll be right there."

Beth met him at the door. "I think our troubles might soon be over." John held his trembling wife until she regained her composure. She explained the whole story about Reid and Susan and the newspaper clippings. John's fair skin flushed a deep red. His neck veins pulsed with rage. "If I get my hands on that guy . . . I swear, I'll . . . "

Grant placed a sobering hand on John's arm. "I know you're angry, son, and you have every right to be. The important thing is that we have a suspect. Since Reid bragged about ruining Beth's tire and has clippings of the fire . . . it looks suspicious."

"The fire—he must be the one."

Grant rubbed his chin. "It doesn't prove he started the fire. There are still too many loose ends. His claim that he'd support Beth if you went to prison gives a clear motive."

John sank into the nearest chair. "This is crazy." In a flash he relived the past year. His engagement and marriage, his bid for seminary, the arrest, his doubts, fears, the loss of their baby, and their struggles overcoming depression. "What do we do now?"

Beth wrapped her arms around John's waist. "We pray."

Grant Delaney was on the phone to John's defense attorney.

The next day, the lawyers presented their findings to the prosecutor. With Susan's signed statements, the police obtained a warrant to search Reid's apartment. Among other things, they found numerous clippings about Beth and John, along with a file of clippings on the furniture store fire. They examined Reid's computer and discovered he had frequented numerous websites on arson.

They questioned Beth and Susan further at the hospital.

Susan had one more confession to make. Reid had been drunk the night of her assault. He'd bragged about how he'd gotten John's fingerprints on the gas can. He'd followed Beth's car to the church parking lot and watched as she greeted John, and they entered the church. While wearing gloves, Reid punctured her tire when no one was looking. He waited behind the bushes for John and Beth to leave the church and followed them to the repair garage.

Susan looked apologetic "When John went inside the shop, Reid put the gas can on John's car. He laughed about how easy it had been. John came to his car and removed the gas can before going back to the shop. That's when Reid grabbed it with a black plastic garbage sack and drove away."

Susan continued, "I told Reid if he didn't tell the police the truth, I would. He went crazy and lunged at my throat. He choked me until I thought I'd pass out. That's when I kicked him." Tears streamed down her swollen cheeks. "He began pounding me with his fists. I screamed and begged him to stop, but he was like a madman. When I fell, he kicked and shoved me down the stairs."

Beth was horrified. "What a monster!"

Susan flinched. "Afterward, he left me lying on the floor while he went to sleep off his drunken stupor. Somehow, I managed to make it to our neighbor's house. I told her I fell down the stairs and she drove me to the hospital."

The detectives confronted Reid at the jail with Susan's testimony. He slumped in a chair while his chained ankles and flip flops complimented his orange jumpsuit. Reid denied it at first, but when he realized they had signed sworn statements from

Susan and her neighbor, as well as Susan's mother, he filled in the rest of the story.

His glazed eyes beamed with pride as he described how he'd posed as a sprinkler system inspector. Clem had given him access to the overhead sprinklers with no qualms. When Reid finished tinkering with the sprinklers, he disappeared. No one realized the system had been deactivated. And no one suspected that Reid was napping in the broom closet until the store closed. The gas can next to him was wrapped in a black plastic bag. Three hours later, Reid sprinkled mattresses, sofas, chairs, and carpets with gasoline. He laughed maniacally as he recalled starting small fires, piling up pictures, wooden bookshelves, and accent pieces.

Reid stared into space. "The store was so old the walls made good kindling. But the smoke was killing me. I had to get out of there!" The detectives listened intently as Reid elaborated. "I left the building and hid the gas can in the bushes. Then I removed my gloves and tossed them in the fire." His breathing quickened as his wild eyes glistened. "I ran up the hill and watched the building turn into an orange ball of flames. Even the rain couldn't stop it."

He told them how he stood frozen with fascination as dozens of fire trucks responded to the blaze. It gave him a euphoric feeling of power. He smiled, "And they just kept coming!"

The detectives stared at the deranged man.

"I called the cops on a burner phone and described John's car leaving the scene. Heck, I'd seen his car many times. When the cops asked my name, I hung up."

"A few days later, I called the police again, from a different phone, giving a description of John's car fleeing the scene— along with his license plate number. I ended the call before they could ask any questions." Reid's dark eyes glowed as he finished his story: "It was so easy; a piece of cake." He leaned towards the detectives. "That way when, John goes to prison, I'll be there to comfort Beth. It all makes perfect sense."

With the new evidence, the prosecutor dropped all charges against John. The DA focused his energy on Reid Harper. Assault and battery charges were the least of Reid's worries now. They upped the charges to attempted murder. That, along with his confession of arson, would keep him imprisoned for years. The stories spread throughout the media, absolving John of any guilt.

The DA issued formal apologies to John and his family on all forms of media.

Cards and letters flooded the editorial columns affirming the Beaumont family's good name. Testimonies of how the company had provided furnishings to various charities over the years surfaced, too. Several local shelters relied on their generous donations every winter. As a result of the publicity, the stores became busier than ever. A crescendo of praise and thanksgiving reached heaven's gates from John and Beth as well as their family and supporters. The Lord faithfully walked them through the fiery trial and exposed the enemy. What the enemy hoped would destroy them, God would use to strengthen them for His call on their lives.

Beth and John sat on their sofa, thanking God for clearing John's name. The front-page newspaper article vindicating John covered the coffee table. As Beth read about Reid's involvement she turned to her husband. A shroud of sorrow covered her face. "I'm so sorry for the pain I've caused you."

John frowned. "What are you talking about?"

"This whole nightmare is really my fault. Reid nearly destroyed you because of me."

John put a protective arm around her shoulder. "He's a sick man. What scares me the most is that he might have harmed you. Maybe it's a good thing that he focused his rage on me instead of you. Besides, it's not your fault he turned out to be a psychopath."

"But if you hadn't met me, none of this would have happened to you."

John looked deep into her troubled eyes. "If I hadn't met you, I'd be a very empty man. No one has ever given me more happiness. I'd go through anything for you."

Beth leaned against his chest. "All I really know is how much I love you."

John nuzzled her hair. "Let's pray. 'Lord, we come with grateful hearts for each other. Help us heal emotionally from the ordeal we have come through this past year. Strengthen us, guide us, and use us to comfort and minister to your people. Put a new song in our hearts as we sing of your mercies that are new every morning. Put a hedge of protection around us as we follow where you lead us. In Jesus' name, Amen.'" John drew her closer. "Maybe our lives will smooth out now that all this is behind us."

She smiled. "Do you think?"

THE END

My heart is steadfast, O God, my heart is
steadfast!
I will sing and make melody!

I will give thanks to you, O Lord, among the
peoples; I will sing praises to you among
the nations.

Psalm 57:7, 9 (ESV)

Notes

CHAPTER 11

i. Isaiah 40:30-31

CHAPTER 17

i. Colossians 3:15

CHAPTER 20

i. 1 Corinthians 13:4-7 (ESV)

CHAPTER 21

i. Psalm 46:10
ii. Psalm 109:1-4 (ESV)
iii. Isaiah 43:1 (ESV)
iv. Isaiah 43:2 (ESV)
v. Isaiah 41:9 (ESV)
vi. Psalm 30:5b

Acknowledgments

1 Thessalonians 5:11, "Therefore encourage one another and build one another up, just as you are doing." (ESV)

I thank God for the encouragers in my life. The people who pray for me and take a chance on me, trust me, comfort me, minister to me, and counsel me, the ones who want to see me succeed in life. The ones who love me when I'm not so lovable.

Ted Genengels: Special thanks to my loving husband, who has always believed in me. As a child, I prayed that God would someday send me a husband who would take me to church. I met Ted just before my senior year of high school. Not only was he a Christian, but he was also adorable. We recently celebrated our 65th wedding anniversary. We have three children and lots of grandkids; some are great. (Well, they all are.) Ted makes the best lattes every morning.

Gigi Exum: My firstborn child calls me every day. If I need anything, she's there in a heartbeat. She has the patience of Job, the kindness of a saint, and is beautiful inside and out. She's given us three wonderful grandsons. She works for DSHS, a perfect fit for a compassionate woman.

Ryan Genengels: My youngest child is kind, gentle, and thoughtful. He is very techy and helps with computer stuff and finds fabulous buys at the Goodwill, like my latest gift, a small Bose speaker that connects to my cell phone. He's a postal worker, musician, and singer/songwriter. He's given us two grandchildren.

Shawn Genengels: My first baby boy has taught me more about life than anyone else. His life has not been easy, but he perseveres. He served six years in the Navy. He is the best mechanic and can fix just about anything. I can't tell you how many brakes he's fixed for needy people. He speaks three languages and has translated on Mexico mission trips. He loves to play pool. He volunteers for a ministry that feeds the hungry. He's given us a grandson and a great-granddaughter.

Sharon Svendsen: My sister, author/teacher, invited me to attend writing classes, conferences, poetry readings, and more. She cheered me on when my stories and articles were published. She survived reading my first rough draft of *Steadfast Love*. I love her very much.

Jackie Murray: An author and friend who edited version after version of this masterpiece, always cheering me on. Tireless, helpful, and steadfast. A real jewel.

Wanda Brunstetter: An author and friend who challenged me to write fiction in addition to nonfiction, years ago. My second book, *Fingerprints on the Altar Rails*, is fiction.

Virginia Holt: My friend and a nun who prayed my first book, *Unfailing Love*, into existence. She also read my first draft of *Steadfast Love*. I miss you Ginny.

Lisa Woolery LeMaster: An author and friend who read my manuscript and gave helpful suggestions.

Ann Krieger, a lifetime friend and prayer partner. You always have my back! We have ministered together and traveled to many places, including Jerusalem and Egypt. You are such a gift!

Thanks also to Ann, Zoanne, Gigi, Betty, Mary, Karen, Diane, Kay, to name a few. There are so many wonderful encouragers who pass through our lives over the years. Pastors, church friends, neighbors, and ministry buddies.

Thanks to my publisher, Torchflame Books, and to Teri, Jori, and Mandi for your patience and guidance.

If I have overlooked anyone, please forgive me. "To err is human, to forgive is divine."

About the Author

CAROL GENENGELS was born in Seattle and raised in the beautiful Pacific Northwest. She enjoyed spending summers at her aunt's beach house playing in the sand and collecting shells.

Her childhood prayer was that God would someday give her a husband who would take her to church. She met Ted, the answer to her prayer, in her senior year of high school. They recently celebrated 65 years of marriage.

She studied Medical Assisting at Olympic College and worked in the medical/mental health care field before retiring. She and her husband, world travelers, have 3 children and several grandchildren.

Carol served in church and community leadership roles and co-founded *A Woman's Touch Ministry in* Silverdale, WA and served as director for fifteen years. Being in the trenches with diverse women gave her compassion to meet them where they are.

Carol authored numerous short stories, poems, devotionals and articles. Her true stories have appeared in several devotionals, including *Chicken Soup for the Soul* books, *God Allows U-Turns* books, God's Rainbow Book (Prayers and Inspiration for Victims of Hurricane Katrina) *Bad Hair Days, Stories for Spirit Filled Believers, Journeys of Friendship*, etc. as well as Woman's

Day, Reminisce, and various other magazines. Her first book, *Unfailing Love,* has blessed many lives. Her next book, *Fingerprints on the Altar Rails,* was well received by her readers. Carol won an award for her newspaper article on *Road Rage.*

Carol and her husband co-founded Grays Harbor's first NAMI (National Alliance on Mental Illness) affiliate in 2007. In 2011 the county awarded them a *Phoenix Award* for their tireless work with persons dealing with mental illness. Carol's article, *A Cry for Help,* published in *The Psychiatric Journal,* June of 06, caught the attention of a psychiatrist in the US legislature. It was used to garner two million dollars towards a mental health bill. Additionally, Carol has testified in the WA state legislature on a bill she and her husband co-sponsored. Carol, active in Toastmasters International, served a term as President of their local affiliate. As an inspirational speaker, Carol has ministered at retreats and conferences. Her greatest joy is seeing women set free to be all that God has created them to be. Carol's favorite scripture is: "Therefore, my beloved brothers, be steadfast, immovable, always abounding in the work of the Lord, knowing that in the Lord your labor is not in vain." 1 Cor.15:58 (ESV)

Connect with Carol online at torchflamebooks.com.

g

Thank You!

Thank you for reading! If you enjoyed this book, please leave a review on Amazon, Goodreads, BookBub, The Story Graph, or anywhere else you like to track your recent reads. Alternatively, you could post online or tell a friend about it. This helps our authors more than you may know.

- The Team at Torchflame Books

Visit torchflamebooks.com to find your next great read.